"I couldn't stop wondering what it would be like to kiss you." This time when David looked at me, there was heat in his gaze.

"Maybe you should find out." I turned around and leaned against the counter. I hoped I looked sexy and inviting, but I probably looked excited and nervous.

He stood up slowly and walked around the kitchen island to stand in front of me. His suit jacket hung open and I could see the muscles under his shirt shift with each step, but it was his eyes that drew me in. Placing a hand on either side of me on the counter he leaned close. I felt as if he was searching my soul, looking for something in particular. As if he had found his answer, he dipped his head and his lips captured mine.

It was slow and careful, as if he was waiting for some sign. When his tongue brushed across my bottom lip I sighed and ran my hands over his chest. I hadn't been kissed in so long I had almost forgotten what it was like—that connection between two people who wanted the same thing: each other.

## By Nichole Chase

SUDDENLY ROYAL
(Royal Series, Book One)
RECKLESSLY ROYAL
(Royal Series, Book Two)
MORTAL OBLIGATION
(Dark Betrayal Trilogy, Book One)
MORTAL DEFIANCE
(Dark Betrayal Trilogy, Book Two)
IMMORTAL GRAVE
(Dark Betrayal Trilogy, Book Three)
FLUKES
(The Flukes Series, Book One)
ON CHRISTMAS HILL
(A Christmas Hill Short Story)

*Forthcoming*

RELUCTANTLY ROYAL
(Royal Series, Book Three)

# RECKLESSLY
# *Royal*

# NICHOLE CHASE

**A V O N**
*An Imprint of* HarperCollins*Publishers*

AVON BOOKS
*An Imprint of* HarperCollins*Publishers*
10 East 53rd Street
New York, New York 10022-5299

Copyright © 2014 by Nichole Chase
Excerpt from *Suddenly Royal* copyright © 2013 by Nichole Chase
ISBN 978-0-06-231747-6
www.avonromance.com

First Avon Books mass market printing: April 2014

Avon Trademark Reg. U.S. Pat. Off. and in Other Countries, Marca Registrada, Hecho en U.S.A.
HarperCollins® is a registered trademark of HarperCollins Publishers.

Printed in the U.S.A.

10 9 8 7 6 5 4 3 2 1

For Jonathan,
my dashing rogue in not so shiny armor.

# ONE

THERE WOULDN'T BE more press outside of Rousseau Manor if Queen Elizabeth herself was planning to parade around in her panties while singing the British national anthem. I peeked out the curtain of the top floor when the doorbell chimed—another delivery of wedding gifts for the soon-to-be-married couple. I took a deep breath and let the curtain fall closed.

I wasn't sure why I was feeling antsy as my brother's wedding drew near. Turning back to the mirror in the guest bathroom, I traced the bags under my eyes with my fingers and sighed. I brushed the stray blond hair out of my face. The blue of my eyes looked pale, almost gray in the sterile bathroom light. I hadn't slept much in the last week, trying to keep the wedding stress from landing on my brother's or Samantha's shoulders. They'd been tying up loose ends at the Future Bird Trust and attending to the immediate needs of their estates and royal duties. I knew they were worried about leaving too much for me and Max, my brother, to handle while they were away for their month-long honeymoon. It annoyed me, even though I knew they were doing it out of love, but it felt like they didn't think I would be able to handle the responsibility.

It wasn't just the lack of sleep that had me down, though. As people RSVP'd and sent in joint gifts I was constantly reminded that I had no date for the wedding; no one guaranteed to dance with me or to sneak away with me if we got bored. It *bothered* me. For the last few years I had all but ignored men, kept them at a distance. I hadn't kissed anyone in so long I was beginning to doubt I ever had. My cousins were having babies and I still had my V card. It was getting to be ridiculous. And as I got older it felt more like a burden than something to be proud of—an embarrassing story to have to explain to a potential lover.

Laughter from down the hall derailed my pity party. I had things to do, and the last thing I wanted to have happen was for Sam to worry about me. Practicing a smile in the mirror, I washed my hands and brushed the hair out of my face. It wasn't that I didn't love Sam or that I minded setting everything up—in fact I loved doing it all— it was just that my loneliness had been brought into sharp relief as lovebirds and cartoon hearts circled my head.

I'd scheduled a spa day for me, Sam, and Jess. It was something to help get us ready for the wedding and, even more importantly, to keep Sam out of the public eye. The country was overbrimming with paparazzi, salivating for wedding pictures. Despite her increasing comfort level with being in the public eye, I didn't want her to be stressed before the wedding. Getting married should be a happy occasion, not something burdened with strangers and roadblocks.

I made my way down the hall and peeked into the doorway and felt my smile become real. Samantha's feet twitched and she muttered curses under her breath as the technician worked. I covered my mouth and tried to not laugh. Jess was silently filming the whole ordeal with her phone. Probably blackmail to counter the video Samantha took at Jess's bachelorette party.

"Suck it up, cupcake!" I walked in and poked one of her flailing legs. "You don't want to look like you have hairy caterpillars attached to your face on your wedding day."

"This is torture!"

"Threading is the best way to go. You're going to look amazing." I patted her knee.

"I'm going to kill you both." Sam turned her head to look at us. "Ouch!"

"My apologies, Duchess." The technician moved to the other eyebrow. "Try to stay still and it will hurt less."

I shook my head but took a couple of steps out of Sam's reach. "Stop being a big baby."

"Just think, after this you still have your bikini waxing!" Jess laughed.

A loud grunt of anger was our only answer.

When the technician finally finished, she left the room to go get the wax ready. I handed Sam a bottle of water and checked our schedule on my phone. I was debating switching the times for the massage and the bikini waxing. Maybe it would be best to do the bikini wax after the massage. That way Sam would be relaxed. Of course, if I did that, it would probably ruin that after-massage glow. Best to leave it the way it was.

"Cathy, when I said I didn't want to go to the clubs or have male strippers, that didn't mean I wanted to have my skin peeled off my body instead." Sam narrowed her eyes at me.

"You said a spa day would be great." I laughed when she threw a pillow at me. "Relax. We're doing fun stuff tomorrow. We're just getting the torture out of the way first."

"Oh, what are we doing?" Jess leaned forward. "Tell me it's something crazy and fun."

"I'm not telling." I shook my head. "Just get through today and it will all be worth it."

"I'm not sure anything is worth what you're putting me through today." Sam mock-glared.

"Wah. Shut it and take it like a woman!" I stood up and clapped my hands together. "Ready to get waxed?"

"No. Definitely not and never will be." Sam shook her head vehemently. "No one's going to be seeing that anyway." Sam looked at me with pleading eyes. She'd gotten really good at them.

"Hello? Honeymoon, private island, your new husband?" Jess leaned back in her seat. "You don't want to look like the bride of Bigfoot."

"Hey!" Sam reached over and shoved Jess's knee.

I snorted. "Alex wouldn't notice. My brother is disgustingly besotted."

"My luck someone would get a picture of me running around in a bikini and title it something unimaginative but equally horrible, like the 'America's Hairy Duchess.'" Sam drank more of her water.

"Oh! What about 'Destitute Duchess Forgoes Wax and Razors'?" Jess laughed.

"Har, har." Sam snorted.

"And that's why we're taking care of it all today." I grabbed Sam's arm. "Enough stalling."

"Let's do this!" Jess stood up and grabbed Sam's other arm.

"You two are cruel and I never should have introduced you." Sam stood up and pulled her arms away from us.

Jess and I placed bets on how Samantha would react to the waxing procedure. I felt sure that Sam would hold it together but Jess didn't agree. Thankfully, Sam didn't burst out of the room naked and half waxed at any point, which is exactly what Jess thought would happen. This meant I won the right to not help Sam if she had to go to the bathroom in the wedding dress. Being crammed in a stall, holding yards of fabric while my sister-in-law relieved herself, really wasn't something I wanted to do if it could be helped. Instead when she came out of the room she went straight to the kitchen for wine. That was something I could get behind.

Over the last two years I had become very comfortable with Rousseau Manor so I headed straight for the wine cellar while Sam and Jess got glasses. A couple of years ago, I wouldn't have known where the kitchen was, much less the wine, but with the reinstatement of the missing royal families I'd become acquainted with Rousseau very well. When Sam took permanent residence at Rousseau it had meant lots of movie nights, cookouts, and shenanigans. I looked toward the cupboard for food, but didn't have to worry. Margie, the cook, had left out a tray of snacks for us to munch on.

In triumph, I held up the bottle of red I had found, while Jess cheered.

"Gimme, gimme, gimme." Sam held her hand out. "This has been a traumatic day. I need something to get me through the rest of it."

"Pansy." I handed her a glass and poured her a hefty amount. "And next is a massage. Not exactly painful."

"Pansy, my ass! Tell me again why I couldn't just get my eyebrows waxed? They feel raw." Sam touched her forehead gently before she drank some of her wine. "And don't even get me started about the torture I just went through. I would have rather been put on the rack in the Tower of London." She winced.

"Threading is the best. Your eyebrows look fantastic." I didn't mention that there would be thousands of people taking her picture or that it would be plastered across every magazine in the world. She was already antsy about the guest list and normal stuff—she didn't need to worry about the media attention.

Samantha's phone beeped and she pulled it out of her pocket. She frowned before typing quickly.

"What's wrong?" I leaned forward to peek at her screen.

"The friend I hired to work at the FBT is getting in early. Apparently he made a mistake booking his ticket and will be here tomorrow."

"Is he staying here?" I sorted through the snacks until I found a carrot stick. "We're doing the bachelorette thing tomorrow."

"I know." Sam frowned. "He was already uncomfortable about staying here, but I don't want to ask him to stay in town."

"Eh. It'll work out." I smiled and shrugged. "It always does."

"So, just a massage now?" Sam looked from me to Jess. "I could use a massage."

"Massage time for everyone." I smiled and rubbed my hands together. Sam wasn't the only one who needed to relax.

"Wait a minute! Why do you guys get massages? I'm the one that's been plucked and skinned alive." Sam frowned. "I should get all three massages myself."

"No way, Princess." I laughed when her face

froze. "What? That's what you'll be in a few days. Good-bye America's Duchess and hello America's Princess."

"And one day you'll be America's Que—" Jess was stopped by the look on Sam's face.

"Nope. Don't go there." Sam shook her head. "One thing at a time. That's a lot to swallow."

"You won't have to worry about that for a long time anyways." I put my hands on the counter.

"It's just a lot to take in." Sam sighed. "It's a lot of responsibility."

"Meh. It's worth it." Jess sat up a little straighter. "You've got Prince Yummy."

"And me!" I lifted my wineglass.

"And Cathy." Jess laughed. "Not to mention a ridiculous amount of money, awesome job, and fabulous friends."

"All true." Sam shook her head. "So you're saying I should stop my bitching."

"Exactly." I laughed.

"Look at us. I'm still in school, barely sleep, and poor Cathy hasn't had a boyfriend the entire time I've known her." Jess tipped her glass toward me.

Sam looked over at me and frowned, but I shrugged it off. "I'm picky."

"We get it, Cathy." Sam sighed. "It's hard to find someone worth the risk."

"What risk? I'm not talking about you finding a husband, just someone to spend a little time with." Jess wiggled her eyebrows. "Take the edge off. How long has it been?"

My cheeks heated and I took a sip of my wine. There was no mistaking what she meant. How had the conversation turned into a discussion about my sex life?

"Jess." Sam set her glass down. "Leave her alone. She has her reasons." I'd confided in Samantha once after a night of drinking when she asked about guys at school. It had been nice to talk to someone—especially my soon-to-be sister-in-law. She hadn't made me feel foolish for being scared of what could happen.

"What?" Jess looked between us before leaning forward. "Oh my God. You mean you haven't . . ."

"No." I shrugged and hoped I could pull off nonchalance, because it was the farthest thing from what I was actually feeling. "Too much at risk. How am I supposed to know if someone wants me for me? And if I just do it to get it over with, what if they try to use it against me? Or to manipulate me?" I thought about the photos of Alex that his ex had released, and shuddered. I'd never be able to understand how he had stayed so calm. I had been a wreck and the pictures weren't even of me. "It's not just my virginity. It could haunt me forever."

"What you need to do is find someone that doesn't care about your title." Jess narrowed her eyes.

"And how do you suggest I do that?" I leaned back in my seat. "Hand out surveys?"

"You need to find someone that isn't impressed by your tiara." Jess leaned forward eagerly. "Someone that maybe even hates your title."

"Oh. That's a great idea." I sat up. "Hi, I'm a princess. I heard you hate royalty. Want to go have sex?"

Sam laughed but Jess seemed unfazed.

"Why not? Take away the title and what are you left with?" Jess asked.

"A sexy blonde with a great sense of humor." Sam wiggled her eyebrows. "It could work."

"Right." I spun the wine in my glass. I had contemplated a one-night stand before, but I hadn't found anyone that inspired that kind of lust. I didn't want it to happen and not enjoy it. That seemed pointless. But I was getting tired of waiting for the right guy to come along . . .

"I'm just saying that if someone happened to show up that was really hot and didn't care for royalty, you should go for it." Jess shot Sam a look.

"What?" I narrowed my eyes.

"Nothing. I'm just saying you need to live a little." Jess smiled.

"You do need to have some fun." Sam popped a piece of cheese into her mouth. "You haven't done anything spontaneous or fun since . . ."

Her voice quieted, but I knew what she meant. I hadn't been to a club or party since the night Sam found out her father was dying. It had been such a scary night for everyone. That had been over a year ago, though. I hadn't done anything but go to school and family functions in that time. Other than my movie nights with Sam and Jess's bachelorette party. But that didn't really count.

"Okay. We need to find you a hottie." Jess leaned on the counter and pursed her lips. "I have a friend studying to be a neurologist. He's cute and driven."

"Um, no. I do not want to be set up with anyone. That's just weird." I shook my head. "No, no, no."

"Why not?" Sam poured more wine into her glass. "We're cool people. We know cool people."

"Yes, because cool people often need to tell people that." I laughed.

Sam snorted. "C'mon. A neurologist? Some people would think that was a serious catch."

"I always thought I wanted someone like Jess's

friend, but I don't know anymore. I just . . ." I pursed my lips. "Maybe you're right. I should just find someone to have fun. Stop worrying about the long term."

"That's not—"

"Exactly!" Jess cut Sam off. "Have some fun! Cut loose!"

"We'll see." I took a sip of my drink before going to rinse my glass and setting it in the sink. "Ready for your massages?"

"Hell yeah!" Sam drank the rest of the wine in her glass. "Time to relax."

"Then come on!" I forced a large smile. Thinking about my love life, or rather the lack of my love life, was depressing. The chances of finding someone who would love me for me were so slim, they practically didn't exist. What Alex had found with Sam was a miracle. I'd be lucky if I found someone who didn't make me want to puke when I saw them.

# TWO

"When I said I wanted to do something crazy, I didn't mean I wanted to become a stripper." Sam stood in the large formal living room, looking at the silver poles in front of her. "Be honest. Did Alex put you up to this?"

"No, but he's going to owe me." I snickered and sat down on the floor to stretch.

"You didn't hire a stripper, did you? That guy in the spandex, currently sitting in my kitchen, is not going to shake his man-pickle in my face, right?" Sam grabbed a bottle of champagne and poured us all a glass. "Because if you did, I'm going to need a lot more to drink. He looks like Gene Simmons on steroids."

I chuckled loudly. "No. I didn't hire a stripper."

"Damn." Jess winked at me.

"I thought this would be fun! Crazy and silly, and not out at clubs or at bars where people could see us." I accepted my flute from Sam and took a swallow.

"This is going to be awesome. Can you imagine Bert's face when I tell him what we did tonight?" Jess bounced on her toes a little. Her new husband would probably be thrilled.

"Did you see the teacher? He could kill us with one punch! This is going to be work! And hard." Sam narrowed her eyes.

"It's a fun class, I made sure." I leaned over, touching my head to my knee. When I sat back up Sam was glaring at me. "What?"

"Okay, Miss I-Can-Touch-My-Head-to-My-Leg. I'm sure this will be a blast." Sam laughed. "If I have a heart attack, tell Alex I loved him."

"Will do." I stretched out over the opposite leg.

"Is it just going to be us?" Jess sat down on the floor and started her own stretches.

"Nope. We have a few more people coming." I leaned forward and brushed the floor with my fingertips.

"Who else?" Sam dropped to the floor next to me.

"Friends." The doorbell rang and I hopped up off the floor. "I'll get it."

I could hear voices through the door and my smile grew. Yanking open the double doors, I threw myself at my cousin, Daniel, my face breaking into a smile. Laughing, he spun me in a circle.

"Cathy!" He kissed my cheek before setting me

back on the ground. We'd become very close over the last couple of years.

"Why don't you twirl with me like that?" Chadwick, Sam's loyal assistant, asked. They'd been openly dating for a year now, and I loved seeing them both so happy.

"Because you don't have all that blond hair to spin around." Daniel made a tsking noise. "You keep cutting it too short."

"Not to mention it's red." Chadwick rolled his eyes. "And I look like a Muppet if I don't cut it." He leaned forward and kissed my cheek.

"You look great." I led them back into the house. "And dapper as always. I'm loving the tie." I flicked the pink plaid silk with my fingers. Chadwick was my favorite shopping buddy.

"I thought you were with the guys!" Sam stood up and hugged Daniel before glaring at Chadwick. "You lied!"

"I most certainly didn't." Chadwick rolled his eyes. "We were there and now we're here."

"Yes. Too much testosterone." Daniel laughed.

"Cathy asked us to come to this first, but there was no way I was going to be here while Sam got waxed." Chadwick shuddered. "Did she hurt anyone?"

"She was very well behaved." I winked at him.

"Oh my. So you were serious about the pole

dancing?" Daniel walked around one of the poles, a hand on his chin. "This could be interesting."

"Very serious. Now go change!" The doorbell rang again. "Got it."

The guest list wasn't very long, but I'd made sure the important people would be there. Sam's surrogate mother, Patricia, arrived with Lady Adriane and Heather, the Duchess of Marion. It might seem weird to invite Adriane, one of my brother's exes, but she and Samantha got along well.

Opening the door, I threw my head back and laughed. All three of them were wearing feathered boas in bright colors.

"We brought one for everybody!" Patricia held up a bag.

"You have no idea just how perfect that is." I hugged them each before leading them back to the room. I pulled a bright pink boa out of the bag and wrapped it around my shoulders. Our instructor had turned up the music and was doing hip gyrations near one of the poles. He totally did look like Gene Simmons, minus the creepy face paint.

"Oh my." Patricia put a hand up to her heart.

"Oh my doesn't cover it." Heather cocked her head to the side. "I think I've been married for too long. I don't remember ever seeing a man move like that."

"You didn't go to the right places." Adriane

wiggled her eyebrows before heading for the center of the room and stretching. I'd told everyone to bring workout clothes so there wouldn't be any wardrobe crisis, and it seemed that constant nagging and list making was paying off. Everyone had brought what they needed for the night.

"Let's get ready to shake this house!" The instructor clapped his hands together, his French accent making it hard to understand him. "Loosen up! Get your blood pumping!"

"What did he say we're going to do to my house?" Samantha leaned toward me.

"Just move!" The music filled the room, making the windows shake. I'd forgotten how much I loved to dance. It didn't take long before I was letting go of Princess Catherine and dancing like Cathy—and it felt good. Free and fun. I bumped butts with Patricia, wrapped a boa around Chadwick, and laughed as Daniel did the YMCA.

I downed another glass of champagne while joking with Jess about the wedding and the new moves we were learning. Tonight was my one chance to relax and have a good time, so I wasn't going to play it safe. There were no reporters or photographers to catch me in a bad light. It was liberating. I could already feel a nice buzz from the alcohol and was enjoying myself more than I had in years. Good friends and fun would do that for a person.

Samantha was watching Patricia wiggle and shake while trying not to laugh, and almost knocked over the table with the snacks and drinks. I saved the bottle of champagne while Jess grabbed the tray of cheese. Deciding it would be better to consume the alcohol than risk it being wasted on the floor, I poured the rest of the bottle into my glass before going back to the dance floor.

Once we were all loosened up, the instructor started teaching us simple swings on the pole. He made sure we put our hands in the right place and were ready to hold our weight. He adjusted my leg before rushing off to help at the pole next to mine. Giggles fought to escape my mouth as I watched Chadwick and Daniel try to push Patricia up the pole. Chadwick's normally perfectly coifed hair was mussed as he tried to coach her into wrapping her legs around the metal shaft. Daniel was making obscene faces while he propped her up with his back.

"I can't do it! I can't do it!" Her voice was high as she gripped the pole tightly. "Stop trying to bend me in *unnatural* ways!"

I couldn't help the laugh that escaped me as I watched the three of them crash back to the ground. Hurrying to their sides, I helped untangle their limbs before helping them off the ground. Patricia was red-cheeked, and Daniel, who had borne the brunt of her weight, made a beeline for the drinks.

"Well, that was the first time I've been under a woman." He took a large gulp of his drink before turning to whisper loudly to Samantha, "And I think it will be the last time too."

Patricia decided to watch the rest of the class while shouting jokes, but the instructor didn't let the rest of us escape. He wasn't a difficult teacher, but he did try to teach us some of the moves instead of letting us just swing around on the pole. I gripped the cold metal firmly in my hands and lifted myself from the ground before leaning backward and letting go so that only my legs were holding my weight.

Sam whistled and I gave her a thumbs-up that was actually a thumbs-down because of the way I was hanging. The thought made me laugh and my grip on the pole loosened, letting me slide down closer to the floor.

"Don't distract me! I'm upside down." I giggled.

"You're also drunk." Sam tilted a little, unsteady on her feet.

"You're just jealous that I can pole dance." I

stuck my tongue out at her, which made her laugh.

I was a bit sloshed, but I wasn't going to tell Sam that. My legs slipped and I slid the rest of the way to the ground, my head stopping my fall. Maybe I was drunker than I thought. The doorbell rang as I scrambled up from my spot on the floor.

"I've got it!" Chadwick took off to the front door, his steps a little too loud.

Backing away from the pole, I took a running jump and grabbed directly in the middle. I used my momentum to swing my legs high in the air. Making sure I had a good grip on the pole, I spread my legs into a split.

"Wow." A deep voice broke into my thoughts and I looked up. A man was standing next to Chadwick, wearing a backpack and carrying a large duffel bag. His dark eyes ran over my body and I shivered, which was a bad thing. My hands slipped and I fell, crashing to the floor with a loud *oof*.

"Are you okay?" Sam ran over and helped me stand up, but I wasn't feeling any pain. In fact, I was feeling awesome. Looking past Sam's shoulder, I smiled at the hottie and waved. He was perfection, from his messy dark hair down to his scuffed boots. And exactly what we needed to end the night with a bang.

"Heeey yooou. I don't remember hiring a stripper, but boy am I glad you showed up." I let Sam help me up to my feet and wondered why she was making a choking sound. I slapped her on the back, worried. "Are you okay?"

"I'm fine. Fine!" Sam barked a laugh. "That's not—"

"Good! Because it looks like I outdid myself!" I turned her around with a flourish to look at the delicious man standing on the stairs. His shirt strained across his chest as he shifted his feet and I found myself thinking about tracing my fingers across those hard lines. I let my eyes run over him instead, taking in the tight plaid shirt, worn jeans, and work boots. There was nothing polished or metropolitan about him. Everything screamed outdoors. And I liked it.

"Cathy," Sam tried to stop me, but I shrugged her off and skipped up the steps.

"What are you supposed to be? A lost lumberjack?" I pulled the heavy bag out of his hands and set it on the ground. "We'll, c'mon! Someone start some music." I gyrated my hips a little and wiggled my eyebrows. "Take it off, bab-ay!"

"If you insist, gorgeous." His American accent

gave me pause as a dim memory tried to fight through the fog in my brain, but it didn't last long. His eyes stayed locked on mine as his calloused fingers worked the top couple of his buttons free. I wasn't sure if it was the alcohol, or just his deep brown eyes, but I was entranced. I didn't even notice when Sam climbed the stairs.

I couldn't look away from him as he slowly unbuttoned his shirt and exposed the skin underneath. The need to touch that tantalizing bit of flesh raced through me, and my fingers twitched. Hypnotized by the color of melted chocolate, I leaned forward. One corner of his mouth turned up into a smirk and it only added to his charm. Where it might have been a turn-off in another man, it simply added to this stripper's appeal. I smiled in response, eager for him to continue.

"God, please don't, David. I'll never be able to look at you again." She covered his hands with her own and laughed, her cheeks a bright red.

"David?" I looked at him, confused, before looking over my shoulder at Jess. She was nodding her head with wide eyes like I was supposed to remember something. "David?" I said the name again, mulling over what that could mean.

I looked down at the bag I had taken from him

and my eyes landed on his boots. It was then that a moment of clarity surged through my mind like a stampede of wild horses and I covered my mouth.

"Oh God." A wave of nausea hit me. "You're Sam's friend."

I promptly turned around and threw up into a potted plant.

# THREE

Sᴜɴʟɪɢʜᴛ sᴛʀᴇᴀᴍᴇᴅ ɪɴ through a crack in the curtains, tracing a fiery path of pain directly across my face.

"Ow." I squeezed my eyes shut. "Ow, ow, ow."

I threw my arm over my eyes and willed myself to die. Never had I ever been so hungover in my life. If it wasn't for my dire need to use the bathroom I wouldn't have moved ever again, but my bladder was not going to let that happen. Rolling over with a groan, I cracked one eye open.

On the table next to the bed was a bottle of water and two small white pills. It was like the Alcohol Gods knew exactly what I needed; or more likely, Chadwick had planned ahead. I picked up the pills and made out the aspirin brand name before tossing them back and drinking the water. With a shaky breath I swung my legs onto the floor and shuffled to the bathroom.

Without thinking, I turned on the light and

whimpered. Flailing around blindly, I hit the switch and leaned against the cool tile of the bathroom wall. Turning so I could press my cheek against the cold surface, I sighed. Why did I drink so much last night? When did I drink enough to make me feel this bad? Sliding across the floor slowly, I made my way to the sink and splashed water on my face. I remembered the bottle of champagne and a couple of drinks. What else had I done?

Looking up into the mirror I traced the puffy circles and shadows under my eyes. Running my fingers up to the top of my head I gingerly probed the knot under my hair. When had that happened? Had someone hit me with a wine bottle at some point? That's what it felt like, but I doubt that had happened.

Opening the medicine cabinet I got out my toothbrush and toothpaste I had stashed there the other day and tried to remember what had happened the night before. I remembered feather boas, Gene Simmons, and Sam knocking a table over. As I tried to get rid of the awful taste in my mouth, the image of a man filled my mind. A stripper? I spit the toothpaste out and felt my brow furrow. He was certainly hot enough to be a stripper, but I hadn't hired anyone to take their clothes off. The press would have a field day if that story got out. So why did I remember a really sexy man standing in Sam's living room?

I dragged my sorry tail back into the guest room and rummaged around in my overnight bag. I refused to turn on the light. My head was pounding and even the memory of the sun made me want to cry. Pulling out a pair of jeans, I slid them on and found a shirt. My head hurt too bad to pull my hair out of my face so instead I left it down.

Grabbing a pair of sunglasses out of my purse, I slid them on and gave myself a pep talk. I had too much to do for the wedding to hide in bed all day. Though it sounded like a really good idea.

I didn't hear anyone else moving about in the family wing as I made my way downstairs, so I hoped that everyone was still asleep. I needed more water and was not ready to talk to anyone. There was a knocked-over plant on the landing of the stairs and I knelt down to scoop up the dirt.

"Want some help?" The deep voice startled me so much that I stumbled off the step I was perched on and my sunglasses fell off my face. I looked up into the dark brown eyes that had haunted my thoughts this morning and gasped. My headache was forgotten as I stood there staring at him. He was leaning against the kitchen doorway, a coffee cup in one hand and a broom handle and dustpan in the other. "It took forever to find a broom in this place."

"I thought you were a dream." I instantly regretted the words.

"You dreamed about me?" His mouth pulled up into a delicious smirk.

"Um, no." I brushed some of the hair out of my face and searched for words. "No. I, um. I don't remember much about last night. It's a bit hazy. And I certainly didn't dream about you."

"Well that's a shame." He winked at me. Setting his cup down on a small table, he handed me the broom and knelt down with the dustpan. "So you don't remember asking me to take my clothes off?"

I stared down into his handsome face while my mouth gaped like a fish. Oh my good God. No wonder I had thought he was a stripper. I had asked him to take his clothes off. If I had been alone I would have beat my head against the wall. An image of Sam stopping his hands fluttered through my mind and my cheeks heated. I really had told him to take his clothes off.

Wrinkles appeared in the corner of his eyes and he chuckled. "I'd say forget about it, but it appears you already have."

"I—I think it's coming back to me now." I swept the dirt into the dustpan and chewed on my lip.

"I'm really sorry. I don't usually drink that much. In fact I don't think I've ever drunk that much before. Ever. And never will again."

He poured the dirt back into the pot. When he stood my eyes lined up with the collar of his shirt, and I tried to not notice the way the material strained across his chest. My gaze trailed upward, over his scruffy jaw, nose, and sharp cheekbones to meet his warm stare.

"David Rhodes." He held his hand out to me, his eyes running over my face.

"Yeah, I remember that now." I wrapped my fingers around his. "I'm Cathy."

"Nice to meet you, Cathy." His fingers squeezed mine and his eyes twinkled with mischief. "Again."

"I'll never live last night down, will I?" I laughed.

"Not if I can help it." His fingers tightened on mine briefly before he let go. "It's not often that a princess orders me to take my clothes off." His voice took on a distant tone.

"I'm just Cathy here." I frowned. I hated being reminded of my title. As if I ever forgot. And the way he had said it—almost like he found the idea distasteful.

"Here?" He raised an eyebrow.

"At Sam's place." I shrugged. "Here I don't have

to be Princess Catherine." Why was I explaining myself to him?

"Because she's American? Or not really royalty?" There was no mistaking the defensive tone.

"Because she's Sam." I narrowed my eyes. My headache was starting to make its presence known once again. "Titles have nothing to do with it."

"Okay." David nodded his head as if I had answered correctly.

"Are you testing me?" I frowned. "Because I have a killer hangover and am not really in the mood."

"I just wanted to make sure you really liked Sam. She talks about you a lot." He shrugged.

"I love Sam." Insulted, I took a step away from him. "She doesn't need you to show up right before her wedding and start taking a poll. She's quite able to take care of herself and really good at keeping assholes in check."

"Looks like she may have taught you a thing or two." Rubbing the back of his neck with his free hand, he smiled sheepishly. "Sorry."

"Sorry that you're an asshole or for insinuating that I would use Sam?" I felt my upper lip twitch.

"Right now, both." He shrugged. "Sam's like my little sister. I just wanted to make sure she really was happy over here. It's really different from back in Minnesota."

"I'm busting my hump to make sure her wedding goes off without a hitch and that she's not bothered by any of the stressful bits." Crossing my arms over my chest I glared at him. "Everyone wants Sam to be happy."

Leaning over, he picked up my sunglasses and offered them to me. "I'm sorry. Truce?"

I took the glasses from him. "Then I hope there is more coffee where you got that." I pointed at his cup. "Because I'm going to need it."

"It so happens that there is a pot full, minus one cup, in the kitchen." He walked over and opened the door he had come through.

The smell of the coffee did not make my stomach turn, which I took as a good sign. Walking to the cabinets I grabbed a mug and poured myself a cup. The stool at the island scraped along the floor as David took a seat. I could feel his eyes on me as I whipped up some foam and made a small bull's-eye on top. I wasn't an artist like my brothers, but I could give a good barista a run for her money. Goose bumps erupted along my arms and I berated myself for caring. Distractions weren't welcome right now, nor were attractive men and their preconceived judgments.

"So," I said turning around. My mother had taught me that anger usually came from confusion, and as much as it killed me to be pleasant when I really felt like a piece of poop, I'd try. For Sam. Not because David was incredibly delicious to look at. "What's your issue with Lilaria?" I was pretty fond of my country and found it hard to imagine anyone could dislike it so quickly.

"I'm not sure I have a problem with Lilaria, exactly." He shrugged. "It's just so different from where Sam and I come from." He looked around awkwardly. "Speaking of Sam, any idea when she'll be up? I need to ask her some questions before the wedding. I doubt I'll have much time to talk to her afterward."

"Let her sleep a little longer. She has a big day ahead of her." I frowned. "And it's really not that different here. She has a family that loves her and she still works with birds."

"Yeah." He looked around the kitchen, and I tried to imagine it from his point of view. Rousseau wasn't the largest home of the royal families, but Alex had told me about the tiny house Sam had shared with Jess.

"How long did it take you to find a broom this morning?" I decided I'd try to make him more comfortable. Maybe that would help his defensive attitude. "I came over to visit not long after Sam moved in. It took us ten minutes to figure out how to use the oven."

"Roughly fifteen minutes." He smiled at me. "Maybe someone will draw me a map."

"I bet Chadwick already has." Turning away from him, I poured myself another cup of coffee. I really needed more water than coffee, but I'd grown accustomed to the stuff since I had been spending so much time with Sam.

"He must have been the one that left the coffee-pot ready for this morning." David lifted his cup and frowned. Standing up, he came to the coffee-pot to pour another cup.

"Him or Margie." I sipped from my cup and tried to ignore how close he was standing next to me.

"Margie?" He looked down at me with his dark eyes and I understood why I had drunkenly asked him to undress. The man was gorgeous.

"Uh, the cook." I took another sip of my drink and forced myself to stop contemplating how the angle of his cheeks highlighted his eyes.

"The cook." He sighed and leaned against the counter. "How many people work here?"

"Not many." I shrugged. "Maybe ten? Too many people make Sam uncomfortable."

"Ten." He shook his head. "That seems like 'many' to me."

"Think of it like a resort. They're just here to keep things going and to make sure you have what you need." I didn't point out that there was twice that many at D'Lynsal, and ten times that many who worked in the palace.

He shifted his shoulders and frowned into his cup. He looked so uncomfortable I felt a twinge of sympathy for him. It was hard to leave your normal life behind and do anything different. And he was here because Sam trusted him with her home and the Future Bird Trust, which had become her baby over the last year.

"You know, it's not so bad." I smiled at him. "You'll be so busy with the FBT you'll hardly notice anything else, but you won't have to worry about washing your clothes or cooking dinner."

"It doesn't sound that bad when you put it that way." Something warm filled his eyes when he looked down at me. "You know, you don't really seem like a princess."

"Wow. You're really bad at compliments, you know that?" I laughed. "Besides, how many princesses do you know?"

"Well, not many." He chuckled. "You, and I guess Sam will be one soon."

"Exactly." I shook my head. "Speaking of the morning grump, she should be up soon." I looked down at my watch. We had a lot to accomplish and very little time to do it in.

"I'm up. There better be more coffee." Sam shuffled into the kitchen, her eyes half lidded. "And if you call me Princess, I will throat-punch you."

In fear for my life, I turned to open the cupboard to get a cup for her and face-planted into David's chest. My coffee splashed onto his shirt and I cringed.

"Yow." He grunted and pulled at his shirt.

"Sorry!" I spun and set my cup down and picked up a rag from the counter. I rubbed at his shirt in an attempt to soak up some of the hot liquid. "Sorry. So sorry!"

"It's okay."

"It's not okay! Are you burned?" Without thinking I lifted his shirt to make sure he didn't have any blisters. As soon as I exposed his skin I gulped. Despite a red mark, his tanned chest and stomach looked perfect. Too perfect. Perfect enough to make me consider suggesting taking the shirt off all the way. You know, so I could rinse it, not just because I suddenly wanted to watch him walk around half naked.

Okay, I could be honest with myself and admit that I liked what I was seeing. Hadn't I already decided I wanted to see him naked last night? Of course, I had been drunk. Heat rushed over my body and I froze, my fingers still on his skin. I may have had too much to drink last night, but I wasn't drunk right now.

"I'm fine." His voice rumbled out of his chest under my touch. His hand caught my wrist with gentle fingers and I looked up into his warm eyes. He smiled at me, even though I had just dumped steaming liquid on him.

"Um, I suppose you want to take care of this yourself." I handed him the rag and turned around to hide my pink cheeks. I had just rubbed all over his chest like some kind of hormonal idiot. I looked for my coffee but it was gone and I scanned the room. Sam's wide eyes watched me over the rim of my cup as she sipped the leftover contents.

"You were taking too long and blocking my way to the pot." She shrugged, but her eyes were amused. Which was very wrong considering that she had just woken up and had only a little coffee. I must have looked like a real idiot.

"Whatever keeps you from killing everyone with your grumpy face." I shrugged and walked over to the sink. When had I become so incredibly clumsy? And since when did I rub all over men in Sam's kitchen? What was wrong with me?

"We're going to need more coffee if we're avoiding death glares." Sam scooted between us and filled a new mug with coffee. "We've got a lot to do."

"I'm going to change." David jerked his head toward the door. "Do you have a little time to talk before you go?"

"Sure." Sam answered. "After coffee."

"Got it." David smiled at us. "See you around, Cathy."

"Bye." I smiled at him awkwardly. As soon as he walked out of the door, Sam burst out laughing. "What?"

"You sure are determined to get his clothes off." She shook her head.

"I am not!" My words were a little too loud. Great. I sounded guilty. "It was an accident."

"Right." She sat down on one of the stools. "That's why you were busy stroking his chest a few minutes ago."

"I was not *stroking* anything. Oh God, I had stroked his chest. I was making sure I hadn't hurt him."

"Uh-huh. Sure." Sam rolled her eyes. "There was definitely no stroking going on in my kitchen just a few minutes ago. Nope. Not at all. And certainly no sexual tension or gooey puppy-dog eyes."

"Shut up and drink your coffee." I glared at her. "I did not give him puppy-dog eyes."

"Whatever you say." She hummed to herself as she poured more creamer in her cup.

My phone beeped and I picked it up. Selene, my assistant, had sent a text to let me know a car was on the way. I had to get back to the palace for a meeting and to check some of the last-minute wedding plans.

"I've got to go." I stood up and stretched. "I'll see you tonight?"

"You know, you really didn't have to do as much for the wedding as you have." Sam frowned.

"Hush. I like doing it." I smiled. "It's fun to see all of the little details come together."

She looked up at me and smiled. "Thank you."

"You're welcome." I rinsed my cup out and grabbed a bottle of water from the fridge. "I need to go. My car should be here any minute."

"Go. I'll see you later." Sam made shooing motions toward the door. "And I won't tell David you think he's hot."

It wasn't very ladylike, but I shot her the bird. If there was one thing I had learned about Sam and Jess over the last year, it was that they loved to see me squirm.

"Love you too," she hollered after me as I pushed through the door. I just laughed. My brother had done well for himself.

# FOUR

$\mathcal{P}$ICKING UP THE flowers, I frowned. They were the wrong color. Again. Selene had even taken pictures to the florist to show them what we were looking for and they still used the wrong flowers.

"Was there a problem getting the ones the duchess requested?" I looked at the woman across the counter from me.

"We couldn't order enough and thought this would be a good alternative." She twisted the paper in her hands.

"You've had the flower order for months." I smiled. Mother had taught me you could get away with a lot more by smiling when you said it, and this woman was already a nervous wreck.

"Yes, ma'am. But there was a problem with the delivery truck and the shipment arrived in poor condition. We were able to receive these on short notice."

"Ah." I nodded my head like I wasn't frustrated. "Well, in that case, they will work just fine."

It wasn't that I was mad. I just wanted everything to be perfect. The last thing I wanted was for Sam to see her flowers and be upset that they weren't what she picked out.

The rest of the appointment went well. The centerpieces were being made and stored in one of the large walk-in refrigerators. Food was being prepared and the bakers had begun working on the cake and cupcakes. I shook my head as I looked at the cupcakes that covered a worktable. Alex and Sam hadn't been able to decide on a cake flavor, so had opted for several different types of cupcakes. It had actually been an ingenious idea, because it meant we could also make separate trays for guests with food allergies.

"The tailor delivered the dresses last night." Selene looked at her clipboard as we walked through the palace. I had tried to get her to use a tablet, but she didn't care for electronics. Of course, she was older than my mother, so it shouldn't surprise me.

"Were there any problems?"

"No. Everything was as it should be." She marked something on her papers before pointing at the main entrance. "Chadwick has requested that we have an extra guard at the front gate. He's worried about the guests' arrival."

"I think Alex already took care of that. Would you double-check for me?"

"Of course." The scribble of her pencil made me smile. Selene had been with me from the time I was old enough to start attending official functions—before my father had passed away.

One of Selene's junior secretaries stopped me with a folder of papers. I flipped through them quickly. Tabitha was a small, petite woman, and while she was thorough, something about her screamed power hungry. It was in the little things, the sharp look in her eyes, the constant volunteering, the way she tried to fit into my schedule. Selene felt that she would make a good replacement for her one day, but I had serious doubts.

"The list is fine, except for this name." I tapped the name of a reporter from America. "He ran a very unflattering piece on the duchess a couple of months ago and I'm not going to let him rip apart their wedding day just for kicks."

"Yes, ma'am. I'll make a note of it." Tabitha bobbed her head and hurried on down the hallway in a different direction.

"It seems like most everything has been taken care of," I said.

"You've done an excellent job of seeing to everything." Selene smiled at me.

"Oh! What about the ring bearer and flower girl? Did their gifts come in? Sam wants to give them to the children at the rehearsal dinner." I flipped through my e-mail on my phone, looking for a confirmation of delivery.

"They are wrapped and in the duchess's room."

Samantha hardly ever used her room at the palace. If she was staying overnight you would find her in Alex's room, even if he wasn't. I'd say it was disgusting the way they loved each other, but to be honest that would just be jealousy talking. I wanted something like what they had but knew better than to think it would really happen to me.

"Excellent. She will be able to use her room? We haven't put everything on the bed, right?" Sam might not agree with me, but she wasn't spending the night with Alex right before they got married. I'd sleep in front of her door if I had to. I wanted him to see her walking down the aisle in her wedding gown and feel the full impact. Most people didn't find true love; they had been lucky. Far luckier than I was likely to be. I'd never be able to trust that someone wanted me for me, not just what I could get them.

"Of course not. She will be able to get in her own bed." Selene cracked a smile. "If you can keep her there." The staff at the palace thought it was funny that Sam snuck into Alex's room and vice versa. Eventually it became a loud secret. No one openly talked about it, but they all knew. Now Sam didn't even try to hide it. She just came and went as she wanted, though the palace's official stance was that they had separate rooms when the media asked.

"I've already bought the super glue and extra door lock." I laughed. Sam had given me an evil look when I told her she had to stay in her room the night before the wedding. I knew it was an old tradition, but it was something we had upheld in our family. Plus, I was a romantic. They'd thank me later.

"Oh, your mother would like to see you tonight before dinner."

"That's fine. I think we can work in a little additional time." Several of the visiting royals and dignitaries would be here soon and a welcome dinner had been set up. We rounded a corner and passed several of the rooms allocated for guests. "Oh, do we have any extra rooms available?"

"I'll have to check. Have we forgotten someone?" She flipped through the pages.

"Sort of. Samantha has a houseguest and he's coming to the wedding." I thought over the floor plan. "If we don't have any guest rooms left, put him in the family wing. David Rhodes."

"He is a close friend of the duchess?" Selene made notes.

"Yes. They went to college together and he will be managing the hands-on portion of the FBT while Alex and Sam are gone." When we got to the small room I used as my office, I kicked my shoes off. I should have worn flats, but sometimes appearances really did matter. At least when I needed to make a good impression. Walking over to the small fridge behind my desk I grabbed another bottle of water. I had already drained the first one. My head was pounding and all I wanted to do was take a nap. "Do we have any aspirin?"

"I'll go get some for you." She set her clipboard down on her desk. "Do you need anything else?"

"Maybe a snack." A little food might help settle my stomach as well. "Nothing heavy, please."

"I'll be right back." She closed the door behind her and I fell into my seat with a sigh. Stupid, stupid, stupid. Why had I drunk so much last night? Rubbing at my temples, I closed my eyes and tried to will the queasy feeling away.

A knock on my door gave me a start that was quickly followed by irritation. I should have an hour free to catch up on e-mails.

"Come in." Sitting up straighter I forced a smile.

"I thought you might need this." Chadwick

smiled at me and held up a sports drink. "Electrolytes."

"I'd kiss you but I might puke if I get up." Sighing, I leaned back in my chair.

"Please don't get up then." He closed the door behind him gently before taking the cap off the drink and handing it to me.

"You're amazing." I sipped at the orange-flavored drink and closed my eyes. Selene was amazing and we got along swimmingly, but there was a maternal feel to our relationship. I supposed that was to be expected when she was the one who explained tampons to me.

"I figured you'd been drinking water all day, but needed something a little better." He sat down in the seat across from me. "You doing okay?"

"Do I look like I'm doing okay?" I frowned.

"Well, you always look marvelous, but to those of us that know you, I can tell you're not feeling well." He propped his leg up on his knee and leaned back in his chair. "Do you remember much of last night?"

"Bits and pieces." I scrunched up my nose. "Very unfortunate pieces."

"I'm proud of you."

"Why?" I frowned. Surely he didn't mean when I asked David to take his clothes off or when

I threw up in a potted plant. "I'm computing at half power today."

"You let yourself have fun last night. I don't remember the last time I saw you so relaxed."

"I relax," I protested. "And really, I'm paying for last night's fun."

"Meditating in the garden is not what I mean. You're twenty-one! You should be having fun." He laughed at my expression. "Maybe not quite that much fun, but you know what I mean."

"Chadwick, you know how busy I am." I started to shake my head but thought better of it. "And I can't afford to have people see me like I was last night."

"You can't afford to not have any fun either." He frowned at me. "I know how hard you've worked on this wedding. I know how hard you work at school. You need to be yourself and not worry about upsetting anyone."

I sighed. There wasn't much arguing with him when he decided to turn into a big brother.

"Don't sigh at me, missy. I'm not telling you to give yourself liver damage. I'm just pointing out that Cathy is just as good as Princess Catherine. You don't have to be one or the other."

I looked at him, considering what he was saying. I just didn't know how to be both. Not anymore.

There was a light tap on the door and Selene came in with a tray and a bottle of aspirin.

"Hello!" She smiled at the redhead sitting across from me.

"How are you, Selene?" Chadwick stood up and moved out of the way so she could set the tray on my desk.

"Very well. I sent you an e-mail this morning with some of the details of next week. Once I have the okay I can send out the schedules." She uncovered the sandwiches while she talked, and I murmured a quiet thanks.

"I'll get to it tonight." Chadwick smiled at her before turning back to me. "I'll see you later, Catherine."

"Get out of here." I hated it when he called me by my whole name. "Thanks for the drink."

"Any time." He winked at me as he left and I shook my head.

I opened my laptop and started work. I need to get things done before the dinner tonight. If I could finish early I might be able to squeeze in a quick nap so I'd be more on my game. I'd be sitting next to the younger brother of another royal family and he was handsy.

# FIVE

THE THRONGS OF people outside were astounding. Even though I had expected it, the size of the crowd was staggering. It made me nervous, and I had grown up with the constant watching eye of the media and public. I couldn't imagine how Sam must feel in this moment. Even Alex looked anxious.

"You look a little pale." I smiled over at my brother.

"I'm not pale." He flashed a wobbly smile.

"You don't look pale, you look like you're going to hurl." Max slapped Alex on the back and laughed. "Should I call for a bucket?"

"Shut up." Alex growled.

"Cold feet?" I turned to look at him.

"Of course not." He pulled at the sleeves of his tux. "Not mine anyways."

"You think Sam won't show up?" I laughed. I couldn't help it. My cocky brother was worried the love of his life would stand him up at the altar. "Sam isn't going to leave you hanging."

"I'm worried about what she'll do when she sees this crowd." Alex peeked out the curtain. I squeezed next to him and looked at the masses.

"Chadwick will keep her calm." I touched his arm.

Alex nodded sharply before wrapping an arm around my shoulders, leaning down, and kissing the top of my head. I smiled. This was something he did when he was nervous but didn't want to say that aloud. It actually worked in his favor, because to those who didn't know him, he appeared completely comfortable.

"When do we get to eat?" Max picked up a cracker from the table and popped it into his mouth. "This isn't going to cut it."

"You just had breakfast." I rolled my eyes.

"A small breakfast." He frowned. "Tiny."

I didn't take his grumpy attitude personally. He hated being in the public eye as much as, if not more than, Sam. The fact that he had agreed to be Alex's best man without a fuss was a big deal. It was a large testament to how much he loved our brother.

"There will be snacks after the ceremony." I walked over to the table and poured myself a glass of water. I needed to go downstairs soon.

"I see the motorcade." Alex's voice was quiet. One of the oldest Lilarian traditions was the ride the royal bride took through the city. Thankfully, Sam was able to do it in a car and not in a coach. However, this had meant she had to get ready at a local home before starting her ride to the palace.

"Get away from the window!" I ran over and pulled on his arm. He let me drag him over to a chair. I pushed his shoulders so that he sat, and I turned to look at Max. "Don't let him peek."

"Sure."

"I mean it, Max! If you let him peek I *will* find out. And I *will* make your life a living hell." I pointed at him.

"Breathe, Cathy. It's going to be fine." He shrugged. "I don't know why it matters anyways."

"Max," I warned. "I have to go."

"Yeah, yeah. You're welcoming her to the palace." Max waved his cracker in the air. "Blah, blah, tradition, blah, blah."

"It's fine, Cathy." Alex gave me a more normal smile. "I promise to not peek." He lifted three fingers into the air.

"Okay. I have to go." I shot Max a glare before darting out of the door. I'd have my hands full with Sam and really needed him to make sure that Alex didn't have any problems.

Selene was hurrying toward me, her clipboard clutched in her hands. When she saw me, her face relaxed. "The duchess has arrived."

"I'm coming." I reached up and touched my tiara. I'd worn a very small one so that it wouldn't in any way compete with what Sam was wearing. I didn't want to wear one at all, but it was expected that I represent my title.

The cheer of the crowd could be heard through the castle walls. Butterflies fluttered in my stomach, which made me worry even more about Sam. If I was nervous, she must be ready to run and hide. No wonder Alex was scared.

As I rounded a corner I ran into the suit-clad shoulder of a man. "Excuse me."

"Cathy?" The deep American accent made me pause.

"David?" How did I manage to keep running into him? I looked up at him and felt my stomach tumble for a completely different reason. The man cleaned up nice. "What are you doing here?"

"I'm lost." He smiled. "Chadwick only gave me a map for Rousseau."

"Catherine." Selene's voice cut into the conversation, reminding me of the time crunch.

"Come on." Grabbing his hand I pulled him with me. It would take too long to explain how to get to the seating outside. His fingers curled around mine and for some reason my mouth pulled up into a smile.

"Where are we going?" He picked up his pace to keep up with me.

"To welcome the duchess into the royal family." I winked at him.

He didn't say anything, but I saw him gulp. I squeezed his fingers to try and reassure him. Mother was waiting at the bottom of the stairs talking with one of her attendants. She looked up as we thundered down, and raised an eyebrow.

"Sorry, I was with Alex." I leaned forward to kiss her cheek. She looked amazing in a pale green dress that showed her support of the Rousseau family. It was a similar shade to the dresses Jess and I wore at Sam's wedding party. Everything had been worked around the colors of the Rousseau family crest. Thankfully, Sam liked green.

"Who is your friend?" She smiled at David.

I let go of his fingers quickly. "Mother, this is David Rhodes, Samantha's friend from Minnesota. He will be working at the FBT and staying at Rousseau while Sam and Alex are away." Angling my body toward David I smiled. "David, this is my mother, Her Royal Majesty, Queen Felecia."

I watched his face as he took in what I was telling him. There was no panic, which I had been expecting. Instead, he bowed his head and gave my mother a small smile.

"It's a pleasure to meet you," he said.

"The pleasure is mine. It's always nice to meet Sam's friends." Mother turned to me and adjusted the neckline of my dress. Years of practice kept me from rolling my eyes. "Are you ready to step outside?"

"Anyone bring a barf bag for Sam?" I joked. Mother shook her head, but I could see the love in her eyes. She was excited that Alex and Sam were finally making it official.

"I wouldn't be surprised if Chadwick doesn't have some stuffed in his pockets." David's eyes shone with mischief. "I don't believe I've ever met someone as well prepared as him."

I laughed. "They are probably color coordinated."

The sound of trumpets announced Samantha's arrival at the front door and I looked at my mom. Time for the show.

"Selene, would you mind showing David to the guest seats? He's sitting with Samantha's family." I wondered if David had been aware of the fact or not. His face had a look of surprise.

"Of course." Selene motioned for David to follow her, but his eyes lingered on me.

"Don't worry, you have a great seat." I turned away from him and took a deep breath. "Showtime."

I moved next to my mother and waited for the footmen to open the doors. The roar of the crowds was insane. I could barely hear myself thinking, but I smiled and waved. This was something the people of our country looked forward to, a time when the country united and our traditions were celebrated.

Well, and there was a healthy dose of curiosity.

Samantha's car idled in front of the stairs and the photographers who had been invited inside the gates snapped pictures at inhuman speed. To my utter relief Sam was laughing in the car. Her face was relaxed and she looked genuinely happy. A thousand pounds of worry lifted from my shoulders and I took a deep breath.

Two footmen dressed in the finest palace livery opened the back door of the sedan and helped Chadwick, Patricia, and Jess out of the car. Jess was wearing a long satin dress similar to mine. Her hair hung loosely down her back and she looked every inch the royal bridesmaid. Stepping to the side, she reached in and took Samantha's bouquet before moving so that Chadwick could step forward. As I watched, my best friend stepped from the car to the collective roar of the crowd.

Goose bumps erupted along my arms and I

had never been more proud of Sam. With a slow turn, she waved to the people inside the gates and peering over the walls. She nodded at the cameras and posed for the photographers. Not once did she look nervous or upset. It was as if she had stepped into her role as princess with ease.

And she looked every inch the part. I had wanted the full effect, jewels, lace, and a train that went for miles, but instead what she wore was so Sam, I couldn't imagine anything more perfect. The dress was simple, the pleated A-line skirt skimmed the ground and the rhinestone belt gave it just enough glam to make it seem like a fairy tale. The dress was technically strapless but we had gotten around that particular requirement with a sheer top that covered her shoulders and had a piece of lace from her mother's wedding veil sewn to the shoulder. She had refused to wear a veil that covered her face—something to do with going into the marriage with her eyes wide open—but she did have a very simple one in the back that matched her train in length.

Jess returned the bouquet to Sam before adjusting the train so that it lay flat. Patricia was a step behind the bride as they climbed the stairs and stopped in front of me and my mother. Sam stopped and curtsied; the entire time, the whir of cameras could be heard.

"Welcome today, to the family of D'Lynsal." Mother stepped forward and kissed each of Sam's cheeks.

The roar of the crowd was deafening and Sam turned to wave, her carefree style exactly what the waiting people wanted. As we entered the palace, we all turned once more, waving at the cameras before closing the doors.

"Oh for the love of all that is holy, I have never been so nervous in my life." Patricia fanned at her face with her hands and Chadwick directed her to a small bench.

"You look amazing." I touched Sam's dress gingerly. "It's absolutely perfect."

"You've seen it a hundred times now!" Sam laughed.

"Yes, but not like this. Not all done up and ready." I felt the tears gathering in my eyes.

"Don't you dare cry!" Sam pointed at me. "Don't. You. Dare."

"I'm not going to cry." My lip wobbled. "Why would I cry?"

"Because you're an adorable, sentimental lady." Sam leaned forward to hug me and I jumped backward.

"Don't hug me! I don't want to get makeup on your dress."

"Oooh. Didn't think of that." Sam stood up and looked down at her skirt. "It's pretty white."

"You look lovely." Mother stepped forward to grasp Sam's free hand. "And you handled that crowd wonderfully."

"Thank you." Sam laughed. "I just imagined they were a class full of students excited about birds."

Jess groaned. "God, you are such a dork."

"Hey, it worked!" She swatted at her friend with her bouquet.

"I'll take it. Whatever gets you through today." I adjusted her veil.

"How is Alex?" Sam looked at me with big eyes. She hadn't seen him since the rehearsal dinner the night before.

"He's waiting on you." I smiled. "Are you ready?"

She took a deep breath. "I'm ready."

"Then let's do this." I looked over at Chadwick, who was talking into an earpiece.

"They're ready." My stomach fluttered in excitement. After all the work, planning, and stress, the moment had come to see if it had all been worth it. And from the smile on Sam's face, I was pretty sure I'd managed to pull it all together.

"Alex is ready?" Sam reached up and touched the tiara on her head and took a slow breath.

"Yes. He is in place." Chadwick took a step in front of Sam. "This is going to be over so quickly, you'll barely be able to remember it."

"And the only thing that matters is you and Alex." Jess touched her friend's shoulder.

"Guys." Sam laughed. "I'm fine. Really. I'm just ready to get this over with and start the reception."

"Did you drug her?" I leaned close to Chadwick and lowered my voice.

"No. Though I did come prepared just in case." He winked at me. "She genuinely woke up this morning ready to go. I'm a little worried that she might drag Patricia down the aisle."

"Good thing the children will be walking in front of her."

"Are you kidding? She might climb right over them." Chadwick flinched.

"I'm not going to murder children on my wedding day." Sam frowned as she fidgeted with the green and purple flowers of her bouquet.

"You mean you'd never murder children, right dear?" Mother asked.

"Oh yeah. Of course." Sam looked up. "Unless they are zombies after my brains. Then all bets are off."

"Thank you for that important information." Mother shook her head, used to Sam's random ramblings. "I have to take my seat." Stepping forward, she grabbed Sam's hand. "I'm truly honored that you're joining our family."

"That means a great deal to me." Sam kissed Mother's cheek briefly and I had to choke back tears. I remembered how scared she had been having lunch with my family so long ago. And now she was comfortable hugging us whenever the thought struck her.

"I'll see you outside." Mother turned and made her way out of sight. She would need enough time to be guided to her seat before we could take our places.

"Flowers, party members, clothing. All check." One of the coordinators looked us over like we were lambs going to slaughter. "You're ready. Remember, when you hit the outdoor stairs, wait for the music. This will be your cue to begin your march."

"Thanks." Sam smiled at the woman.

The children bearing the ring and a small flower basket were escorted into the room next to the outer door with the rest of us. Leo smiled at Sam while digging in one nostril with determination.

"You look pretty." Violet smiled up at Sam.

"Thank you, but I think you look much prettier." Sam knelt down and tweaked the little girl's nose. "I especially like the flowers in your hair."

"You can wear them if you want. I don't care." She reached up to pull at the leaves and flowers worked into her hair.

"No, no. I think it looks too pretty on you to take off now." Sam stilled the little girl's hand. "Besides, I heard that only the special flower girls are allowed to wear such pretty things in their hair."

"Oh. Well, I am special." Violet smiled at Sam, showing the gap between her two front teeth. My tiny cousin was just over two years old at this point and said everything that was on her mind.

"That you are." Sam stood up and looked at Leo. "Have you found what you're looking for?"

"I lost a popcorn kernel." He tilted his head backward. "Can you see it?"

"How did a popcorn kernel get up your nose?" I knelt down in front of him while his nanny made panicking motions behind his back.

"I was hungry!" He put his hands on his hips and glared at me. "I can't walk if I can't breathe!"

"Okay. Look up and let me check." He tilted his head so far back that he lost his balance and almost fell over a gilded chair. I grabbed his arm before he hit the ground, and held on to my irritation. Who had given the kids popcorn as a snack?

"Be still, Leo." I squinted to try and see if

there was anything within picking distance. Sure enough, there was a golden corn kernel wedged tightly in his nasal passage. "For the love of . . ."

"He really has corn in his nose?" Sam covered her mouth and I knew she was trying not to laugh.

"Yes. He has popcorn stuck in his nose." I frowned at the little boy. "How did this happen?"

"I don't know." He shrugged.

"You don't know how you got a popcorn kernel stuck in your nose?" Sam asked. "Seems like something that I would remember."

"Well," he said. "I tried to eat it but it hurt my teeth. So I thought maybe it was a rock, not popcorn. I sniffed it to see if it smelled like a rock, but it went up my nose!" He pointed at his face. "Then the harder I tried to get it the worse it got! Now I'm going to die from not being able to breathe. Maybe Chadwick should carry the rings." He looked at Sam's assistant with hope.

"Leo, please tell me you didn't put that in your nose just so you could get out of being the ring bearer." I shook my head.

"No." He crossed his arms. "I thought it was a rock. But maybe I shouldn't have to carry that silly pillow now."

"Anyone have a pair of tweezers?" I shook my head and looked around hopefully.

"I can get some." Chadwick ran from the room.

"Leo, no more sticking things in your nose, okay?" I frowned at him. "Not even your finger."

"Why?" He pursed his lips angrily.

"Because you could put something in there that could hurt you."

"Nothing can hurt me. I'm Superman." He winked at me and I had to fight not to laugh.

"Well, I'm pretty sure that the man of steel never tried to cook popcorn in his nose."

"Oh! Could he cook it in his nose?" Violet bopped happily next to me. "That would be cool."

"No, but it could hurt him." Chadwick burst into the room and handed me a small set of silver tweezers.

Gritting my teeth I reached into his nostril with the tool. It didn't take long, but I was relieved to have the little kernel out of danger's way. Tossing the kernel and the tweezers into the trash, I gratefully took the hand sanitizer Chadwick proffered. Jess handed me my bouquet and I smiled at our group.

The wedding party wasn't large, which was perfect. Sam wouldn't have a ton of people who didn't mean something to her surrounding her on her wedding day. I admired her sense of self and the way she stood up for what she wanted. This would be the first royal wedding that had not taken place in the palace chapel in hundreds of years. When Mother had started talking about plans, Sam had cleared her throat and very quietly said no. There had been only two things Sam had insisted on for her wedding day: getting married outside and having a piece of her mother's veil incorporated into her dress.

The rest she let us handle. I'd done my best to make sure she was involved, but when it boiled down to it, she just wanted to get married, have her family present, and have a good time. That had meant I'd had a lot of fun with the details, which she would probably never notice—and I was really okay with that.

As we moved into formation, we heard the opening music and I rocked on my feet a little. We would be entering the church in a somewhat different formation than Sam was used to seeing at weddings. Accompanied by Patricia, Sam would walk behind the person officiating and the two children, while Jess and I would follow behind.

"You've got this." I winked at Sam as she took a deep breath.

"As long as Alex is at the end of the aisle, nothing else matters." She smiled.

"He'll be the one bouncing on his heels and craning his neck to see you." I laughed. Despite my smile, my heart clenched a little as I wondered if I would ever have that kind of love.

As the doors opened, Samantha laughed at my joke. It hadn't really been my intention, but I knew instantly that the pictures of her happiness would make the cover of every magazine. She practically vibrated with eagerness, and there was no way of faking that anticipation.

The voices of the children's chorus, accompanied by a string ensemble, filled the air, and the show had begun. There were cameras and professional photographers hidden around the setting in ways that I hoped would keep them from being too obvious.

I couldn't see Sam as she moved down the stairs and across the lawn, but I could see the expressions on the guests' faces. And they were in awe. Sam would never see the effect she had on people or the way she filled her new role so perfectly, but it was obvious to those of us on the sidelines. She was meant for Alex in a way that no one else would ever be able to match. And while I would never be able to explain how happy that made me, it also reminded me of my own loneliness.

Garlands of flowers hung from the trees and the aisle was lined with flowered plants that gave the entire area a fairy-tale feel—with my brother playing the part of Prince Charming. I watched as he broke protocol and peeked over his shoulder to see Sam. The look in his eyes and the smile that broke across his face made me giggle. You would never have known there were a thousand people packed into the palace lawn by the look in his eyes.

The formal exchange of the daughter to the waiting groom had been modified for Patricia. Just a few words in Lilarian had been swapped so that it honored Sam's late parents and her relationship with Patricia. There had been a lot of debate in the tabloids and gossip websites about how they were going to handle the situation, but I doubted that anyone would be able to find fault in the way it was presented.

When Alex took Sam's hand, tears formed in my eyes and I couldn't help it. For the world, today wasn't just about their wedding—it was about Sam, America's Duchess becoming a princess. But for Sam and Alex, nothing mattered today except for their marriage. And that was exactly how it should be.

I took my spot next to Jess, keeping careful attention on Violet, and watched as my brother promised to cherish and protect my best friend.

The entire ceremony went smoothly except for Sam's soft giggle when she said a word wrong. It wasn't until they were pronounced man and wife that the script changed.

To the cheers and applause of the audience, Alex dipped Sam backward and kissed her soundly. I covered my mouth as I laughed, my eyes darting to where my mother sat. Her broad smile was unmistakable as my aunt leaned next to her and whispered. When Alex finally let Sam up for air her cheeks were pink and a content smile brightened her face.

As they stepped down from the dais, Jess moved forward to straighten Sam's train and to return the wedding bouquet. At the bottom of the stairs, Alex bowed and Sam curtsied to Mother before making the long walk back to the palace. I could see them laughing as they walked, waving to friends and familiar faces. As I stepped carefully down the stairs a pair of warm eyes caught my attention.

David watched me with a small smile, but there was something in his eyes I hadn't noticed in another man's gaze before. Hunger. Just good, old-fashioned lust, and it sent a shiver down my spine. His eyes traveled over the tight-fitting satin of my dress and back to the barely noticeable cleavage.

I might never have a relationship like Sam and Alex. Hell, I might never find that type of love. But I could find someone to make my blood run hot for one night.

The last boy I had dated had treated me like a trophy, showing me off at parties. Even his kissing had been more like battle than something passionate; as if he was trying to lay claim to me, instead of loving everything I am.

Most girls wanted a man who made them feel like a princess, but I wanted one who made me feel like a woman.

And I think I'd just figured out who that was going to be. I'd just have to convince him as well.

# SIX

**M**USIC SPILLED OUT of the ballroom and into the night air on the patio. People milled about, chatting and munching on tiny crab cakes and crackers with cheese. There wasn't a cloud in the sky and the stars twinkled high above the leafy trees along the stone patio.

I took a deep breath, enjoying the crisp spring air and the space away from everyone who was dancing. After spending time relaxing and cutting loose at the bachelorette party, it felt constraining to be Princess Catherine while everyone else had fun. I had danced with dignitaries, with Max, and even with Chadwick. I'd danced with "friends" and distant cousins. I'd made small talk with people who thought they knew me and I managed to not barf at their annoying jokes. When I had seen Kyle—the disgusting worm of an ex-friend— making his way across the room toward me, I'd decided it was time to make an exit. A fast one.

So instead of playing Perfect Princess Catherine, I was outside, leaning against the railing, sipping ice water.

Trying to come up with a plan for seducing the one man who seemed to detest my title, but craved my body.

David was the polar opposite of my old pal Kyle, or Jake, my last boyfriend. They had wanted my virginity, but only because they saw it as a status symbol. Something to brag about to their friends. "Hey guys, I deflowered a princess last night."

I sighed and drank some more water. Okay, they probably would have come up with some much more crude than *deflower*.

"Are you hiding?" a little voice asked near my hip.

I looked down at the little boy with red hair and smiled. I couldn't remember the little guy's name, but I knew that he was Duke Thysmer's great-grandson. Another one of the royal families that had been returned to their title and lands.

"A little bit," I said.

"I thought so." He moved to the rail next to me and stood on his tiptoes to look over the edge. "Me too. I don't like the music."

"And why's that?" My lips twitched. "I heard

someone say that this is one of the best bands available."

"Yuck. They don't play anything fun. It's all old people music." He scrunched up his nose.

"I hated this type of music when I was your age too."

"Yeah? Don't you still hate it?" He looked up at me with curiosity.

"Nope." I shook my head.

"Why not?"

"Dancing." I set my glass down and turned to look at him directly.

"Dancing?" He made a face. "Like gross dancing?"

I laughed. "What's gross dancing?"

"Like them." He jerked his head toward the spot where Sam and Alex swayed in the center of the dance floor.

"Well, that dancing is nice too, but what about . . . the funky chicken?"

His giggle lifted my spirits. "You don't do the funky chicken!"

"Of course I do!" I put a hand to my chest. "Why wouldn't I do the funky chicken?"

"You're too princess-y!" He giggled again.

"Oh yeah? I bet you can't do it."

"Can too!" He laughed.

"Nah-uh. Don't believe it. You're too little." I narrowed my eyes. "You're too small."

"I really can! See?" Tucking his hands under his arms he flapped his elbows like wings and bucked his head.

It took every drop of willpower not to burst out laughing. "You're okay."

"You can't do any better."

"Of course I can!" Folding my arms against my body I flapped my fake wings and clucked. I took a few steps, bobbing up and down.

The little boy wrapped his arms around his stomach and laughed loudly. I clucked at him and he laughed harder, his little eyes squeezing shut.

"Those are some impressive moves." David's voice froze me in place. "Especially to that fantastic classical music."

"She's so funny!" The little boy pointed at me.

I turned to meet his eyes with my hands still tucked into my armpits. I couldn't have planned a more embarrassing way to see him. Okay, that's not true. I could ask him to take his clothes off. Again. Or spill coffee all over his suit. Yeah. I guess this was just par for the course.

"We were just trying to liven up the night." I shrugged.

"Looks like you're doing a great job." David knelt down and smiled at the little boy. "Have you tried the hokey-pokey yet?"

"Is that the one where you put your leg in and

shake your booty?" He gave a little wiggle to demonstrate.

It was David's turn to laugh. "That's the one."

"Marty!" a woman's voice called. "Martin!"

"Uh-oh." The little boy looked past David.

"Marty, I've been looking for you everywhere." A redheaded woman ran through the open double doors, her soft pink dress fluttering in the wind. "I told you to stay at the table. The table! Does this look like the table?"

"Sorry, Mama." He smiled, but didn't look very worried. "But look! The princess knows the chicken dance!"

"Marty was just helping spice up the night." I smiled at the woman. "You're Meredith, right? We haven't been introduced before." I held my hand out to her and almost pulled it right back. Hopefully she wouldn't think about the fact that my fingers had just been shoved in my armpits.

"It's a pleasure to meet you, Princess Catherine." She stood up and shook my hand. Brushing some of her long hair back over her shoulder she smiled at everyone. "When Marty disappeared I almost had a heart attack. I hope he didn't bother you."

"He was delightful." I reached out and ruffled his hair. "Was your grandfather able to make the trip?" Duke Thysmer was in his seventies and not traveling much.

"Yes. I was getting him some water for his medicine when Marty decided to disappear." She gave the boy a stern look.

"Sorry, Mama." He looked down at his feet.

"Get in there and tell your grandfather you're sorry for scaring *him*." She raised an eyebrow and I smiled. Meredith must have been very young when she had Marty, but she had the motherly expressions down pat. Once the young boy had disappeared back into the ballroom, she turned and smiled at us. Her eyes ran over David in appreciation. "Hi, I'm Meredith."

"Forgive me. David, this is Lady Meredith of Thysmer." Seeing her curvaceous figure shift so that every angle was somehow highlighted made my stomach turn. She wasn't doing anything wrong or outlandish, but damn if she wasn't the type of woman that turned heads. I remembered hearing once that she was an actress, so it only made sense that she knew how to show off her good angles. "Meredith, this is David Rhodes, a close friend of Duche— I mean Princess Samantha."

"Lovely to meet you." Meredith held her hand out and David shook it gently.

"Nice to meet you." He smiled, but let go of her hand quickly.

"I'm going to go in and make sure he's actually doing what he's supposed to. You two enjoy the night air." With a grin, she whirled away and disappeared in the throngs of people.

"She's a duchess?" David turned and looked at me.

"Her grandfather is a duke, but her official title is Lady Meredith." I bit my bottom lip. "She must've been really young when she had Marty."

"I didn't see anyone with her. Is Marty's father not in the picture?"

I frowned. Was he fishing for her relationship status? "No. I don't think he has ever played a large role in their family. She has been single for as long as I've known her."

"That's rough." He frowned. "So, the boy, will he inherit the title as well?"

"Yes. Since he is the firstborn and only grand-child."

"Your family tree is pretty confusing." One side of his mouth pulled up at the corner and I felt relieved. He seemed more interested in our family than in Meredith's dating life.

"Oh, you have no idea. This is just the tip of the iceberg." I took a step closer to him and hoped that he had already forgotten the chicken dance. "Meredith is part of the royal tree, but so far removed that she isn't truly related any longer. Much like Sam."

"I think I remember hearing the name Thysmer before." David stuck his hands in his pockets. "It was in a lot of articles about Sam."

"They were the other family that had their title reinstated." I smiled. "We don't see Meredith often. She attends university in England. In fact, this was the first time I've actually met her or her son."

"He looked like a handful." He laughed.

"I think you're right," I said.

"But he did get you dancing." His eyes ran over my dress and then back to my face. "I would think you'd have an endless line of people wanting to dance with you."

"Look at you. You're getting better at the compliments." My mouth twitched and I hoped I wasn't grinning like an idiot.

"Well, then I saw you doing the funky chicken and it all made sense." His lips quivered as he fought a laugh.

"Hey! I'll have you know, I do a great funky chicken." I poked him in the chest and his hand shot up to grasp mine. His thumb ran over the back of my hand and I took a deep breath.

"Why don't you show me what other types of dances you know."

Had he just hinted at more than dancing? Did I care? Hell no.

"Lead the way," I said.

Wrapping my hand through his arm, he led me back into the ballroom and onto the dance floor. With one hand on my waist he guided me through the other dancers in a slow waltz.

As we glided around the floor I was shocked to see Max dancing with Meredith. His eyes were locked on her mouth and she was talking softly, her lips curved into a gentle smile. I had never seen Max pay so much attention to a woman. He'd had lovers in the past, but it had always been obvious that they were a momentary distraction. What really intrigued me was how different the two were. Meredith with her flair for acting and Max with his deep desire to stay as far out of the public eye as possible.

Shaking my head I looked back at David and smiled. "I wouldn't have thought you would be a dancer."

"Now, that's not true." His eyes twinkled. "I seem to remember you telling me to shake it the other night."

Heat rushed to my cheeks. "I knew I'd never live that down."

"Are you kidding me? I should write home and tell my best friend." He laughed but my back stiffened. "I'm joking, Cathy."

I didn't respond, trying to fight down the dread of what would happen if he really did write home about my drunken episode. His fingers tightened on my waist and he pulled me a little closer.

"Cathy, I'm serious. It was a joke." He leaned down so his lips were close to my ear. "I know how hard it is to keep your life out of the news. I've seen how difficult it has been on Sam."

"I'm not normally like that." I met his eyes briefly before looking away.

"Yeah, I get that." His hand touched my chin to get my attention. "Which is a shame. I liked the grumpy Cathy who poured coffee all over me and the happy, forward woman who told me to take my clothes off."

"Shh!" My eyes almost bugged out of my head.

A chuckle rumbled out of his chest. "No one is paying the slightest bit of attention to us."

"That's not true." I shook my head. "There is always someone watching. Always."

"Every person in this room is watching Alex spin Sam around the dance floor like Fred Astaire and Ginger Rogers."

"They do look amazing." I craned my neck so I could see my brother. Sam had removed her train, making her dress much more manageable.

"I have to admit, seeing Samantha these last

couple of days has really been a surprise. She fits in here so well—like she's always been a duchess." David's eyes took on a faraway look. "It wasn't that long ago that we were eating two-day-old cold pizza while going over projects. Or stomping through a field, searching for a bird. She never cared about her nails or makeup." He paused for a minute, thinking. "But now, she's so . . . polished. It was always there, but it's like you guys took her and shined her up."

"She still stomps through fields, chews her nails, and will just as quickly punch someone in the nose than deal with their crap. You're seeing wedding Samantha." I chuckled. "And you missed the very scary primping part of the process."

"I'm imagining a bucket of water where you guys are scrubbing her with giant brushes while she cusses at you."

"That's not too far from the truth." I laughed, remembering the eyebrow threading.

"Much better."

"Excuse me?" I looked up at him confused.

"You relaxed." With the hand on the small of my back he rubbed gently with his thumb. "I didn't mean to upset you."

"No, it's not your fault." I shook my head.

"You're right though. I shouldn't have to separate Cathy and Princess Catherine."

"Then don't." He shrugged like it was the easiest thing in the world.

I sighed but didn't respond. It was almost impossible to explain how I had to manage being two different people. I didn't even want to think about it.

The music stopped and David guided us from the dance floor. His hand stayed on my back, his touch sending goose bumps over my skin.

"Would you like something to drink?" He leaned close so that his warm breath washed over my cheek.

"A water would be nice."

"No more alcohol?" His smirk was understandable.

"I think I've had my share for the year." I smiled. "Maybe the next five years."

"Well, there goes my plan for getting you drunk." He winked at me.

"You do remember what happened to the potted plant, right?" I shuddered.

"That's a good point." Picking up a glass of water he turned and handed it to me.

"So how long are you going to be staying in Lilaria?" I sipped from my cup.

"I'm not sure." He spun the wine in his glass with a look of disappointment.

"I'm sorry. I didn't mean to pry." I touched his arm gently.

"I'm not upset about that—I'd just much rather have a beer than a glass of wine." He looked at the glass with sad eyes.

"Well, that I think I can fix." I looked around the room. Things were calming down, Sam was still dancing with Alex while teasing Daniel for stepping on her dress. "Come on." Grabbing his hand I pulled him along behind me.

"Where are you taking me?" He set his wineglass down on a table as we walked.

"Does it matter?" I looked back at him and raised an eyebrow.

"No." He shifted his fingers so they laced with mine.

"Okay, then." I winked at him and pulled him with me.

We went through the servers' entrance and through the kitchen. David didn't say a word, just followed as I wove through the counters. Taking a small hallway, I led him into a smaller, much quieter kitchen that served the family wing. Opening one of the refrigerators I tossed him a bottle of beer before digging through the freezer for my favorite ice cream. He sat down at the island while I found a spoon for my frozen treat.

"How many kitchens are there?" He took a sip of his beer.

"Three," I said. "The large one for formal functions, the employee kitchen, and this is the family kitchen."

"And you have a cook who takes care of your stuff in here?"

"Two master chefs that rotate and their assistant staff." I frowned. "To be fair, we often host dignitaries or visiting royals in the family wing. So it's more often than not, there are additions to our family meals."

"So, your family wing isn't really so much about family." He wiped some of the condensation from his bottle with his thumb. "And more about making certain people feel special."

"It's our home." I sat up straighter, annoyed. "We're not the only family that has guest rooms or visitors."

"True." He shrugged. "Just seems so foreign to me. It would be annoying to have to get dressed just to go get a snack. Or what if you forget something in your office?"

"Well, I'm not normally hanging out in my room naked, so it's not a big deal." I laughed. It really didn't seem like a big deal to me. I hadn't known anything else.

"That's a shame." Heat followed his gaze over my body and I bit my lip. I was starting to feel nervous about my plan to seduce him—what did I know about seducing a man? Then again, maybe it was going to be easier than I thought.

I smiled up at him from under my eyelashes. "Does that mean you hang out in your room naked?"

"It's been known to happen." He laughed. "Especially if I can't find a clean towel after a shower."

The thought of him standing there while water rolled down his body made me suck in a breath. Yep. That was a sight I wouldn't mind. Not in the least.

"You're teasing me."

"Nope. I hate to do laundry. You have to gather it all up, then wash it, then dry it, then fold it. And to add insult to injury, once you've done all of that you still have to put it up in the closet." He spun the liquid in his bottle slowly. "I'd rather do the dishes than the laundry."

"I started doing my own laundry in college." I laughed. "I didn't know I needed to read the labels. Needless to say I lost a lot of things because I didn't realize they had to be dry-cleaned."

"It must have been a weird transition."

"I love it. For so long I didn't get to do the regular stuff. I was expected to ask people to do things for me like I was helpless. I hated it. I hate asking for help." I scraped the bottom of the ice cream bowl with my spoon. "Now I get to be independent and make time for things that everyone else does."

"On top of being a full-time student and a full-time princess?" He cocked his head to the side. "When do you sleep?"

"How did you know I was a full-time student?" I raised one eyebrow.

"I might have asked Sam a few questions." He ducked his head and smiled.

"And why would you do that, Dr. Rhodes?" I couldn't help the grin that pulled at my mouth. I stood up and set my bowl and spoon in the sink.

"I couldn't stop wondering what it would be like to kiss you." This time when he looked at me, there was heat in his gaze.

"Maybe you should find out." I turned around and leaned against the counter. I hoped I looked sexy and inviting, but I probably looked excited and nervous.

He stood up slowly and walked around the kitchen island to stand in front of me. His suit jacket hung open and I could see the muscles under his shirt shift with each step, but it was his eyes that drew me in. Placing a hand on either side of me on the counter he leaned close. I felt as if he was searching my soul, looking for something in particular. As if he had found his answer, he dipped his head and his lips captured mine.

It was slow and careful, as if he was waiting for some sign. When his tongue brushed across my bottom lip I sighed and ran my hands over his chest. I hadn't been kissed in so long I had almost forgotten what it was like—that connection between two people who wanted the same thing: each other.

One of his hands moved from the counter to grasp my hip, pulling me tightly against his body. I melted into him, delighting in the way we fit together. Twining my arms around his neck I let my mouth dance with his, tasting and exploring. His hand on my hip moved to cup my ass, gently massaging as he pulled me even tighter against him. I could feel the growing bulge in his pants and it excited me to know that I was the cause.

I pulled my arms away and slid them under his jacket, pulling his button-up shirt out of his pants and running my hand along his back. His mouth left mine to trail kisses along my neck and

I sighed with pleasure. When his hand moved to cup my breast, I groaned and pushed against him, wanting more. As his kisses moved lower and lower I let my head fall back and was lost in the sensation. His lips skimmed the top of my dress, his warm breath collecting in my cleavage as he inhaled raggedly.

Looking up into my eyes, he touched my cheek. "I'm sorry. I got carried away."

"I'm not sorry." There was no way I was going to let him get away now. I laced my fingers in his hair and pulled his head back to mine. I craved his kiss like a dying woman in the desert.

His hands weren't as gentle this time, touching and exploring my body as I did his. I had made up my mind and I knew what I wanted. I wanted David. With shaky hands I reached for his belt but he stopped me.

"Is there somewhere else we can go?"

Sucking in air I realized that we were still in the kitchen. While it was unlikely anyone would be coming up here anytime soon, it wasn't a risk I was willing to take.

"Yes." Taking his hand I started to pull him along, but he stopped me with a kiss. His tongue hungrily explored my mouth. We stumbled through the kitchen like that, locked in each other's arms as we looked for the door. My back pressed against the cool wood and I moaned when he used one leg to push mine apart and planted himself against my hot center.

His lips left mine and he nipped at my earlobe while I tried to peek out into the hallway. Once I knew the coast was clear I opened the door and pulled him with me to my room. When we were inside I closed the door and tried to calm my racing heart. Xavier, my dog, lifted his head from where he was lying and then went right back to sleep. I had never brought a man into my rooms before. At least not a man that I intended on seducing. Apparently my dog didn't care half as much as I did.

David didn't seem to notice my hesitation. He moved behind me, his hands running over my waist while his lips brushed along my bare shoulders. I leaned into him, enjoying the feel of his manhood pressed against me through the thin material of my dress. When his hands moved up to cup my breasts I moaned.

"I want to see you." I whispered the words, needing to see the desire in his eyes to give me the bravery to go forward.

Gently he turned me around so that I was facing him and I stared into his heat-filled eyes.

His hands slid up my bare arms, over my shoulders, and along my neck to cup my face. Tilting my chin upward he studied my face with hooded eyes.

"You always get what you want, don't you, Princess?" His deep voice rumbled underneath my hand on his chest.

God, I hoped so. Because right this moment there was nothing I wanted more than David's skin pressed against mine.

"Undress me." The words came out husky and I prayed he'd do it. I was scared that if I did it myself he would see my shaky fingers.

His dark eyes flashed and he reached behind me to slowly pull the zipper down. Carefully he slid the material off, exposing me in my underwear and shoes. I felt even more naked knowing that he was seeing me in my strapless bra and garter belt.

David let his gaze rake over me and I could feel it like a hot touch. With sharp movements he pulled his jacket off and threw it over a chair before undoing his tie. I watched with short breaths as he knelt in front of me, his messy hair obscuring his face as he pulled one shoe off and then the other. I reached down and unhooked the garters so that he would be able to remove the stockings, but he didn't roll them down as I expected. Instead, he nuzzled between my legs and my knees went weak. My head fell back against the door and I thought I'd faint.

His hands cupped my cheeks, while his mouth pressed hot kisses through the material of my panties. When he finally stood up, he lifted me into his arms and carried me to my bed. After lying me down on the soft duvet, he undid his pants, letting them fall to the floor, followed by his shirt.

I had been right when I thought that he would be a delicious visual treat naked. The man was an Adonis, with the kind of muscles a man got from hard labor, not lifting weights in front of a mirror. When he crawled onto the bed, covering my body with his, I froze for half a second before sinking into his kiss. When he shifted so that his leg was between mine, my heart stilled.

I was really doing this, finally getting rid of the virgin baggage. And with a hottie who made me laugh. So why did I suddenly feel worried I was making a wrong decision? Was I rethinking this?

With deft hands he undid my bra and his warm mouth found one peak. My doubts dissolved in a rush of pleasure and I closed my eyes to enjoy the sensation. No one had ever touched me the way David was touching me. I let my hands run over his shoulders and down his back. When he leaned up to capture my mouth once more I let my fingers slide over his abdomen and down to his hardened shaft. He sucked in a breath and murmured in my ear something I didn't quite understand.

His hand followed the same path mine had and his fingers stroked gently along the growing wet spot between my legs. When he moved the fabric out of the way and touched the delicate skin my breathing accelerated. I focused on his kiss as he teased me open and gently slipped one finger inside.

I couldn't stop the sharp intake of breath or the way my body froze in shock. It wasn't that I hadn't done the same thing myself before, but it was entirely different to have it done by someone else. I tensed, unsure if I liked the sensation or not. It was different and slightly uncomfortable.

"Cathy?" David pulled back and looked at me, worry creasing his brow.

"Yes?" I took a deep breath and tried to not look relieved when he pulled his hand away.

"Are you . . . is this your first time?" His voice sounded odd, surprise laced with frustration.

My heart stopped in my chest as I looked at his face. What had I done wrong that he had figured it out?

# SEVEN

$\mathcal{I}$ DIDN'T SAY ANYTHING at first. I didn't know how to respond. Was it really a bad thing that I was a virgin? That I hadn't taken that step yet?

"Does it matter?" I fought the urge to cover myself up.

"Of course it matters." Sitting up, he ran a hand through his hair.

"Why?" I sat up and pulled a pillow over my chest. Shame was beginning to smother the flames of lust.

"You can't—you shouldn't just give that away." He stood up and pulled his pants on. His excitement was still evident, even though anger laced his words. "That's reckless!"

"It's mine, isn't it? I can do whatever the hell I want to with it!" I stood up and pulled the blanket with me so it saved the little bit of modesty I had left.

"Why the hell would you give it to *me*?" He held his arms open.

What was I supposed to say? That he had made me laugh? That he had treated me like a normal person? Or how about the fact that just the sight of him made me want to pant? I couldn't tell him that. I still couldn't believe I'd gotten him into my bed at all. And now . . .

Now it was all falling apart. Turning into the worst nightmare ever. Well, no, that wasn't quite true. At least I knew he wouldn't sell the story to tabloids.

Sam would kill him and find a swamp to hide his mangled body.

But here I was, naked in front of a man that I wanted, and he was rejecting me. Shame burned through my body and tears rushed to my eyes.

"Cathy." He took a step forward and I took one in retreat. "I'm just saying that this isn't something you should just give away. If you've waited this long it should be with someone that is special."

"I've waited long enough to know that I will likely end up with someone that only wants me for what I can give them." My voice rose and I stomped to the door. "You were different! I thought you just wanted *me*."

"I did!" He reached for my arm but I shook him off.

"I didn't realize that my *virginity* would be so damn disgusting."

"It's not—"

"Look, don't worry about it. I'm leaving." I opened the door and started to walk out.

"No!" He took three steps forward and pushed the door closed. "You're not going out there like that." If I hadn't known better I would have thought his words had seemed possessive.

I looked at him confused, unsure why he would care if I left, until I realized I was still wrapped in the blanket. And then to my utter embarrassment I realized it was my room.

"Get out." I jerked the material closer.

"Fine." He picked up his shirt. "But this isn't over, Cathy. We're going to talk."

"Not likely." I turned my face away from him, scared that he would see the tears gathered in my eyes.

"I didn't mean to upset you." He pulled his shirt back on before letting his arms hang limply at his sides.

"Just go." I shook my head. Nothing he said was going to make any of this better.

"I'm leaving, but for what it's worth I did want you for you." He started to say something and then thought better of it. "Good night."

He pulled the door shut behind him and I leaned against the wall. Hot tears ran down my cheeks and I gripped the blanket tighter around me. Humiliation flowed over my body and I couldn't believe I had actually tried to seduce someone and he had run from me faster than a kid from a haunted house.

Walking to the en suite I dropped the blanket and turned on the shower. If I was going to be this miserable I might as well drown my mortification under the rain showerhead.

What was I supposed to do with myself at this point? I wasn't interested in sex anymore, which was for sure. Was I supposed to just get dressed and crawl back into bed? After the shower I threw on some of my most comfortable nightclothes and sat down on the small couch in the corner and opened my laptop. There was no way I was going to get any sleep at this point, so I decided I'd get a jump on things for tomorrow.

There would be cleanup from the wedding, media attention to deal with, and the tasks I'd taken on while Sam and Alex would be gone. I answered e-mails, forwarded things to Selene, and uploaded some of the pictures I had taken from the night. I even sent a message to Selene to see if she could schedule a lunch with Meredith and

Marty while they were in town. It would be nice to make them feel a bit more involved with the family. Especially since they spent the majority of their time in another country.

I'm not sure when I fell asleep, but I woke to the soft shuffling of feet in my room, and the stream of sunlight coming through the windows. I wiped at the drool on my cheek and turned to see who was in my apartment. Selene was straightening my bed and had David's jacket draped over her arm.

"Um." I sat up and blinked the crust out of my eyes. I hadn't realized he had left it the night before.

"Good morning." Selene smiled at me. "I got your e-mails first thing and will see if Meredith has any free time. I believe she and her son are staying for a little while to tour the capital."

"Oh, thank you." Scrubbing at my face I watched her and tried to figure out how to explain the jacket. "David must have left that last night after we finished talking."

"Of course." She leaned over and picked up my dress from the ground and laid it on my bed. "I'll be sure to get it back to him and see to it that your dress is cleaned."

"Yes, I'd like to be able to wear that one again." It had been very flattering. Of course, it would also always be linked in my mind to the night a man ran screaming from my bed.

"Certainly. It looked lovely on you." She gave me a gentle smile. "I'm glad to see you've made a new friend. You haven't had much time to relax. Is there anything you'd like to talk about?"

"Er—no." I frowned. Well, she knew. Or at least thought she knew what must have happened last night. And in all honesty, I still wasn't sure what had happened. Well, some parts were crystal clear: David's kisses, the way his mouth felt against my skin, and his laughter. Then there were other parts that were clear, like the disdain on his face when he realized I was a virgin or the shame I had felt when he backed away from me. If I never saw him again, it would be too soon.

"Okay. Well, your morning is pretty empty. If you have something you'd like to do, let me know and we'll get it taken care of. Or if you'd rather just relax, that's a good plan too." Selene smiled.

"I think I'd like to read for a little while. I can't remember the last time I read for fun." Samantha had given me several books that she thought I would enjoy. Getting up, I walked over to my bedside table and pulled the drawer open. *Vain* by Fisher Amelie looked up at me and I touched the pretty cover. A distraction would be a welcome thing this morning. "Would you let me know an hour before our next appointment?"

"Of course," Selene said. "I'll be back in a little while."

"Thank you." I took the book back to my little sofa and curled up under a blanket. I read the intriguing synopsis, opened the book, and got down to business. By the time two hours had rolled around, I was so engrossed I could barely think of anything else. I hated Sophie, the main character, before pitying her. Then I fell in love with her and the hero just as quickly.

There was a knock at my door, but I was in the middle of a particularly gripping paragraph and didn't want to get up. "Come in!"

I didn't look up until I was finished and that was when I realized that David had entered my room, not Selene. He was wearing jeans and another of his damn flannel shirts and had tucked his hands into his pockets. He looked determined and frustrated. Maybe even a little nervous.

I stared at him, wondering why he was here. What could he possibly have to say that hadn't been already said? My virginity freaked him out and he'd apologized. Yeah, that pretty much summed up everything we had to say to each other.

However, my mouth was apparently not on the same wavelength as my brain. "You left your jacket. Selene said she would get it back to you." I shifted in my seat so that my feet were touching the floor. That's when I remembered I was wearing an old pair of pajamas.

"She brought it to me." He rocked back on his feet. "How are you—"

"What do you—" I shook my head as our words overlapped. He smiled, and I'll be damned if it didn't do that funny thing to my heart. "Did you need something?"

His mouth twitched and I could tell he was doing that thing where he tried to decide what to say. "I think we should go out on a date."

"What?" My eyebrows pulled together and I frowned.

"A date. Like to the movies or grab some food." He shrugged one shoulder and gave me a half smile.

"The movies?" I stared at him dumbfounded. Go to a movie theater?

"Or whatever you do in Lilaria on dates." He scratched at his chin. "I'm willing to do something else."

I looked down at my bare feet sticking out of the faded night pants and thought about it. Just the idea made my stomach do flips. Could I have a normal night with him after he had turned away from me? After he had seen me mostly naked?

"You're asking me out on a date?" My brain refused to completely compute what was happening.

"I'd like to see you again." His head bobbed a little as if he was agreeing with what he had said. "I'd like to get to know you better."

Maybe it was that last sentence. Or perhaps it was the fact that I really had enjoyed talking with him last night. It could even be the fact that he looked so damn adorable standing there asking me for a date. But my mouth once again took over and my answer burst forth without thought.

"I'd like that."

"Good." A grin broke out on his face. "Tonight?"

"Um, I have to check my schedule." I frowned.

"You know, with any other girl I might think you were trying to find an excuse, but you probably really do have to check your calendar." He chuckled, but I caught the nervous hint underneath.

"I'm not trying to find an excuse." I rolled my eyes. "Free time is sometimes hard to come by."

"Yeah, I've noticed." He smiled sheepishly. "About last night—"

"No." I shook my head adamantly. "Let's just forget last night."

"There are some things a man can't forget." He looked at me with deep eyes. "But we can start over—try things from the beginning."

"This means we're not going to talk about the whole stripping mishap, right?" I stood up and held out my hand.

"Oh, now that isn't something anyone can forget." He wrapped his fingers around mine. "Hi, I'm David Rhodes."

"Hi, David. I'm Cathy."

"Nice pj's." His eyes ran over my body and I wondered if he was imagining what was underneath.

"I wasn't exactly expecting company." I frowned.

"Would you have dressed up if you'd known I was coming?" He still had my hand wrapped in his.

"Well, you've already seen me puke in a potted plant and hungover the next day." I shrugged. "This is actually an improvement."

"Even hungover, you were gorgeous." He winked and finally let go of my hand.

"Wow." I couldn't help but laugh. "Are you practicing these compliments in the mirror at night?"

"I can't reveal my secrets." He tucked his hands back into his pockets.

There was a knock on the door and I looked past David as Selene stuck her head inside.

"My apologies. I didn't realize you had a guest." She started to duck out, but stopped long enough to add something. "Our next appointment is in an hour."

"Thank you. I'll be ready soon." I nodded at her as she closed the door quietly.

"Well, I'll let you get dressed," David said.

"I have a meeting with some of the officials working on my new charity." I smiled. I was really looking forward to meeting with the investors. The program I wanted to start targeted schools that had cut art training out of the budget. Art was something that I was passionate about and I didn't want children to miss out on the opportunity to express their creativity.

"I'd like to hear about it." He walked to the door before stopping to smile at me. "Should I call your secretary and make an appointment?"

"No." I giggled. "Chadwick is helping you while Sam is gone, right?"

"Yeah." He shook his head. "That man is intimidating. I think he has planned out my bathroom schedule."

"I'll have Selene find out when we both have free time."

"Hopefully soon." He opened the door, smiled at me, and then closed it behind him.

"Hopefully," I whispered. The oddest feeling swamped over me. Fear, excitement, and pure adrenaline. If I didn't know any better I felt like I wanted to giggle and squeal. Instead I acted like the adult I was and got dressed while I danced around the room to music from my mp3 player. Giddiness had me shaking my booty in the mirror. I hadn't ever been this excited by the thought of a date before.

That was, until a thought hit me like a ton of bricks. What if he had only asked me out because he felt sorry for me? The pathetic princess stuck in a tower that he needed to rescue? It could be that he didn't want to see me again at all and was just doing what he thought was right. After all, he had left me naked and panting last night without seeming bothered.

# EIGHT

KICKING THE SHOES off in the car I slumped in my seat and closed my eyes. I had never had such a strong urge to punch someone as I did while listening to the idiot bankers asking what their return would be for something like the art program.

"Well, that went well." Selene humphed from her seat. "What is it your new sister says? Those men were a bunch of asshats."

A laugh burst out of my mouth and I peeked one eye open to see her grin as she flipped through her files.

"That's it exactly." I sat up. "Why did they even come? I mean, what did they expect? A percentage of crayon drawings? Finger paintings to hang in their offices? *That* I could take care of, but a financial return?"

"You made a compelling argument." Selene looked at me over the top of her glasses. "Stretching a child's imagination leads to new products, intellectual property, and more local resources."

I blew a raspberry. "Fat lot of good it did me."

"You know how this works," she said. "They come in all gung-ho or completely distant."

"I know it's annoying." I closed my eyes again. "They just want to be able to say they had a meeting with a princess."

"Well, I'm sure that's a big point for some of them." She shrugged. "But then again, you know that you can use your status to make good things happen. That comes with the job."

I sighed. It was the same conversation we'd had countless times over the years. Only this time I didn't feel placated by the simple observations. I was tired of being Princess Catherine. It was completely ridiculous that it took my title to get people to invest in our children.

Right now, I was looking forward to going back to D'Lynsal and finishing the book I had started earlier. My eyes popped open when I remembered that David would be just a short drive away at Rousseau. Even if I wasn't sure if he wanted a date with me or he felt sorry for me, I had told him I'd try to find time. The worst thing that could happen would be an uncomfortable night that ended in him feeling better and me right back where I already was.

"Selene?"

"Yes?"

"When do I have another dinner free?" I looked down at my nails and picked at a cuticle.

"Thursday, I believe." She raised an eyebrow. "Is there something you'd like me to schedule?"

"I was thinking about going to see a movie."

"Tell me which one and I'll have it screened at the palace for you." She picked up her pen.

"No, I'd like to go out." I paused, looking for words that wouldn't make me sound like an excited girl. "With a friend."

"I see. And is this friend trustworthy?"

"I think so." I looked up at her and frowned. "Why?"

"I know that Princess Samantha trusts him, but you don't know him very well." She said the words quietly and I tried to see the worry beneath her disappointed tone. It obviously hadn't taken much of a jump to figure I was referring to David.

"That's what I'm trying to correct," I responded. "I'd like to know more about him."

"Okay, then." She nodded her head but not without a grin. "I'll check with Chadwick and see what we can work out."

"Thank you."

By the time we pulled up to D'Lynsal, I was

more than ready for a hot bath and my bed. My apartment at the palace was great, but despite what I had said to David, it didn't feel like home the way our family estate did. The palace was meant to house visitors, showcase our culture and history, while giving the country a place to look toward during tough times.

After I turned eighteen I had the apartments updated to my tastes, which had been fun but weird. People had complained in tabloids about the fact that I was wrecking historical objects. Others cheered on my need to modernize the palace. In truth I was just tired of the rose petal pink wallpaper and green carpet. I'm sure that had been the height of fashion at some point, but I couldn't stand it a moment longer.

D'Lynsal, however, was ours. It was the home we didn't have to share with the media. There were no flyers or press releases if I decided I wanted to change a paint color or update a light feature. Some of my fondest memories were running through these halls or fighting with Alex and Max. Seemed odd when you thought about it, but the best part of being a child was that we had nothing more to worry about other than dessert and getting out of events we thought would be boring. The older we had gotten, the harder it had become to avoid those important functions.

And now I even looked forward to some of them. Well, not many. At least not as much as I was looking forward to seeing David again—despite the butterflies that came with the thought. I still couldn't believe that he had come back to ask me on a date after what had happened that night. Not that I had a great deal of experience with men, but I didn't think that many of them would have tried to find a way to make it okay. In fact the men, or I should say boys, that I had spent my youth around would never have even thought to stop when they realized I was a virgin. Most of them would have felt it was an even better score—which was exactly why I was still a virgin.

The driver came around and opened the door for Selene and me, helping carry my bags up the steps and passing them on to some of the household staff. I hadn't put my shoes back on when we climbed out of the vehicle, completely comfortable at our home. There was a small fire in the great room, even though it was summertime. The evenings could have a chill in the air despite the time of year. Dropping my shoes onto a small footstool, I curled up onto the settee and watched the flames jump.

It felt like it had been years since I had last

curled up in this same position. Here in this spot, I could remember my father sitting in a nearby chair while reading a book and mother working on paperwork. She had never been able to take time off—even on the weekends or late at night. Father had thought it was because of the way she had grown up watching her father do the exact same. It was one of the reasons our father had pushed for us to have hobbies, to do things that we wanted, and kept us from performing royal duties until we were older.

The ache that accompanied my thoughts was familiar but manageable. No matter how long it had been since I'd last seen his face, I'd miss him like the accident had happened the day before. Now though, I also remembered the happiness and good times, not just the pain.

"What are you doing, monster?" Max mussed my hair before plopping down into Dad's seat.

"Relaxing." I curled up even tighter into a ball so my feet would be closer to the warmth.

"You? Relaxing?" Max picked up one of the magazines on the table and raised an eyebrow.

"Yes, I'm relaxing. Why is that weird?" I craned my neck so I could look at him.

"Because," he said. "You're like Mom. Always working on something."

"That's not true. I take time off." I scrunched my nose.

"Sometimes." He shrugged while looking at the magazine in his hands. "But even then you're working in your head. You don't ever turn it off."

"Turn what off?" My voice rose a bit and I frowned.

"The list." He looked at me with an amused expression.

"List? Are you drunk?" I rolled my eyes.

"No, I'm not drunk." He reached out with his foot and pushed the seat I was curled up on. "The list. The one where you're mentally checking things off, planning what to do next, and accepting more responsibility."

"Not everyone can get away with hiding in an office or studio all day." My sneer was obvious.

"Sure they can." He laughed. "You just have to not care what everyone else wants."

"That's not as easy for some people." I closed my eyes, not wanting to let him ruin my peace. "Other people have to pick up the slack, in case you didn't know."

"Right. Thanks for that."

"You're an ass."

"Well, say something else that we already know."

"You're a terrible Sudoku player." I laughed.

"Now that's just cruel." Max fake-groaned. "What is the point of those puzzles anyways?"

"I don't know, genius. You'd think those would be fun for you and your giant brain."

"My giant brain is geared for painting, creative things. Numbers make me sick." He frowned.

"And yet you can't get enough of computer games." I rolled over so I was lying on my stomach and looking at him. "You're such a nerd."

"Everyone needs a distraction." He wiggled his eyebrows at me. "Looked like you found yourself one."

"What?" I hoped my expression didn't give away my surprise. I should have known that more people would have noticed me and David sneaking away.

"Sam's friend. The bloke with the dark hair who can't find a razor."

"Really? Are you going to tease me about a guy like we're teenagers?" I rolled my eyes.

"Yes, yes I am." He chuckled. "Care to say what happened after you disappeared?"

"Absolutely not." I'd die if anyone found out the truth. It was almost better that they think I'd had a one-night stand. I wouldn't be the first in the family to scratch an itch.

"I thought that might be your response." Max stretched in his seat. "Just be careful there."

"What do you mean?" Why was everyone warning me about David? It was starting to piss me off. It wasn't like he had chased me. I'd been the one doing the seducing. I think, anyways.

"Don't get bent out of shape." It was his turn to roll his eyes. "I just meant that he's not used to everything we put up with. It's a lot for people to adjust to. You know how hard it's been for Sam."

"David is a smart man."

"He is." He laughed at my expression. "What? You didn't think I'd do my research when I saw him sneaking off with my baby sister?"

"I'm not a baby."

"You'll always be the baby in the house." He shrugged. "I'm just saying that you might need to prep him for what dating you would entail."

"Right, I'll draft up a list for him in the morning." I rolled my eyes. I wanted to get to know David better, not scare him away.

"Well, I'm calling it a night. I have to meet the local council in the morning for lunch since Alex is away."

"Oh, that sounds fun." I smirked. That would be torture for him.

"Trade?" Max stood up.

"Yeah, I'm going to pass." I laughed.

"You're opening a bird sanctuary tomorrow, right?" Max frowned. "Photographs, speeches, all that good stuff. I guess I'd hate that just as much."

"Yep." I laid my head down and stared at the flames. "Back to work in the morning."

"Right." He leaned down and kissed the top of my head. "Good night, sister."

" 'Night." I yawned loudly. It was definitely time for bed.

# NINE

THE NEXT MORNING came early and in ugly fashion. The beautiful weather from the wedding had passed and storms were forecast for the rest of the week. Sighing, I climbed out of bed and got ready for the day's schedule. I opted for an outfit that would allow me to wear boots. With the amount of rain that had fallen the night before, I would sink in the mud if I wore heels.

Selene was ready downstairs with umbrellas, my briefcase, and her ever-present clipboard. "This will probably be a little shorter than we planned since the weather isn't cooperating."

"Do we have food scheduled for the event? We'll need to give the visitors and staff something to do inside." I thought about it for a moment. "We don't want them to feel slighted by not staying long enough."

"True. We had light breakfast fare planned, but I will call and see if we get something a little more substantial. We'll also need to adjust the photo ops." Selene pulled her phone out of her pocket. It was one of the few pieces of electronics that she had adjusted to using.

"Let me know if I can do anything to help." I whispered the words quietly. She nodded her head as she rapidly spoke Lilarian into the phone.

I pulled out my phone and checked the weather before sending a text to Chadwick. I figured he would be present for the event since Sam would want a firsthand account even if she was on her honeymoon.

**Me:** Is there room inside for everyone today?
**Chadwick:** David has moved some birds inside and is going to do a demonstration to amuse people so we're not walking through the rain to tour.

My heart thudded in my chest. I was going to see him much sooner than I had thought.

**Me:** David will be there?
**Chadwick:** Yes.

I didn't say anything in response. I hadn't expected to see David today. Would that be awkward? I looked down at the skirt, sweater, and jacket I had chosen to wear. Cute but efficient. I took a deep breath.

**Chadwick:** Why? ;)
**Me:** Will be nice to have help. And wink at yourself.
**Chadwick:** Just saying that if he played for my team, Daniel would need to be worried.
**Me:** LOL

I turned the screen off and looked at Selene. "Ready?"

"Yes." She opened an umbrella and stepped out the door. She rubbed her chest with her free hand before motioning for me to follow her out. Her face looked tight, but I knew she developed heartburn from time to time, so I didn't think much of it. I kept my head under cover so that my hair wouldn't look like a mess when I arrived. There wouldn't be time to prep once there; I'd jump straight into my diplomatic role. Shaking hands, smiling for photos, and making small talk. It should be fun.

The sanctuary was in a town near Rousseau and about an hour drive from D'Lynsal. Which meant I had some time to look over other information. The building was on an old farm that had been donated by a family with a love for birds. It would mostly cater to animals that would not be able to be reintroduced to the wild, and in time would be used as an educational tool. Growing up with two older brothers had left me with a fondness for the outdoors, even though I was just as happy in an evening gown.

I scrolled through the website, checked out the resident birds, the people running the business, and the footnotes about people who had helped design the habitats. Turned out Dr. David Rhodes had his hands on a lot of projects. There was even a page with his credentials and a paragraph detailing why he had chosen to work with raptors.

It felt a bit like cheating to read the information, but then again, I knew he could just as likely pull up stuff about me on the Internet. And hadn't he confessed to asking questions about me? Only Sam was gone so I couldn't bug her for information. I could ask Jess, but that would lead to more questions from her and I'd never get away without divulging what had happened the other night.

By the time we pulled up to the farm, I had found out that David was the oldest son of a family from southern Georgia in the United States and that he was also the first in his family to attend college. Like a super spy I had found his pages on social media—even though they were mostly bare—and seen pictures of his family. It looked like his youngest sister might have a disability, but there was no way of telling for sure from just the picture. His other sister was in college and it looked like she was very studious. That didn't surprise me in the least. David radiated book smarts. It was in little things, like the way he chose his words carefully, or the manner in which he said certain words. He took pride in his education and I couldn't fault him for that.

The photographers were outside, even in the rain, waiting to catch a shot of us as we unloaded from the car. It was a mess outside and I was glad I'd chosen to wear my boots even if we were going to be inside.

The building was adorable and practically screamed Sam. Very rustic, but with sophistication in the details that let you know the animals would be well taken care of by the people inside. David was standing on the porch, looking extremely uncomfortable as people snapped his picture in his first official FBT production. He was wearing his standard plaid shirt and jeans, and work boots.

There was something extremely sexy in the combination, though I wasn't sure it was an appropriate outfit for this event. Hell, who really cared?

"Welcome to Victory Hall." David stepped forward to shake my hand, which meant I had to leave the safety of my umbrella. I squeezed his fingers tightly so that he knew he wasn't alone in this fiasco.

"When I said I wanted a date, I didn't think it would be with the entire contingent of the country's press," David leaned forward and whispered in my ear.

My heart fluttered at the mention of our date but my laugh was halfhearted. If he only knew, that was exactly what he had done when he asked me to the movies.

He gently took my arm and led me inside while Chadwick ushered the press in. The volume in the room increased tenfold as everyone took up an empty spot and divested themselves of their wet coats.

There were several workers inside and one of them hushed us so that we wouldn't scare the birds. It amused me to see the photographers immediately start whispering as the older woman stared them down. A table for refreshments was set up in the welcoming room, but David didn't stop, instead leading us all back where there was a room that would obviously be used for presentations. David motioned for me to take a seat at the front of the room, which I did, careful to make sure no one could see up my skirt. It was long, but you never knew what kind of angles pictures would be taken from. I'd seen photographers slide across a room on their back to try and capture that one-of-a-kind shot of something.

"Welcome to Victory Hall. We're all very glad to have you here." David smiled around the room. "Please forgive my need to speak in English. Despite the programs I bought, my mastery of Lilarian is still an embarrassment."

The room smiled and chuckled, which seemed to ease some of the tension in David's shoulders.

"As some of you might have heard, the Duchess of Rousseau was married this past weekend, which means I've been called in to help run Victory while she is away." There were twitters from some of the people at the thought that someone might have missed the royal wedding. "This means that instead of seeing her smiling face, you're going to have to listen to me blather on. Luckily, the lovely Princess Catherine has come to make sure I don't make a complete fool of myself."

"No promises!" I mock-whispered, and the group of people laughed.

David's shoulders slumped. "Well, folks, in that case, I apologize ahead of time."

I smiled, trying to not laugh. He was much better at working a room than I would have thought.

"Victory Hall was established as a place to bring injured animals for rehabilitation. However, it was also the Duchess Samantha's—"

"Princess!" one of the reporters interrupted.

"Er, yes. It was also Princess Samantha's plan to use this facility as a means of education. Schools will be able to travel here to learn more about our feathered friends, while also learning how to make sure they don't end up needing our help."

He walked over to a stand where a large owl sat on a fake tree, and picked up his gloves. With careful movements he lifted the bird to his arm and turned slowly so that the audience could get a good look.

"This is Sax, a Eurasian eagle owl, and I'm not ashamed to tell you, he's the largest owl I've ever worked with. Sax here is heavier than a great horned owl from the States and has a larger wingspan. The female eagle owls can weigh anywhere from four to nine pounds, and let me tell you, that is one heavy bird. Sax here weighs a nice four pounds and that's partly because he has a steady diet here at Victory."

Gently he coaxed Sax to open one of his wings

and I watched with sad eyes. I might not have a degree in ornithology like Sam and Alex, but I could tell there was something terribly wrong.

"Sax was shot by a hunter who didn't want him on his land." David looked at the owl quietly. "The saddest part is that Sax was only doing what he's meant to do. Now he will never be able to fly again."

Carefully he replaced Sax on his perch and looked out at the audience. "That's what Victory Hall is trying to correct. Misinformation is killing these animals. We hope that with more education and hands-on learning experiences we will be able to teach our children why these creatures are so important. We're also hoping that if a farmer has trouble with a problematic bird, they can come to us and we can find a better solution."

"There are farmers still poisoning many raptors," I spoke up. "Some of them don't know how much harm they are causing, while others don't care. Organizations like the FBT and their subsidiary groups like Victory Hall play a vital role in the defense of these creatures." There were some murmurs from the people seated near me.

"Princess Catherine is correct." David smiled at me and my heart did a little flip. "Why don't you come help me introduce our next guest?"

I could only hope that I wasn't smiling like an

idiot, because I felt like a bubbly girl on the inside. Even though I knew there was probably a script for today, I didn't care.

"Of course." I may have unintentionally added a little more wiggle to my walk than normal and had to tone it down as I climbed the stairs to the platform. "What do you have?"

"Let's get you a glove." He leaned close as he helped me slide my hand into the leather protection. "Wouldn't want anything to hurt your pretty skin." His voice was low, but I couldn't help the blush that spread up my cheeks as I heard the whir of cameras.

"I didn't realize you were such a flirt." I whispered back.

"I practiced in the mirror last night." He winked at me before turning back to the audience.

"Tina, can you bring me Loki?" David turned and smiled at the woman near the edge of the stage.

"And just what is Loki?" I looked at the giant glove he had fit on my arm. I'd handled birds since I was a child, but that didn't mean all birds were the same. I secretly prayed that he wasn't bringing a vulture out for me to hold.

"There's the fearsome bird." He motioned to where Tina walked back into the room. She was holding a tiny owl.

"Aw." I smiled at the itty-bitty thing as he transferred the bird to my wrist.

"This is a little owl," David explained. When the audience laughed he shot them all a smile. "Really. Apparently the scientist that day wasn't feeling very inspired, so this guy is literally a little owl. *Athene noctua.*" He said the Latin name with ease.

I looked at the tiny guy on my wrist and couldn't help the goofy grin that pulled at my cheeks. He was adorable. His little head turned this way and that as he scanned the room and I reached up with my other hand to scratch the top of his head. Just as I got close, his head spun and he nipped. I barely missed losing the tip of my finger to the little beast.

There were gasps in the room that quickly turned to nervous laughs when I tsked at the bird. "That was not very nice, Loki, but I can see where you got your name!"

"Are you okay, Cathy?" David reached for my hand, examining my fingers while the photographers sat up in their seat and snapped pictures.

Not only had he addressed me by my nickname, he had taken my hand in his with a familiarity that people didn't normally see with me. It wasn't that I was cold, but I was always careful with how I interacted with men.

"I'm fine." I didn't snatch my hand back or make a big deal about any of it. If there was an issue Selene could play it off that we were friends through Sam. Which was exactly the truth. The fact that we had seen each other naked and had plans for a date was no one's business. Besides, I liked the way worry wrinkled his brow as he checked my fingers. "Really, no blood."

"I should have warned you." His jaw tightened. "I'm still learning these birds."

I could tell what he was thinking, that he shouldn't be doing this presentation until he was fully ready. Unfortunately that wasn't how things worked in my world. We were often thrown into situations where we had to "fake it until we made it."

"Well, goes to show you that I don't have the proper training for handling these gorgeous creatures." I smiled at the cameras. "Of course, that doesn't stop me from admiring their beauty."

Tina moved onto the stage to take Loki from me and I removed the glove. "Thank you for making sure I was all right, David. A real live knight in shining armor."

His mouth twitched and I wondered what he was deciding not to say. I found myself intrigued just as much by what he left unsaid as by what he decided was worth saying.

# TEN

"So, that was weird." David sat at a table with his feet propped up.

"Really?" I shook my head. "That was pretty tame."

"All of those people with the billion questions and pictures were a tame version of what you normally deal with?" David raised an eyebrow before scratching his chin. "I've faced down a brown bear and didn't sweat as much as I did today."

Chadwick snorted. "It's a totally different beast."

"Nice." I lifted my water bottle to toast his pun.

"I am learning that." David let out a rush of air. "I'm still surprised Sam asked me to do this. I might know birds, but you need to know even more about people, and that is a knowledge I seriously lack."

"Are you kidding? You did great." I smiled at him. "They thought you were charming."

"Apparently, they weren't the only ones." Chadwick faked a cough. "Sorry, something caught in my throat."

"Yeah, right." I rolled my eyes, but David grinned at me. "You should get that checked out."

"I did. It's hereditary. Apparently my father is a smart-ass too."

David choked on his soda and started coughing. I slapped him on the back and tried not to laugh.

"Catherine, are you about ready?" Selene asked. As much as I loved Selene, there were times when I wished I had someone younger working with me, like Chadwick. Someone who made me laugh and eased some of the serious strain on my everyday life. Naturally, trading her loyalty and dedication wasn't an option.

"Of course." When I got up, Chadwick and David both stood, which made me shake my head. "Sit down, you two. It's not like I'm so frail I can't walk to the door by myself."

"It has nothing to do with being frail and everything to do with respect." David moved so that he was standing next to me. "You handled those reporters with ease."

"You didn't do too shabby yourself." I smiled up at him. "You think Sam chose the wrong person, but she got it right."

"We'll see." He opened the door to the break room. "I think Chadwick is working with Selene to find us some free time."

"Good." It was so natural it happened without thought. I stood on my tiptoes and pressed a soft kiss to his cheek. When the realization of what I had done hit me, I froze. He turned to look me in the eyes, my hand still on his chest, and I wondered if he was going to kiss me back. It was so easy, that sense of normal he gave me, but at the same time, electric and hot. It was real and unforced. Not like being with a boy in school because you traveled in the same circles or could understand each other's lifestyles.

This was something else; this was honest-to-God attraction.

The moment probably lasted no more than just that—a moment—but it felt like an eternity as we stared into each other's eyes. Somehow, this moment was even more intimate than having his head pressed between my legs. Of course, that thought sent shivers over my skin and blood rushing to my cheeks.

Clearing my throat, I stepped back. "See you soon."

He didn't say anything, just nodded his head with a small smile.

"I've called and rescheduled the afternoon tea with Duke Challins." Selene looked at me from the corner of her eye as we walked to the car.

"We're running late?" I looked down at my ever-present watch and frowned. "We're an hour behind." I waved at the people outside as we walked down the steps.

"I didn't want to interrupt while you were enjoying yourself." She smiled as we slid into our waiting car.

"You?" I looked at her questioningly. "You thought I should skip an official event?"

"I did." Selene shot me a look that only a mother should be able to give. "I thought you should be happy."

"I'm happy." I frowned briefly before schooling my features back into something content.

"No, you've been existing. You do what is expected of you, what should make you happy, and always put everyone else first." She set her clipboard down and brushed at her skirt. "It's time to focus on you, Cathy."

"I'm in school for something I love. I'm reading a book!" I snorted. "I go shopping!"

"You're going to school where there are expectations of your grades, assignments, and even what you'll do with your degree." Selene frowned. "You go shopping for clothes to wear to formal functions, to do charity work. You buy clothes that you won't wear because you don't go to clubs or parties anymore—not that I'm saying you should." She sighed. "I'm saying you should have some fun, make some mistakes, live a little more."

"You're saying I should be reckless?" I almost threw my hands in the air. Hadn't David just accused me of that, and now Selene—the Prim and Proper Fan Club president—was telling me to go be crazy. Okay, not crazy. But to cut loose.

"Absolutely not." She shook her head. "No drugs, or craziness. Nothing that could hurt you. And by all means don't get pregnant." She looked at me over her glasses and I felt my eyes widen. I sputtered but she held up her hand. "While I have a feeling that David is a gentleman, it's easy to forget yourselves when involved in certain things—"

"Selene!" I gasped. "We didn't—I mean I wanted—it didn't happen. Nothing happened."

"Catherine." There was that sharp mother tone again. I quieted instantly. No matter how old you were, it triggered something inside you that made you put your hands in your lap and look at the other person expectantly. "It doesn't matter. No, that's not true. If you're saying what I think you're saying then I think even more of your new friend. But what I said stands; be careful."

"Yes, ma'am." I took a deep breath. "Have fun. Don't be reckless. Wear party clothes."

Selene reached over and pretended to slap my knee, much the way she had when I was younger and refused to cross my legs. "Stop that. Have fun. Don't overthink it. You loosened up a lot today. It's good."

"So, if I loosen up some more can we maybe cut some more appointments?" I wiggled my eyebrows.

"I think I've reached my quota of rule breaking for the day." She sat back and picked up her clipboard.

"Well, a girl can dream."

She shook her head but didn't look back up at me. "You should be dreaming up things to say to Lady Nancy. She's going to try to rope you into her charity auction again."

"If I give her any more heirlooms my mother will skin me." I sighed.

"You know that's not what she wants," Selene tsked.

"You just told me to live a little. If I donate any more of my time, I'm going to need a clone to brush my teeth and shower." I sighed as I flipped through the e-mails on my phone. "You and I both know she just wants me to work with her oldest son."

"Phillip wouldn't be a terrible choice."

"You say that like it's the fifteen hundreds and I have to marry to support my family in some way." I ground my teeth. "If I ever get married it will be for love. Something of my own—something that belongs to no one but me and the other person, but most of all not to the crown." I frowned. "I give enough of myself as it is."

"I only meant that Phillip is a very nice young man." Selene rubbed at her chest briefly.

"He is nice. And boring." I frowned. "Indigestion, again?"

"Yes." She took a shallow breath and made an uncomfortable face. "It's been bothering me all day, but don't worry. I'm fine and won't slow us down."

I watched her without responding. I'd known Selene my entire life. She was the type of person who worked from home while sick with the flu, even though she should be sleeping. She never stopped.

"Maybe we should cancel today and head back," I offered. "You don't look like you feel well." In fact she looked pale. As I watched, her clipboard fell from her fingers to the floor of the car and she slumped against the door, her eyes rolling backward. "Selene!"

I undid my safety belt and pushed her into a lying position. "Mark! We need to get to a hospital!" I pounded on the glass between the front and back. He rolled it down even as he accelerated.

"Are you hurt, ma'am?" His voice was calm, but nothing rattled Mark. That's why he was my escort wherever we went.

"Something is wrong with Selene." My fingers felt along her neck in an attempt to find a pulse. Panic gripped me as I cursed not having better medical knowledge. It felt like hours passed before I was able to find the thready beat of her heart under my touch. Her pulse was there, but it wasn't good. She murmured something unintelligible to me, but I couldn't figure out what it was. "I think she's had a heart attack."

"Yes, ma'am." I could hear him talking into his communication device, letting the security guards in the next vehicle know what was happening. "Princess, do you want me to stop and let Jameson help? He was an EMT in the military."

"No! Keep going." My hands shook as I touched her face. Selene was like my mother in more ways than I cared to count. To see her so ill was killing me. "Put him on speaker in the car. Let me talk to him."

"Yes, ma'am." It only took a few pushes of buttons on his steering wheel before Jameson was piped in over the speakers.

"Your Highness, is she responsive?"

"She's mumbling, but it's incoherent. What do I do?" I could hear the panic in my voice, so I took a deep breath. Freaking out was not going to help Selene.

"There is a medical pack in the front seat. Mark, pass it back to Catherine, please." Jameson's voice stayed even, as if he was reciting instructions to a practice class. "Catherine, can you get her to take an aspirin?"

"Not sure, but I'll try." Taking the bag I dumped the contents on the floor and grabbed the small bottle of pills. I popped the lid and dumped two pills into my palm before grabbing my bottle of water.

I twisted the lid off and held the pills up to Selene's mouth. "Open up. You have to take these."

Selene shook her head, but I wasn't about to back down. "Now! You'll do it right now even if I have to pry your mouth open."

"Annoying." Selene's voice was thick, but there was no denying the word.

"Yeah, I am." I pushed the pills between her lips and held the bottle up for her to drink.

"Did she take it?" Jameson asked.

"Yes."

"How is she sitting?"

"I've got her laid out on the front bench." The car was a little larger than normal, with big windows so that people would be able to view us at one of the scheduled stops.

"Prop her up and bend her knees some. We want her heart to work as little as possible."

"Got it." Yanking my light jacket off I tucked it under her head and then lifted her feet; scooting them back so her knees were bent.

"Good. We're not far from the hospital." Jameson told me.

"What else should I do?" I found Selene's hand and squeezed it. Her palms were clammy and she was still so pale I worried she would die right before my eyes at any minute.

"You've done all you can at this point." There was a muffled sound as Jameson spoke to someone in his car. "Mark, take the next turn. The authorities have cleared that one-way road for us."

"Tell them thank you." I said the words automatically. It wasn't that I didn't appreciate their help, but that my worry had stopped my brain.

The only thing that mattered was getting Selene taken care of, and quickly.

"Please hang in there." I brushed the hair out of her face. "You're going to be fine. You're too tough to let something like this get you down. Okay?"

"Fine." Her voice was so weak I could barely make out the word, but I knew what she meant. She'd be fine. Selene was always fine.

*God, please let her be okay.*

# ELEVEN

THE WAITING ROOM was bright and cheerful.
Flowers sat on every table, surrounded by magazines about home decorating and health and fit-
ness. Paintings of beautiful places lined the walls
in an attempt to take away the worry of those left
feeling helpless.

I wanted to rip every painting off the wall and
stomp on them until they were unrecognizable.

Helpless was not a place I liked to be. I'd rather
have been in the operating room passing scalpels
than pacing back and forth between a painting of
an Irish cliff and the image of a waterfall.

Max was watching me from his seat with a
worried look, and that irritated me too.

"What?" I growled the word, stopping mid-
stride to stare at him. "Why are you looking at me
like that?"

"I'm worried about you." He held a cup of hot
tea in a white foam cup.

"Don't worry about me. Worry about Selene." I shook my head. "She's the one whose heart is literally in the hands of strangers right now."

"I checked, Cath. These doctors know what they are doing." His words were quiet, soft, as if speaking to a person on the edge.

"I know." I threw myself into a chair. "It's just really frightening."

"I can't imagine how scary it would have been." He reached out and squeezed my hand.

"It was." Tears formed in my eyes and I sniffed. "I've never been that scared before. Not even with . . ." I couldn't finish that sentence. With Dad there had been no fear, just pain and overwhelming grief. By the time we knew he had been thrown from his horse, he was already gone. It had been instantaneous.

"I get it." Max kept hold of my hand. He might be the sibling that hid from our family the most, but he was still my big brother. And my big brothers were always there for me. In fact, we'd had to have Mother call Alex and tell him not to come home.

Excruciating hours passed as we waited. Mark had brought us dinner at one point, but neither of us ate much. When Tabitha, Selene's secretary, showed up to help, it took all of my willpower not to burst into tears. I was relieved to have help with everything that had to be seen to, but at the same time, it was so very wrong to see someone else handling Selene's clipboard.

When the doctor came out to speak to me, I could barely contain myself. I needed to know what was happening, how she would be—when she would be out.

"We've been able to clear the blockages and are closing up now. She did really well through the surgery and I think she will make a full recovery." The doctor smiled at me. "I know you've been worried, but you did the best thing for her by bringing her here. She has a pretty long road to recovery though. This was a major surgery and she will need time off."

"Of course. I'll see to it that she wants for nothing." I nodded my head.

"She will need to drastically cut back on her stress levels. I'm willing to bet that she is a workaholic."

"We'll make sure she's not overdoing it." Tabitha spoke up from beside me.

I turned to look at her, surprised that she had said anything. Selene would never have interjected during a conversation that didn't directly relate to her. Then again, Tabitha was much closer to my age and not as formal. Knowing that she had worked closely with Selene for two years now kept me from becoming angry. She was probably just as worried as I was about Selene. I should have asked how she was handling the news, not just worrying about myself and my friend. Tabitha had just been called on to fill some very big shoes.

"You're absolutely correct, Doctor. Selene works in her sleep. But we'll find a way to keep her calm and in a place where she can heal." I held my hand out to shake. "Thank you so much for your great care. I can't begin to explain how much I appreciate all of your time and hard work. Selene is like family to me."

"I'm happy to help, and even happier to be able to report good news." He shook my hand and smiled warmly. "The worst part is over. Now you just need to keep her in bed so she can heal."

I almost snorted. He was right, but he was wrong. Selene was out of danger's direct path, but I was about to be in for the fight of my life. Keeping that woman down and relaxed would be a near-impossible job.

As the doctor left I slumped back into a seat as relief washed over my body like a tidal wave. Every muscle went limp and I could barely hold my eyes open.

"Tabitha, can you find me a hotel room nearby?"

"Yes, ma'am." Tabitha picked up her phone and began pressing buttons on the screen. "Are you sure you wouldn't rather go back to D'Lynsal? It's only an hour away by helicopter."

"I think my sister wants to be near her friend." Max touched my shoulder in support. "Plus it would be irresponsible to use the helicopter just because we were tired." The reprimand in his words was gentle but clear. We were a wealthy family, but that didn't mean we didn't have to answer for the use of certain things.

"Of course. I apologize." Tabitha bent her head. "I was just thinking of what was best for Princess Catherine."

"Thanks, but I want to be near Selene." I couldn't help the yawn that followed my words. "And could you make sure someone takes care of Xavier, my dog, while I'm here. I had planned on going back to the palace tomorrow."

"Yes, ma'am. And I've found a suitable establishment a few minutes from the hospital. I can have the team check it out right now."

"Send one car ahead of us." Max pulled me to my feet. "Please make sure that there are rooms for me and my team as well. I will be staying with my sister."

"Of course, sir."

I waited until I had seen Selene before I would leave. She was still unconscious, but knowing that she was stable and in good hands helped me let go for a while.

Max was waiting for me outside the hospital room when I was ready to leave. "There are reporters outside."

"Of course there are." If I'd had the energy I would have snarled, but at this point I just wanted to sleep and to be left alone. "They just can't wait to get more pictures."

Max wrapped his arm around me and squeezed me against his side. "Keep your head down and I'll get you to the car before making a statement."

"No, you don't have to do that." I shook my head. Talking to the press was physically painful for Max.

"Hush." He leaned down and whispered in my ear as we walked past hospital staff. "I can handle this, Cath. I'm not twelve anymore. Stop being so damn tough and let someone else take care of things for a little while."

I looked up at him and felt my eyes well up for the eighteenth time that day. Max might be my older brother, but for all royal duties, Alex and I tended to keep him tucked safely away. That's what happens when your brother finds out about his father's death during a press conference. But right now, it wasn't surprised and hurt green eyes looking at me. It was the eyes of a grown man ready to protect his sister. And right now, I felt like I needed a little protecting.

"Okay."

"I'd rub it in that you let me win, but I think I'll let it slide this time."

"Oh yeah. Way to let it slide." I elbowed him in the ribs. "I'll see you at the hotel."

"Be safe." He let his arm drop from my shoulders and met the press as I made a quick getaway with my security team.

Jameson moved so quickly past the cameras and reporters that I had to lengthen my stride. The car ride was silent, except for Tabitha tapping on her phone. There was no small talk, no friendly glances or comforting words—and I was thankful for that. I had nothing left to give, much less to build a relationship of any kind with Tabitha.

The hotel was large and the doormen didn't blink an eye at royalty entering their building. Tabitha took care of the check-in and led our group up to a penthouse. I looked around the entryway blankly. I had seen everything in the apartment before to some extent or another. Three bedrooms;

a small, boring living room; a kitchen and eating area. Nothing exciting.

"I thought you might like the bedroom off to the right. There is a large tub and I had the maids draw you a bath." Tabitha walked over to the door and opened it with a flourish. "I sent Mark to D'Lynsal to bring you some clothes. If there is anything in particular you need, let me know and I will pass the information along."

"There is always a bag of extra clothes in the car." I sighed quietly. "But thank you. This just means I won't have to worry about ironing."

"I went through the bag and you only had one dress, and a pair of jeans." Tabitha frowned. "I thought we might be here longer than a day."

"You're right." She had gone through my bag? Without asking? My instant ire probably had more to do with my sleep-deprived state than anything else. I reeled in my anger and counted to five. "But next time, please ask before you go through my things."

"Of course, ma'am. I apologize." Tabitha bobbed her head. "I was just trying to not bother you with unimportant things."

"My privacy is very important." I shook my head. "I'm going to take that bath and then go to bed. If Max needs me or something changes with

Selene, wake me; otherwise, I'd like to sleep for a few hours."

"Yes, ma'am." Tabitha turned and walked over to the kitchen table without a curtsy or head bob.

It wasn't that I needed that show of respect, nor did I really want it, but it felt odd to work with someone so new who treated me as if she'd known me forever. Selene came and went as she pleased, had a way of telling me something in a motherly fashion while still maintaining protocol. Apparently working with Tabitha was going to be a very different experience. Sighing, I shook my head and went into the room. When I shut the door I closed my eyes and pinched the bridge of my nose.

My head was pounding, but it was probably from the stress. Stripping my clothes off, I made my way to the bathroom and felt my first smile in hours. The smell of lavender and the warm water went a long way to easing the tension in my neck and shoulders.

By the time the water was cold, I could barely hold my eyes open. Thankfully there was a fresh housecoat hanging on a hook from the door. I barely took the time to dry off before wrapping myself in the thick softness of the bathrobe. I shuffled to the bed and flopped onto the down comforter and was fast asleep before I realized I had closed my eyes.

It felt like it had been only moments when Max's voice woke me. Groggily I looked at the clock in confusion. Why was he making so much noise at midnight? I scrubbed at my eyes and tucked the robe closer to my body. One leg was almost frozen because I hadn't taken the time to climb under the blankets. Sitting up, I pulled the robe tight and looked around my temporary room. There was a small clock sitting on the bedside table and I blinked. The little red dot on the side said it was p.m., not a.m.

"For the love of all that is holy!" I jumped out of bed and dashed across the room to yank the door open. "Why did you let me sleep so late? How is Selene?"

My eyes scanned the room for Tabitha but landed on David instead. He was sitting on the small sofa with a book perched on his leg, but his eyes were trained on me. It was in that moment that I realized I was still wearing a bathrobe that was barely held shut by the loose belt.

"Good morning." His deep voice sent goose bumps over my skin. Everything in the room seemed to disappear, and for a moment it was just the two of us staring at each other.

"What are you doing here?" I asked.

"Hi," Chadwick piped up from his seat at the dining room table. His laptop was open and he shot a smile over the screen. "Nice to see you too."

"Chadwick! Why did you let me sleep so late?" I started to put my hands on my hips as I glared at him, but thought better of it. Instead I pulled my belt a little tighter and glared at my friend.

"I was *instructed* to let you recuperate after your trying day." He stressed the one word in such a way that it became a language of its own.

"Where is she?" I looked around the room for Tabitha but she was nowhere to be seen.

"I believe she's taken it upon herself to contact your appointments and reschedule. She's also sent a message to Samantha."

"She what?" My voice dropped to a whisper and I could feel my temper brewing just under the surface. "Why? Why would she bother Sam?"

"She just wanted to alert the princess of the unfortunate events." Chadwick raised an eyebrow. "Of course, Sam and Alex were ready to come back to help out, but I've made them promise to wait until they could speak with you directly."

"Is that why you're here?" My eyes shot from Chadwick to David and back.

"Well, partly." Chadwick shrugged. "David

and I were worried about Selene . . . and you." He closed his laptop gently. "And I wanted to have a talk with Tabitha about contacting my charges directly. That's against protocol."

"There is a protocol for who can contact Sam?" David asked from his seat. He had closed his book and was watching the exchange between Chadwick and me with interest.

"Yes. All correspondences should be delivered through me or my staff. Tabitha should know this." Chadwick leaned back in his chair. "I've never said anything before, but she's—"

"Overzealous?" I sighed. The last thing I needed right now was an assistant who couldn't manage her job. Trying to find another that I could trust during a time like this would be nearly impossible. "I was going to call Alex today. He's known Selene longer than I have and figured that he would want more information. There was no need for her to upset either of them on their honeymoon."

"Especially considering how recently Sam lost her father," David spoke up. "I know she seems tough, but she's sensitive."

"We know," Chadwick and I responded at the same time.

"I forget that she's been here for so long. It still

seems weird that she is royal. You guys got to see the transformation firsthand. For me, she'll always be the girl that got crapped on by a vulture." David shrugged.

"Sam got crapped on by a vulture?" I laughed loudly. "Oh, now that's a story I need to hear."

"I'll save it for our date." He smiled at me and my knees went a little wobbly. It didn't sound like he was upset about our date. "Whenever you're ready for one, that is."

Oh, I was ready. Until I remembered Selene and the help she would need. "It might have to be pushed back a little."

"You two are a little disgusting, you know that?" Chadwick said. "I think I might drown in the pheromones floating around. And your scheduled interlude is not going to need to be pushed back." Only he would be able to get away with such a comment without getting sacked. "I spoke with the doctors this morning and Selene is doing very well. She's sleeping a lot, but they expect her to heal quickly. And if you think you're going to be nursing her back to health, think again. I've seen how you cook, and your chicken noodle soup would land her back in the hospital."

"Hey!" This time I did put one hand on my hip while I stared him down. Despite my pose, I was too happy to hear Selene was doing well to be truly offended by his jab at my cooking skills. "It's not that bad. Okay, it's bad, but it wouldn't land her in the hospital. You can live on my cooking!"

"Of course." Chadwick opened his computer back up. "If you also order takeout every night."

David chuckled. "It can't be that bad."

"It's not!" I sat down in the chair across from him.

"Oh really? Why don't you tell him how you make macaroni and cheese?" Chadwick never looked up from whatever he was working on.

"I'm never telling Sam anything again." I shook my head. Apparently my new sister had shared my cooking mishap.

"How do you mess up macaroni and cheese? You just boil noodles and add the cheese!" David leaned forward in his seat, a twinkle in his eye letting me know that he enjoyed seeing me shift in discomfort.

"It's not a big deal." I picked at the terry-cloth robe and didn't meet his eyes. "I added the wrong stuff."

"Oh, Catherine. Don't lie. You didn't add the wrong stuff. You boiled the wrong stuff." Chadwick snorted.

"You forgot the water?"

I met David's confused eyes and shook my

head. "No. I skipped water completely and boiled the pasta in milk." Sighing I decided to go ahead and tell the whole story. "Not only did I boil the milk, I refused to not eat my food just because it smelled weird, and ended up with food poisoning. I missed my first two days of classes."

Chadwick was trying so hard to stifle his giggles that he ended up snorting loudly.

"But I make a mean cup of coffee." I added in my defense.

"This is important information." David scratched his chin. "I've just learned that I shouldn't eat anything you cook; and you're so stubborn that you would rather make yourself sick than admit defeat."

"I've gotten much better at cooking." David's eyes shifted to over my shoulder and I turned just in time to see Chadwick touching his nose in agreement. "But yes. I am that stubborn."

"Good to know." David's eyes ran over my body to where my leg peeked out from under my robe.

"I should really find some clothes." I stood up, careful to keep the material in place.

Chadwick stood up from his seat and grabbed a bag that was hidden behind a chair. "I believe this is yours."

"Thank you." I took the bag and headed to my room. Before I closed the door I looked at David and then Chadwick. "How long are you two staying?"

"I've moved our schedule around so that David could attend some of his meetings in town." Chadwick didn't have to tell me why. I knew he was worried about leaving me with Tabitha. And as much as I loved having him here, Tabitha and I would be fine. We just needed to find our groove.

"Once I'm ready I'm going to the hospital. You're welcome to come with me." I meant the offer for both of them, but it was David I looked at when asking. "It would be nice to have a friend along."

"I'd like that." He flashed that charming smile and my heart picked up just a little more.

When I closed the bedroom door I caught a glimpse of my hair and makeup-free face in a mirror and frowned. I needed to do something about that and quickly. Reporters would be camped outside the hospital waiting for my arrival. Not to mention David would be with me. I was vain enough to admit that I wanted to look nice for him. So I threw my bag on the bed and got started. As a royal there were certain things expected of me, and looking nice was one of them. I enjoyed yoga pants and T-shirts as much as the next girl, but it would send the wrong image to people if I showed up to visit a beloved aide looking like I had just been to the gym.

I also didn't want to look too professional or serious, so a suit or dress was out of the question. Instead I opted for a designer top and jacket to pair with jeans and my boots. The key to packing an emergency bag was to include pieces that would work well for different occasions and things that you could mix and match.

And if there was one thing I knew how to do, it was to look the part of a princess.

# TWELVE

With Sam and Alex out of the country and on a private island, the paparazzi had nothing better to do than hound me and Max. It was frustrating, but also a part of life I'd come to expect. There would always be someone wanting my picture, and there would always be another person hoping for something embarrassing.

Security had been deployed at the hospital to make sure patients were able to enter and leave as needed without being harassed. It was a sad day when you had to tell television vans to move out of the ambulance lane, but today was one of those days.

Chadwick and David had ridden in a separate car, while Tabitha, Max, and I rode together. I hadn't been able to find time to speak with my new, temporary assistant, but I would soon.

"I think you should take a minute to address the crowd." Tabitha flashed me a large smile. Her sweet voice made the words sound innocent, but I didn't like being told what I should and shouldn't do.

"I had planned on it." I shot Max a look and he shrugged.

"Excellent. I'm sending you some key points now. Check your e-mail."

I froze, unable to find words for a moment. I knew she was trying to be helpful, but that was a bit over the line. "Thank you, but I already know what I am going to say."

"You should look them over, just in case. These cover every contingency or possible question." She explained her reasoning slowly and I felt myself growing even more annoyed. I wasn't stupid, I just didn't need her help for this.

"Tabitha, I know you mean well, but I've been speaking to the media for a very long time." I ground my teeth before continuing. "The only thing they need to know is that Selene is in good hands and making positive movement toward recovery. I'll express our pain and sorrow at seeing such a close friend in so much pain and then walk on. Nothing else matters at this point."

"I released a statement explaining that you saved Selene's life in the car, so it's well known that you were a big part of her survival. I'm sure there will be questions about what you did."

"You what?" My voice was much louder than I had intended. Max stilled in his seat and I could see the anger working behind his eyes. "You released a statement without consulting me?"

"I didn't want to bother you, but time was of the essence. Besides, it's my job to do that stuff." Tabitha cocked her head to the side. "Don't worry, I made sure that you looked good."

"That I looked good?" My hands shook in my lap. I was so angry I was vibrating in my seat. I'm sure she meant well, but this was inexcusable. I opened my mouth to tell her off, but Max beat me to it.

"Your job is to do what Her Royal Highness directs you to do." Max's deep voice cut through the car. "Your job is to make sure she's awake at a time she sets. Your job is to follow her orders and to make prudent suggestions when the time calls for it. Your job is *not* to make assumptions or to do what you think is right without asking Catherine first."

Silence filled the car and I tried to keep the shock from my face. Max was never one to mince words, but I'd never heard him correct someone so thoroughly.

"I apologize." Tabitha frowned, her eyes going

wide. "I was only trying to handle things the way Selene would."

"Selene and I have worked together for a long time now and have a better sense of each other." I searched for diplomatic words. "Suggesting that I saved Selene's life is not true. It also diverts the attention from those who truly deserve the praise; like the doctors, nurses, and other staff. They are the ones who saved Selene and they are the ones who will benefit from the praise. It would instill trust from the surrounding community in their medical team. Pretending that I saved Selene will do nothing for me, but make me look as if I'm asking for a pat on the back, when all I really care about is my friend healing." I took a deep breath. "Besides all of that, if Jameson had not walked me through it over the speakerphone, I would have had no idea what to do for Selene."

"I see." Tabitha adjusted her skirt and I fought the urge to shake her. She was hurt by being corrected, but if she had come to me first, all of this would have been avoided. Her chin jutted forward and her eyes took on a hard gleam.

Not only had I just responded to her mistake as kindly as possible, I was not taking out my anger on her. Despite my growing desire to do so. For a brief moment I had a mental image of Sam's face if Tabitha had done this to her. It went a long way to cooling my anger. Watching my new sister tear her a new asshole would be satisfying. Too bad I didn't have it in me to do it as well. All I could hope was that the media would understand that she was new to her current position and take that into consideration.

Mark was out of the car and opening my door as soon as we pulled up to the hospital. The press moved close as I exited the vehicle with Max's help.

"Princess Catherine, how is your aide?"

"Princess, will your friend make it?"

"Highness, how does it feel to know you saved your assistant's life?"

Taking a deep breath, I turned and pulled my sunglasses off so that the reporters would be able to see the honesty in my eyes as I responded to their questions. Max moved to stand behind me, but what was truly surprising was that David had also moved to flank me. The logical part of my mind knew that people would draw conclusions about his relationship with me, based solely on the fact he was standing near me. The emotional part of my brain simply enjoyed the fact that he was showing his support for me during a difficult time.

"The last day has been very trying for everyone involved. My dear friend Selene is still recuperating after a very serious health issue and surgery, but seems to be doing much better. All of the credit for her current situation belongs to the wonderful doctors, nurses, and staff that work here. I'll never be able to thank them enough." I smiled softly, careful not to show any teeth. "I'd also like to thank everyone for their prayers and well wishes. They mean a great deal to all of us." I waited for a moment, while the photographers took pictures.

After a moment, Max guided me through the automatic doors and past the throngs of people that had gathered inside to see my statement. It was mainly people waiting to see doctors or waiting on family members to have their appointments. Tabitha walked beside and slightly behind me as we made our way down the hallways. She was quiet and I wasn't sure if I cared that she was upset. No, that wasn't true. I didn't want her to hurt or be angry, but I also wanted her to stop trying to be Selene.

Just thinking of my longtime assistant sent a pang through my heart. The closer we got to Selene the more anxious I felt. Talking to the media didn't make me sweat, but the worry for my friend made me feel short of breath.

There was a guard at her door, which I appreciated. Selene wasn't royalty, but because she worked so closely with me she could easily be targeted by royal stalkers, news reporters, treasure hunters, and random nosy people. A nurse was taking notes when we walked in and motioned for us to be quiet. Selene was sleeping and I was shocked by how frail she looked lying in the hospital bed. It was painful to see and I turned around to hug Max, but bumped into David instead.

His arms didn't hesitate as they wrapped around me, and the warmth of his chest seeped through his shirt to warm my cheek. With one hand he tucked my head under his chin and murmured reassuring words that I didn't quite understand in his deep Southern American accent. It was sweet, though, to have him comfort me when he barely knew me.

But he was trying—trying to get to know me, even after I had hastily thrown myself at him. And I liked what I was learning about him.

Once I had myself under control I let go of David and turned to watch the nurse change the IV bag before checking Selene's pulse.

"She's doing really well," the nurse told me in Lilarian.

"Will she wake?" I moved to touch her arm.

"Oh yes. She's just tired. Her body needs rest." The nurse smiled at me before bobbing a quick curtsy. "Your friend is in good hands here."

"I have no doubts." I turned back to Selene and sat down in the chair next to the bed. "There are a ton of flowers in here. I didn't realize you had so many friends." The joke was my sad attempt to keep from crying, even though it was true. There were so many flowers stuck around the cramped room, it felt more like a floral shop than a critical care unit.

"Stop frowning." Selene's voice was a weak croak. She rolled her head to the side and looked at me with half-lidded eyes.

"Hey there." I smiled down at my longtime friend. "I'm glad to see you're feeling better."

"That is a matter of opinion." She frowned. "I feel like I was hit by a wine truck."

"A wine truck?"

"Drunk and hurt." Her eyes fluttered shut for a minute. "Sorry. Still tired."

"Sleep. I'll be here." I squeezed her hand.

I turned the television to something other than the news and sat for a while, holding my friend's hand while she snored softly. It wasn't until the third episode of a nature show came on that she stirred in her bed.

"Go eat." Her voice took on a stern sound.

"What?" My eyebrows lifted.

"You don't eat when you're worried. Eat something." Her head rolled to the side gently. "Real food."

"Yes, ma'am." I couldn't help my chuckle. Even now when she was recovering from a near-death experience she was trying to take care of me. I leaned over and kissed her forehead but she didn't stir. She was already sound asleep once again.

"Cath, I'm going to go. I have some engagements to take care of, but I believe Chadwick and David will be staying for a little while." Max touched my shoulder. Leaning down he whispered in my ear, "Maybe your new friend is hungry too. Chadwick could stay and watch Selene while you eat."

"Thanks." I reached up and touched his hand. I had a feeling that Max was picking up even more slack now that this had happened with Selene.

"Be careful with Tabitha." With that last sentence, he squeezed my shoulder and left the room.

"Want to find the cafeteria?" David asked.

"Sure." It was well after lunch and I still hadn't eaten. Selene was right, I lost all interest in food when I was worried or stressed, but I'd try to eat something.

Chadwick settled into my seat as I left with

David. I realized this was the first time we had been alone since he had asked for our date. Well, if you didn't count the bodyguards following a few steps behind or the fact that Tabitha was probably lurking somewhere just out of eyesight.

"So does this count as a date?"

"I'm not sure." He scratched his chin again and I wondered if he realized he did that when he was thinking. "Not exactly an ideal place."

"Nah. There's food, flowers, and zombies everywhere."

"Are zombies a qualification for a good date?" He chuckled.

"Well, I hear that scary movies give you a reason to fake being scared and cuddle close." I batted my eyes at him and he laughed.

"I have a feeling that you would be the last person in the theater to be scared."

"I said fake being scared," I replied. "Of course I wouldn't be scared. A good axe to the head of the zombie and you're fine."

"Wow. That's a bit violent, Your Highness." His shoulder bumped into mine and I realized he was as close to me as he could be without actually having his arm around my shoulders.

"Well, a good shovel would work too. Something with reach, but not too long. You don't want to waste time swinging something longer than you are tall." I mimed swinging a bat.

"You've done your fair share of research on this, I see."

"I grew up with two older brothers. They thought it would be funny to scare their little sister with horror movies, but the joke was on them. I wasn't the one up with nightmares." I nodded my head.

"No, I bet you slept with an arsenal next to your bed."

"A big polo stick. They never snuck into my room again." I laughed, remembering them running and tripping over each other as I swung my weapon. Mother had been furious, but Father had simply winked at me.

"Despite everything, it seems like you had some really normal moments growing up."

"Despite everything." I snorted. "There was a lot of normal in my life. I just also had to learn how to behave when visiting dignitaries stayed at our home." I shrugged. "Sort of like when other people are on their best behavior because Aunt Beatrice comes for the holidays."

"Okay, I can see that, I think." He pointed to a sign leading to the cafeteria. "Our food, madam."

"Excellent. I was in the mood for cold turkey and day-old salad." I rubbed my hands together.

"I do aim to please."

We took our trays from the end of the line and pretended not to notice the people staring at us as we chose our food and drinks. I was used to ignoring everyone, but I could tell David had to work at it. When we reached the cash register at the end of the line, I pulled one of my cards from my pocket, but David stopped me.

"I've got it." He ducked his head so that he could whisper in my ear. "What kind of man lets his date pay for dinner?"

"So it *is* a date," I whispered back.

He didn't respond for a minute, just looked down into my eyes thoughtfully. "Any time I get to spend with you is special."

My heart clenched and my stomach did this weird flip, but I couldn't make fun of that compliment. If there was one thing I'd grown to expect from David, it was sincerity, and I knew he meant what he had just said.

I smiled as we walked to a corner table, away from the majority of the people catching lunch or dinner during their break and the sad faces of people waiting on friends or family.

"So tell me about your family. Mine's no secret but I don't know much about yours." I dug into my salad with my fork.

"Not much, huh?" He watched me with a smile.

"Well, you asked Sam about me." I shrugged.

"True." He took a bite of his food before starting. "I'm the oldest of three kids. My family still lives in Georgia, which is pretty much slap at the bottom of the states."

I knew exactly where Georgia was—geography was a necessity in my life—but I motioned for him to go on.

"Our town was tiny and most people didn't go to college. Lots of farm work in the area, but I had a love of animals and wanted to do more. My youngest sister, Liberty Anne, is eleven, and like me she loves animals. She has a therapy horse that is her whole world." His eyes lit up. "She is autistic, but it's as if a light turns on when she's riding Whipper. She tells us that it's magic."

"It's amazing what an animal can do for a person." I nodded my head. "Art does that too. It can give a child a way to express themselves that they normally wouldn't. It's part of why I'm working on my art program for schools."

"Yes, and that's why I want to do something for the animals." He took another bite of his food. "Liberty helped show me how special, beautiful, and magic they can be. I want to stop the senseless killing. I know that education isn't the only thing we need, but it will help. No more poisoning or killing birds just because farmers and hunters don't want competition."

"A noble cause." I smiled at him. My family had a long history with animals and it said a lot about his personality that he wanted to protect them. "What about the rest of your family?"

"I have one other sister, Christi. She's in her third year of school. She's going to be a fantastic engineer. Numbers just come to her naturally." He shook his head. "That's something I was always jealous of."

"She's in her third year? So she's, what, twenty-one?" I dug around on my plate. "You're pretty spread out in age."

"A little. I just turned twenty-seven and Liberty Anne is adopted." He pointed his fork at me. "Was that your sneaky way of finding out how old I am?"

"Maybe." I laughed. "You're really young for having a doctorate."

"I finished early." He shrugged. "I took advanced classes in high school and didn't see the point in taking summers off in college."

"I wish I could take more classes over the summer, but I have to help with engagements. The summer is always extremely busy for our family." I sighed. "Not that I want to be done early."

"Why not?" David had almost finished his sandwich.

"I only have so many years to spend at university before I have to take up a more formal position with the family."

"Being a princess isn't a formal position?" He laughed.

"I mean more responsibility. I'll be taking over a lot more duties and my art history degree will mainly be used for charity work." I shrugged. "It's not a bad deal. I can accomplish a lot of good stuff."

"What would you do with your degree if you didn't have to focus on royal stuff?"

"I'd like to curate exhibits, and I think I've found a way I can do that while maintaining my royal duties."

"That sounds promising." He pushed his plate away from him and leaned forward on the table.

"We have a ton of art that is kept in the palace. Some of it can never leave, but there are pieces that would be perfect for a traveling show. Plus I could use the funds for charity, which would go toward my school art fund." I frowned. "I really need a good name for the charity. It might help get the investors more interested."

"It's amazing what a good name and logo can

do for someone," David said thoughtfully. "I'll think about it. Maybe we could brainstorm on our next date."

"Already want another date, huh?" I couldn't help my smile.

"Well, it hasn't been horrible if you don't count the zombies." His eyes ran over my face and I felt my heart grow lighter.

"Don't worry. I'd protect you." I reached over to pat his hand, but he captured it and brought it to his lips. "What was that for?"

"Your smile."

"Be honest. Did you buy a book of compliments?" My breathing increased and I could feel the heat in my cheeks. Just his touch sent my body into overdrive.

"I'll never tell." He winked.

"Fine. I'll let you keep your secrets."

The sound of a camera clicking caught my attention and I looked at the window to see several photographers taking pictures from the hallway. "Shit."

"What?"

"We're being photographed and they saw you do that." I frowned and turned back to my food. "Don't look at them. They want a full face shot if they can manage it."

"What does it matter?" There was a defensive look in his eyes.

"Don't you remember what happened to Sam?" I leaned forward and lowered my voice. "The paparazzi almost killed her; wrecked her car and chased her through the streets while her father was dying."

"I'm not a duke." He narrowed his eyes. "Or is that the issue?"

"You've got to be kidding me." I sat back in my seat. I'd really been enjoying myself up until this moment. "I wouldn't care if your mom was the bearded woman at a circus, but I do care that you would think so little of me."

"Whoa. Let's back up." He held his hands in the air. "I shouldn't have accused you of that. Mainly I don't think I'd have the same problem as Sam. I'm no one."

"Yeah, Sam thought that about herself too." I shook my head. "What do they teach you at that school?"

"Okay. I'm not a nobody. I'm just not someone that would be of interest." He shrugged.

"If you're dating me, you will be someone of interest." I cringed. "That sounds incredibly egotistical but that's not how I mean it. Because of who my family is my entire life is subject to observation. There are people just waiting to dissect every picture of me."

"Okay, you're saying that if I'm dating you, people will want to take pictures of us together." He frowned and stared at the table for a minute, his mouth pulling to his side as he thought it over.

"Not just us together." I shook my head before grabbing my plate and standing up. "C'mon. We'll talk somewhere else."

He followed me without question and when I looked back at him I could see the wheels still turning behind his eyes.

The attention of the press had amplified the curiosity of the staff and other people in the cafeteria. We dumped our trays and let the security detail clear our path. We made our way back to the room Selene was in, but when I noticed an empty hallway, I pulled David along with me.

"Look, I like you." Blunt was the only way to handle this type of situation. "But if we date— even just one date to the movies, or a quick lunch in a hospital cafeteria, you're going to become tabloid fodder. Strangers meet and decide to date all the time. People have one-night stands all the time. Couples break up or decide to go their separate ways all the time. But with me? Or anyone in my family? All of that makes front-page news."

"I get that, Cathy." He lifted my chin.

"Your face will be everywhere, on everything, plastered across social media. If you decide that this doesn't work for you, it will pop up whenever someone searches your name on the Internet."

"I know." His voice was so calm, there was no way he could understand what I was explaining.

"It's not fair to you, because you don't even have a chance to get to know me to decide if all of that craziness is worth it."

"I think it is."

"I mean, you could decide that I'm a silly— Wait. What did you say?" I frowned.

"I decided that it was worth it." He smiled at my shocked expression. "Look, if we try this out and it doesn't work, then fine. We'll go our separate ways and I'll deal with what happens. But I think we should give it a shot."

He thought I was worth it? "But you don't know me yet."

"I know enough." His thumb traced my bottom lip. "I know I want to know more."

My heart pounded and I wondered if it was possible for a person to die just from the look in someone's eyes, because at this moment I was pretty sure I was well on my way to melting into a puddle of goo.

"I'd really like that."

"Then let's take this one day at a time. We will deal with reporters and nosy tabloids if we have to, but for now let's just take some time to learn more about each other." He dipped his head down lower so that his lips were near mine. And photographers or innocent bystanders be damned, I wanted to kiss him again. The inclination was even stronger now that I'd spent more time with him, and it took every ounce of self-control I possessed to keep from crushing my mouth against his.

I nodded my head. With his hands on me, I probably would have agreed to go streaking down the hall. There was something special about the way his eyes met mine, the way his hands felt on my skin. It hit me like a ton of bricks when I realized that it was because he saw me, the woman, not the princess. I never thought that would happen, and the feeling was intoxicating.

# THIRTEEN

SELENE SLEPT MOST of the time I was in her room, but the few times she was awake did a lot to ease the pain in my heart. I'd been thinking—when not distracted by David's gorgeous eyes—that I needed to cut back her schedule. She wasn't a young woman and maybe it was time for her assistant to take a step up.

"Would you like me to cancel the appointments for tomorrow?" Tabitha was sitting on a stool in the corner of the cramped room.

"Are there any in the area?" I looked over at the other woman. David and Chadwick had left an hour or so before, but not until they absolutely had to. Victory Hall opened to the public tomorrow and David had to be there no matter what else was happening.

"There is a school art program visit, which is about half an hour away."

"What time?" I looked at my watch. It was getting late.

"Just before lunch. Selene's notes mention eating with the head of the department." Tabitha tsked under her breath.

"That would be the L'vere School. I really shouldn't miss that." I sighed. "The clothes that you had brought from D'Lynsal will be appropriate for that engagement."

"I tried to cover all bases." She smiled at me, and for the first time I realized that she wasn't just pretty, but someone who could turn heads.

"You did wonderful," I said. "Thank you."

"You're very welcome." She looked up at me. "I hope that I can fill Selene's shoes while she is recovering."

"They're big shoes. Literally. Her feet are huge." I laughed, but Tabitha's smile was small. "Truly though, you've done a great job for having this dumped on your shoulders."

She beamed at me. "Thank you."

"Of course." I picked up my bag from the ground and stood. "What's the press situation right now? Are they still packed outside?"

"The last I checked, there were still a good many. We could try leaving out the back." Tabitha stood and collected her own stuff.

"I think that would be a good alternative for tonight." Leaning over, I kissed Selene on the head.

"Sleep well and don't drive the staff crazy while I'm gone."

"I'll call for another member of the staff to sit with Selene while you are gone tomorrow."

"Thank you." I followed Tabitha out of the room.

"It's a shame that she has no family." The words were flippant, and guilt slammed into my chest. My steps hesitated and I almost went back to the room. Someone who had devoted her life to me lay in a hospital bed. The only thing that kept me going was the knowledge that she wouldn't forgive me for letting down the schoolchildren.

"She has a family," I retorted, and resumed walking. My steps were a little faster and heavy. "Selene has been part of my family for as long as I can remember."

"I meant blood relatives."

"Blood doesn't make someone family." I frowned. "Love is what makes a family."

"Of course." Tabitha didn't look up from her phone as she typed out some long message.

I shook my head. I knew that Selene's dedication to my family had been part of the reason that she'd never had one of her own. When someone kept the same schedule that we did, they were afflicted with the same problems—sometimes even

more so. It was almost impossible to meet someone who would understand what we did and how
much time it took.

We followed the guards to a rear entrance, and
before the door had even opened I could hear the
commotion outside.

"How did they know?" I looked at Mike, my
security guard.

"I'm not sure, ma'am. It's possible that they
staked out all of the entrances." He shrugged. "I'll
never understand these people."

"Agreed." I shared a small smile with him. If
there was one thing the media managed to do
for our stalked group, it was to unite us against a
common enemy.

"Perhaps you should say a few words," Tabitha
suggested.

"The words I want to say would not be very
polite," I mumbled.

"Just a quick bit." Tabitha strode out of the
doors, leaving me to follow in her wake.

She stopped, blocking my way to the car, and
turned as if waiting for me to make a statement. I
ground my teeth but flashed a smile.

"Thank you all for your concern over Selene.
I'm happy to report that she is recovering and I
have the utmost faith in the staff here." I looked

around at the cameras quickly. "I'm sure that she will be astounded by all of her well-wishers when she wakes in the morning."

There were chuckles all around and I used that to my advantage. Mike's large bulk cleared the path by sheer presence and I climbed into the car as quickly as possible.

Tabitha smiled at me as she slid into the seat next to me. "Perfect."

"I don't need you to tell me if I say the right or wrong thing," I snapped.

Her head jerked back with my words. "I'm sorry, ma'am. I just meant that you gave them exactly what they needed."

"What they need is to leave a sick woman alone." I watched out the window as we drove away, a fake smile on my lips as I cursed my life.

"I hate to point this out, but they are here because you're here. They want you, or your brother, not Selene. If you truly don't want to worry about them bothering her, you could take up some more of your engagements."

"Keep my distance?" That drew my attention back to Tabitha. "We just talked about how I was her only family."

"Yes, but if you're not making stops there, then the media attention will dissipate."

"I don't know." I frowned. Someone needed to be there with Selene. She shouldn't be alone at a time like this. "I'll give it some thought. Maybe we can work out some kind of middle ground."

"It's definitely worth a thought." Tabitha looked at me with direct eyes. "I just want what is best for the both of you."

"It's my hope that she'll be well enough to go home soon. That will cut down on the media."

"That's true." Tabitha looked back down at her phone.

I had thought Selene's clipboard was annoying, but I was finding that Tabitha's use of her phone was insane. I was starting to wonder if she was playing some type of Tetris-style fruit game, or planning world domination. As much as she played on the thing, she could be controlling MI6 for all I knew.

"For now let's focus on taking care of the appointments that are in the area and reschedule the rest. I don't want to be far if Selene needs me."

"It's admirable that you care so much for her. I know she cares for you a great deal." Tabitha looked up and smiled at me.

"It's mutual." The thought warmed my heart. I hated that just a day before I had thought about having a younger assistant. At this point, I'd give anything to have Selene and her clipboard sitting next to me as we figured out the details for a speech or how to engage a particularly difficult audience.

"Well, if we narrow down everything to an hour driving distance, you'll still be able to hit several of the important events." She flipped through the clipboard. "I hope you don't mind, but I took the liberty of putting Selene's notes into my phone. It just makes it easier to sync my calendars together."

"That's fine. I've been trying to convince her to do that for a while." I watched the lights going by and smiled to myself. "You'd think I was trying to get her to write stuff in blood."

"She's the same way in the office." Tabitha chuckled. "Our filing system is a scary beast. So much paper and folders floating around. We have a special first-aid kit for paper cuts."

That drew an unexpected laugh from me. "I bet you guys hate it."

"Well, it would be nice to switch everything over, but we'd all tell you that her system works. And she always says—"

"If it isn't broken, don't fix it," I finished.

"Exactly." Tabitha set her phone down and looked at me seriously. "And that's exactly what I came bumbling in and did. I'm sorry for overstepping boundaries. I truly did mean well."

"No, it's okay. This is a trying situation for all of us." I sighed. "I should have been more patient. I'm sorry."

"No, you were right. I came in, clipboard blazing, and tried to be a superhero. But you don't need a superhero."

"I don't know, I don't think I'd turn Captain America away." I smiled.

"Well, it looks like you already have a knight in shining armor." Tabitha wiggled her eyebrows.

I laughed. I couldn't help it. "I don't know about that."

"Well, he could save this damsel any day." She held up her hands when I turned quickly to look at her. "Just saying that he would look good riding in on a white horse."

"David would look good riding in on a donkey."

She tittered loudly, which made me laugh. She had a horrible laugh, but it felt honest and sincere. "I think you're right. You should snap that up."

"We'll see." I looked back out the window. We were almost back to the hotel and I still needed to do some work before bed.

Her phone beeped and I could hear her clicking away in response. I wanted to ask her who she was talking with, but there was no polite way to approach that subject. And in all honesty, it could have absolutely nothing to do with me. She could be talking to her family, canceling plans with her family or a significant other.

"I should have asked before now, but do you need time to handle anything back at the palace? You had to leave on really short notice." I offered an apologetic smile. "I don't even know if you have any family or children."

"No children." She smiled. "And my boyfriend understands that this is my job. If he didn't understand, he wouldn't be my boyfriend."

"I can understand that." I nodded my head. "But if you need to catch up on anything, I'll be fine. I can manage on my own."

"Of course you can!" She sat up straighter. "But I really am okay. Everything that I was working on in the office is being handled by one of the other assistants. Being ready for the unexpected is part of our job." She leaned forward conspiratorially. "In fact, we've all gotten kind of stale. It's good to shake it up a little from time to time. Though I wish it hadn't been at Selene's expense."

"Too bad she didn't just go on vacation, huh?"

"I don't think she's ever gone on vacation, has she?" Tabitha widened her eyes. "I've only been working with her for a couple of years, but I can't remember her taking off more than a weekend."

"You're right. Which is probably why she's in a hospital from a heart attack right now."

Once we were to the hotel, we made our way back up to the room in companionable silence. Max was sound asleep and snoring on the couch when we opened the door. Knowing that he was probably exhausted from his day in the limelight, I made a quiet sign to Tabitha, who smiled and mouthed good night before disappearing back out the door. I wasn't sure where her room was located, but it was probably nearby.

I took my shoes off and went to the kitchen to grab a snack and get something to drink. The fridge wasn't stocked the way it would be at home, but there were a few things like fruit and cheese on a covered dish. I ignored the soda and opted for water instead. Quietly I padded back across the giant room and sat in the big armchair next to Max. The television was going and the news was showing a story about a wounded soldier who had returned home just in time to see his twin daughters being born. It was a bittersweet story but at least it had a happy ending.

The next story almost made me spit my grape across the room. The stupid title at the bottom of the screen said, "Royal Love," and the story started out with an image of Sam and Alex running around on a beach. Those jerks had found the island and were using aircraft to video my brother's honeymoon. I leaned forward and glared at the smiling reporter as she joked about the fun the two seemed to be having on their getaway. Getaway. Like it wasn't their honeymoon, but just a random trip that didn't matter.

Oh, then they showed Samantha in her wedding dress, smiling for the cameras. She was gorgeous and it would have made my heart swell if it hadn't been used by the very reporter I had told Tabitha to not allow into the wedding. Had he just stolen the picture or bought the rights? It figured that he would be the one hounding them on their honeymoon. Speaking of that, there was now a picture of them kissing on the beach, and I blanched.

"Blech." I turned the channel. No matter how old I got, no matter how much I adored Sam, Alex was still my brother and I didn't want to see him playing grabby-ass with anyone.

The next channel was some type of soap opera and I watched for a minute as the actress slapped some man wearing a tuxedo. Heh. I've wanted to do that before. I picked up a piece of cheese from the tray I had brought with me and looked it over.

It smelled off so I set it to the side and stuck to the fruit.

"Are you really going to watch that?" Max's groggy voice interrupted the string of verbal abuse coming from the television.

"I don't think so," I replied. "I just wanted to know why she hit him."

"That's how they get you." He rolled over on the couch and covered his head with a pillow. "At least turn it down."

"You have a room." I pointed to the side opposite of my room. "With a bed and everything."

"Can't. I'm waiting on a phone call." His voice was muffled. "If I go to my room I won't wake up for it."

"Who is calling you this late?"

"'Merica." The word was garbled.

"Who?" I frowned.

"America." Sitting up, he threw the pillow on the floor. "You're not going to let me sleep, are you?"

"Nope." I shook my head and passed him the fruit tray. "Who is calling you from America?"

"Bird crap." He grabbed a couple of apple slices.

"Bird crap is calling you from America?" I giggled.

"Ha ha. Dork. People are calling me about bird crap. Future Bird Trust. Blah, blah, blah." He stretched. "Something about starting an American branch."

"Can't Chadwick handle that?" I bit into another grape.

"I wish. It's the president's wife, which means she needs to speak to someone other than an assistant. Though Chadwick could tell her more about that stuff than I can. It's just a formality at this point." He frowned at his apple. "What is it they call her? The first lady? What would they call the husband of a president? The first man? That sounds idiotic. Hello, I'd like to introduce you to Bob, the first man."

"It is a bit silly, but I can see why they need a title." I shrugged. "It's a little harder when you don't have royalty, huh?"

"Right. Because that makes life so much easier." He bit into his apple. "I hope Sam comes back knocked up."

I choked on my water and had to wipe up the little that dribbled down my chin. "What? Why?"

"Put that crown a little further away from me." He smiled. "The last thing I want to ever be is king."

"Um, I'm pretty sure that Sam isn't ready to be a mom yet." I frowned. "In fact, I'd be surprised if she didn't have an entire suitcase of birth control packed and next to their bed."

He snorted. "She'll be a great mom. And the kid would be cute. Even if Alex is the dad." Old habits like picking on your sibling died hard, no matter how old you were.

"No doubt. I'd love to be an aunt." I smiled thinking about it. "Now I'm going to have aunt fever."

"Is that like baby fever?"

"Yeah, but when you can give the baby back to the parents."

"I like that idea. I can't imagine being a parent. Can you? We don't have any time to ourselves now. It would be hellish to have to split the little bit we do have with another living, breathing, needy thing."

"Wow." I shook my head. "Let's hope you don't knock anyone up any time soon."

"Let's hope I don't knock anyone up ever." He shook his head. "I honestly can't imagine passing all of this baggage on to someone else."

I sat there stunned for a minute. Sure, I had thought about having children before, but hadn't really thought about the fact that they would have to go through what I had. Then again, they would be further removed from the crown than Max and I. It wouldn't be quite so bad.

"It's what you make of it." I shrugged. "If you

do have kids, it doesn't mean they have to be in the spotlight. The world is changing. You could make sure they had a normal childhood."

"Our children will never have a normal childhood." He looked at me with pity.

"Well, no one is really normal, now are they?" I picked up the remote and flipped through the channels. I didn't want to continue that conversation. Having a child was a part of a normal life I wanted for myself. "Oh! Zombies."

"Great. Phone calls, babies, and now zombies. My own personal horror movie." Max leaned back on the couch.

I threw a grape at him. "It's your fault I like them."

"I'll always regret that." He picked up the grape and ate it.

"Ew. You don't know whose butt has been on that couch." My nose wrinkled in horror.

"And I don't care." He smiled. "Good grape."

Shaking my head, I turned back to the TV and watched as the hero used a bow and arrows to take out a stampede of the undead. Now this was a good way to relax after a long day.

# FOURTEEN

$\mathcal{T}$HE SCHOOL I attended the next day was a miracle of good feelings. The children were excited, the staff was kind, and best of all, everyone seemed genuinely interested in my art program.

Tabitha was great about updating me on Selene's condition and making sure I had the papers I needed for the pitch I was giving to the school administrators. After accepting the different drawings that the children presented to me and seeing the classroom with the new supplies that I had funded, I was escorted back to my car and on my way to the hospital.

"That went really well!" I smiled at Tabitha, relieved. "It's nice to see why I'm doing this, not just fighting with investors."

"I can only imagine how frustrating it is to deal with people that just don't get something you're passionate about." Tabitha typed a few things on her phone as she talked. "And the kids love you. When you sat down and painted at that one table with the kids, I thought they were going to go crazy."

"They were really well behaved." I smiled. "And it was fun. I haven't taken the time to paint a rainbow in forever." I laughed at the thought.

"I think they're going to auction off the painting at their next school fund-raiser for the program."

"Oh Lord. No one's going to want to buy that." I shook my head. "But I guess every bit counts."

"That was the prettiest rainbow I've ever seen." Tabitha looked up at me with a straight face.

Laughter burst out of my mouth, which made her do her weird chuckle-snort.

"There is a reason I went into art history and not studio art the way Max did." I shrugged. "Alex is good too, but I'm the weakest link when it comes to that talent."

"Well, it was a beautiful rainbow. And a nice daisy to boot." She smiled before turning back to her phone. "I'm sure someone will want to hang it on their refrigerator."

I snorted. "Only because I signed my name at the bottom."

"Would you mind making one more stop before we get to the hospital? There is an event taking place a couple of blocks away."

"What is it?" I didn't want to stay away from Selene any longer than I needed to.

"You were scheduled to reveal a plaque at a local animal hospital, but I originally told them you might not make it."

"What is it for?" I asked.

"They have donated over two hundred thousand man-hours to animal care."

"I suppose we could stop by briefly." I frowned. That certainly deserved recognition; I just hated not being with Selene. "I want to get back to Selene quickly."

"Excellent. I will give them a call and let them know." Tabitha dialed a number quickly and explained we would be making it after all. I shoved my frustration out of the way and put on my "princess face."

When we pulled up, there was a large crowd of people waiting outside and a ton of reporters.

"I thought we had originally canceled?"

"I'm betting they thought you might show up since you did the school event." Tabitha shrugged.

Jameson opened the car door and helped me out before lending a hand to Tabitha. I smiled for the cameras briefly before letting Tabitha lead me up the stairs. I noticed that she was smiling for the cameras as well and thought that was odd, but dismissed it. She was probably not used to being around all of these cameras. Her job had mainly kept her in offices until now.

"Welcome, Your Highness. It's an honor to have you here today!" An older man in a pristine doctor's coat shook my hand. He smelled faintly of bleach and I had a feeling he'd taken a lot of time to make sure he looked nice. Between that, his bow tie, and the goofy grin on his face, I was instantly charmed. "I'm Dr. McRae."

"A pleasure." I shook his hand. "I'm sorry to arrive on such short notice."

"Completely understandable, ma'am." He bobbed his head. "I was sorry to hear about your assistant."

"Catherine, please, and thank you." I smiled. "I think they want us to take a picture together."

"Oh! Yes, that would be wonderful." He turned and stood next to me, his hands held in front of him.

We smiled and looked from camera to camera, letting them all get an image or two before going inside. Thankfully there were only two photographers inside and they were more interested in official pictures of me unveiling the plaque.

"It's over here, ma'am." The veterinarian motioned for me to follow him. "Thank you so much for coming to do this. It's an honor."

A red velvet cloth covered an easel, and the staff and their families were gathered around in anticipation.

I moved so that I was standing on the opposite side of the plaque and waited, smiling at the cameras as people took my picture or video.

"I'm humbled to have Princess Catherine here today to help celebrate this huge achievement. I owe my staff and their family a million thanks for all they've done for the animal community." He smiled around the room as people clapped. "Even without the plaque, I hope you all know the amount of good you've done this year."

I clapped with the rest of the room, agreeing wholeheartedly with what he was saying. The amount of man-hours they had put into their community was worth more than a plaque, but at least they were being recognized.

"I'm honored to be in a room with so many kindhearted people. I know that what you've done to help these animals and their families was a labor of love that required a lot of sacrifice on your part. So on behalf of my family and this community, I thank you." I tugged the cloth from the plaque in one fell swoop and rolled it up in my arms.

People oohed and aahed. People clapped. And

of course there were more pictures. I posed with everyone and took the time to shake the hands of the staff. I ate little sandwiches and drank tea. Not once did I glance at my watch to check the time, despite my desire to be with my friend. By the time Tabitha finally came to rescue me, I had been at the veterinary clinic for four hours. It wasn't that I regretted the time spent with the people and it wasn't as if I hadn't enjoyed talking with everyone.

But I had a friend in the hospital, with no family to keep her company. My need to get back to her was pressing on my chest by the time we got back in the car.

"That went well." Tabitha smiled at me. "They were so glad to see you."

I took a deep breath, trying to choose my words so that they didn't come across wrong. "I'm glad we went, but next time, I need you to step in and get us out of there a little faster."

"I thought you were enjoying yourself."

"I was . . . but that's part of my job—to spend time with people and make them feel important—because they are important. I need you to cut in and keep me on schedule. Otherwise it looks like I'm rude for leaving and I'll be stuck there for days."

"Maybe we could work out a signal. That way I know when you're ready." She chewed on her lip for a minute. "Maybe you could look at your watch."

"No, if I do that people will think I'm counting down until I can leave. That would seem rude."

"I'm sorry I didn't think about this. I just knew we didn't have anything else on the schedule." Tabitha sat back in her seat and played with her phone. I was starting to understand why Selene disliked cell phones. Tabitha never put hers away. It was like part of her body and she couldn't think without it.

"No, I told you that I wanted to see Selene. She's been alone for hours now." I frowned. "Perhaps you should put Selene time into your calendar. That way there are no questions."

"Of course." She nodded her head with a smile.

There were reporters outside of the hospital still, but I merely waved and pushed through the throngs. There would be no more official speeches from me today.

The staff smiled at me as I walked through the halls and one of the nurses even gave me a small wave. The fact that they were treating me like someone returning to see a family member warmed my heart. It also went a long way toward easing the tension in my shoulders. It was time to turn Princess Catherine off and just be Cathy for a little while.

"Hello?" I whispered the word quietly as I peeked into the door of Selene's room.

"Took you long enough." Chadwick's voice replied.

I sighed in relief when I realized Selene hadn't been alone this whole time. "What are you doing here?"

"We had an event in the area for the FBT and figured we would drop by to see how Selene was doing."

"We?" I turned to look around the room and realized that David was leaning against the wall. "Hi."

"Hi." His eyes traveled over my body and I felt it like a hot touch. It didn't help that the memory of what it really felt like to have his hands on me was seared into my brain.

I turned to look at Selene and smiled when I realized her eyes were open. "How are you?" I moved to her bedside and grabbed her hand.

"Alive." She squeezed my fingers. "Did you make it to all of the appointments today?"

"No, but we got two in." I smiled. "Tabitha wouldn't let me out of all of them." I turned to see where my temporary assistant was, but she was nowhere in sight.

"They sent Tabitha to help you?" Selene's brow furrowed.

"Yes." I watched her closely, surprised by her reaction. I'd always been under the impression that she was grooming Tabitha to be her replacement.

"I'm sure she'll do a fine job." Selene closed her eyes for a moment. "I'm sorry. This pain medicine makes it difficult for me to stay awake. I'm tired of being in this bed."

"And that, my friend, is exactly why they have you on that medicine. To keep your butt in bed!" I shook my head and she laughed gently.

"You've been telling them my bad habits."

"Of course I have." I leaned forward and lowered my voice. "You have to cut back. You've been doing too much."

"I'm doing the exact same thing you're doing." She looked away from me. We both knew that was a lie. She did much more than I did and she was more than twice my age.

"It's killing you." I frowned. "We need to find another way of handling things. Perhaps hiring an assistant for you."

"We'll talk when I get out of here."

"And when is that exactly?"

"Maybe a week. Depends on how I'm doing." She started to shift and her face flinched in pain.

"What about physical therapy?"

"Oh, those bastards were in here earlier. I don't want to talk about them." She shook her head.

I laughed. Prim and proper Selene had just called someone a bastard. That was well worth a laugh. Even Chadwick was chuckling.

"Wow. Okay," I finally responded.

"Don't tell her that they will be back every day for months," Chadwick stage-whispered.

Selene whimpered. "Oh, that's just horrible."

"It'll be fine. We'll get some great ones to come to D'Lynsal to work with you." I patted her shoulder gently, still bothered by how weak she looked.

"Nonsense. I'll go back home and they can visit me there." Her words were a whisper as her eyes fluttered closed.

"Get some rest." I kissed her forehead. "You're coming home with me no matter what you want."

"You're so stubborn, you know that?"

"Of course I do. I modeled myself after you." I laughed.

She made a disappointed *hm* sound before her breathing evened out and she was asleep. I sat back in my chair and watched her for a minute. It was a relief to talk to her, to know that she really was on the mend.

"I need to step out and make some phone calls." Chadwick stood up. "Would you like me to bring you some food?"

"That would be great." I smiled at him. "You know what I'll eat."

"David, would you like something?" Chadwick turned to look at the man in the corner.

"Sure." He shrugged and pushed off the wall. "Whatever is fine."

"Then I'll be back in a little bit."

"Thank you," David and I said at the same time.

"Of course." Chadwick winked at one of us, but I wasn't sure who exactly it was meant for.

When he was gone, David took the empty seat next to me and leaned forward so that his elbows were braced on his knees. Having him near me sent my blood pressure up. I was keenly aware of how his long body folded up to sit in the chair, how his hair hung in his eyes, and how the stubble along his jaw screamed to be kissed.

"Long day?" His deep voice drew me out of my thoughts.

"What?" Whoops. I'd been caught ogling.

"Did you have a long day?" His smile was

slow as he cut his eyes at me. I had definitely been caught checking him out.

"Long day." I nodded and hoped my blush wasn't noticeable in the dim light. "You?"

"Not so bad really." He turned so he could see me better. "I think I'm starting to understand a little more about the FBT and I still get to work with the birds, so that's a big plus."

"That's good. I know it was a hard transition for Sam to not work with the animals every day." I enjoyed how easy it was to talk to David. If you were to look at us, you would probably think that we didn't have much in common, but that didn't seem to matter.

"Where's Tabitha? The one with the phone?" He looked around the room like she might be lurking in the shadows.

"I honestly have no idea. She always seems to disappear." I pursed my lips. "I'm kind of glad though. It's weird to have someone new spend so much time with me."

"Tell me about it." David frowned.

"See, I'd kill to have Chadwick right now. I can't imagine it being weird. He's so . . ." I searched for the right word. "Comfortable. You don't have to be anything but who you are around him. And he is always on top of things. You never have to worry that he will leave you hanging or say something inappropriate."

"I get it. It's not Chadwick, exactly." He smiled. "The guy is hilarious. It's just having someone at all. You know what I mean?"

"I know what you mean, but I can't relate. There have always been people working around me, helping me keep up with everything, or bodyguards making sure I was safe."

"We had help on the farm. People that worked the crops and tended to some of the cattle. But they were employees. Don't get me wrong, we liked them. Hell, Dad always gave them bonuses at the holidays and if they had nowhere to go, Mama invited them for dinner. But the way Chadwick and Selene work with you? So closely? It's very intimate."

"Intimate. That's a good word for it." I leaned back in my chair. "They sometimes know us better than we know ourselves."

"How's it working out with Tabitha? Seems like you two are getting along a little better."

"It's a learning experience. We have to figure each other out and work around that. It's been— challenging, but I think we're getting the hang of it." I thought about it. "I'm not sure it would work as a permanent solution, but for now, it's fine."

"That's something, considering how quickly everything happened." He leaned back in his chair and folded his arms behind his head. "Speaking of which, I was thinking about our date."

"Okay, shoot." My heart dropped. He was going to cancel. With everything that had happened, you couldn't ask for a better excuse. I stilled my face in an attempt to hide my disappointment.

"I think we should still go." He put his hands back down on his legs. "At first I thought maybe we should postpone it, but since Selene is doing so well, it might be nice to have a little fun. Relax after a stressful week. If that's okay with you."

"Oh." Relief and a little jolt of electricity flooded through my body. He really did want to have a date with me. "That would be nice."

"Nice?" He made a face. "We don't have to go if you've changed your mind."

"No! I thought—" I shook my head. "I'm looking forward to going."

"What did you think?" He leaned closer, his face curious.

"Nothing." I shook my head.

"That means it was something." He smiled. "Out with it."

"No, not now." I shot a glance over to where Selene was still sleeping.

"Okay, but you're not escaping." He winked at me and my heart fluttered.

Chadwick walked in with a soft knock on the door. He was carrying two bags of food that smelled delicious. "There is an empty break room down the hall. The nurses said we could use it for dinner."

"That was nice of them." I took the bag he held out.

"Yep. Now go eat. I'll sit with Selene." Chadwick shooed me out of my seat.

"Are you sure? I know you have a long drive home." I took the bag hesitantly.

"I'm positive." He pointed at David. "You. Her. Go eat."

"You don't have to tell me twice." David held up his hands.

"I like him." Chadwick winked at me. "He doesn't argue as much as Samantha."

David slapped Chadwick on the shoulder. "I'll try harder."

"That wasn't a challenge," Chadwick tsked. He started unloading his bag of food onto the little table next to the bed.

The smell of the food made my stomach rumble and I decided I didn't need any more urging either. David opened the door and we followed Chadwick's directions to the break room.

I took the food out of the bag while David purchased two drinks out of the machine in the corner. I wasn't sure how Chadwick had managed to get us Chinese food, but I wasn't going to complain. Since there were no plates, I undid the boxes so they lay flat. We'd just have to share.

I sat down and broke apart my chopsticks and picked up a piece of lemon chicken.

"No forks?" David looked around, worried.

"I didn't see any." I smiled. "Don't like chopsticks?"

"I'll just avoid the rice." He sat down and propped the sticks clumsily between his fingers. I tried not to laugh when he picked up a piece of chicken, but when it shot across the table I couldn't help it.

"Here." I reached across the table and repositioned his fingers. "Try this."

"I'm still going to fling food at you." He shook his head. "I'm terrible with these things."

With careful fingers, he picked up a piece of chicken and managed to get it in his mouth. "I'd be better off just stabbing the chicken."

I laughed. "Whatever works."

"There have to be forks in here somewhere." Getting up, he rummaged through the cabinets. "Aha!" He held up a box of plastic utensils.

"Lucky." I chuckled, but declined the fork he offered me.

"Good. Now spill." He sat back down.

"What do you mean?" I looked at him innocently.

"Why did you think I was going to cancel?" He took a bite of rice, but kept his eyes trained on my face.

"I thought you were going to cancel." I spit the words out before I could rethink it. "Because . . ."

"Why?" He looked confused and I felt like the biggest idiot.

I took a deep breath. "You know, considering that we haven't gone on our actual date yet, we sure have talked about it a lot."

"I don't know. Seems like this might actually be date number two." He cocked his head to the side. "And I've enjoyed getting to know you any way I can. Now, back to the question."

"Damn." I muttered, even though I was feeling tingly from his admission.

"C'mon." He raised one eyebrow and flashed that slow smile that I was a sucker for.

"I was worried that you were only taking me on a date out of a sense of chivalry." I bit my lip and looked down at the floor.

"You thought what?" He reached out and

tucked some of my hair behind my ear. "You thought I was taking you out to appease my sense of guilt?"

I didn't respond, just met his eyes and held my breath.

"Let me explain something." He set his fork down and I knew he meant business. "I don't feel guilty about what happened that night. In fact, leaving you that night was one of the hardest things I've ever done."

"Then why did you?" The shame from that night rushed back and I leaned a little further away from him.

"Cathy, you deserve more than a one-night stand or a quick tumble in the sheets." His eyes narrowed and his voice dropped an octave. "You deserve to have it all—to experience it all. One step at a time. The teasing touches, the almosts but not quite. And then I want to make love to you. Not scratch an itch or check something off the list. I want you ready and willing, begging me for what you need."

The food I was planning on eating was halfway to my mouth when I froze. I had no words, only thoughts of how he might leave me begging.

"Um." That was the only working syllable I could squeeze out of my lips.

"And most importantly, I want you to decide that you want me to be your first for the right reasons." He paused. "That you want me as much as I want you. All of you, not just your body."

"I—I didn't think that would be an option for me." I set my food down and decided to be a big girl. "That's why I thought a one-night stand would be the way to go."

"I'm not saying that a lot of girls don't use that very tactic, but wouldn't you rather it be with someone you like? You could decide you hate me, or that I drive you crazy. Then you'd regret it and I don't want that." One of his eyebrows rose as his eyes traveled over me. "Well, I want something, but not for you to hate me."

"You're making me blush on purpose." I shook my head.

"I'm just getting started," he replied. His smile grew and I looked down at my makeshift plate.

"Okay, so this is our second date then?" I shook my head before popping my food in my mouth. "This is a pretty weird conversation, don't you think?"

"Nah. I'm sure there have been weirder ones."

"Like what?"

"Killing zombies, for one."

"Okay, so my track record for date conversation isn't so great." I laughed.

"Actually, it's fun and different." His smile went all the way to his eyes. "You're different."

"That's a good thing, I guess."

"It's a good thing."

"Well, you're not so bad yourself." I narrowed my eyes and decided to change the subject. I wasn't sure what would happen if he kept talking about making me beg. "When you talk about yourself, anyways. If you want me to get to know you, you're going to have to divulge more information."

"Ask away." He motioned with his fork for me to go on.

"If Sam hadn't asked you to come to the FBT, what would you be doing?"

"Looking for a job." He chuckled. "No, really. You'd think a doctorate would guarantee a job, but most of the good positions are filled by lifers."

"Lifers?" I asked.

"People that snap up a great position and never leave." He frowned. "I did have an offer from a university, but I'm not ready to go straight into teaching full-time."

"That makes sense. Want to see and do a little more first." I nodded my head.

"Exactly. Then I can decide where I really want to be." I finished off the last of the chicken and moved on to the noodles. "It must be hard for you to not have a choice."

"I have a choice," I argued. "Well, with some limitations, but really, most people have limitations and certain expectations. Being a princess is my job. I love it most of the time, but everyone has bad days or days you just don't want to go to work. Then there are bad parts to every job, and you just have to work around them. This week has been tough. I thought I was going to go insane at a plaque unveiling. It was for a great cause and the people were wonderful, but all I could think about was getting back to make sure Selene was okay."

"That's understandable." He nodded in understanding. "I love working with birds, but that doesn't mean there aren't days when I want to beat my head against a wall."

"Exactly. Today was one of those days." I frowned. "The media has been ridiculous. They've even calmed down when it comes to Sam and Alex, except for the wedding, but lately they are everywhere. I don't usually rate this much attention."

"That is a lot to deal with, but you're a pro." He reached out and touched my hand. "I've been watching and I can see how you work the crowd. It's so natural, I imagine most people don't notice when you turn it on. Turn on the princess."

"That's exactly what I do," I said. In less than a week, David had noticed more about me than most people. "I turn on Princess Catherine and do my duty." I shook my head. "That makes it sound like I don't enjoy it and I normally do. But I have to be so careful and follow certain protocols. There are days that I just want to be Cathy."

"I get it." He frowned. "I don't mind teaching, actually enjoy it when the students are interested, but that doesn't mean I don't want to just be David. It's why I turned down the professorship."

"I think you're going to like the FBT. You'll get the best of both worlds." I stood up and started cleaning up the trash while he got a rag to clean off the table. "I think we've left Chadwick alone long enough. Who knows what type of things he's planned for you."

"Scary." His voice was odd as he turned and looked at me. "I'm thinking . . ."

"You're right. That is scary." I threw the trash away and watched him as he walked toward me.

"We agreed that this was our second date, right?" His hand cupped my face while his thumb rubbed along my cheek.

"Yes." My voice came out husky as he leaned a little closer.

"Then I think a kiss is in order," he said. His

free hand moved to cup my hip and pulled me a little closer. "I've been dying to since the other night."

I went willingly, eager to taste his kiss once again. He didn't rush the moment, dragging out the wait as his lips neared mine, but still didn't touch. His breath washed over my face and I leaned forward even more. When his lips finally touched mine, it was the softest whisper of a kiss, brushing against my lips like a feather's touch. While his lips moved slowly, there was a barely contained heat behind his touch. His fingers tightened on my hip and his other hand dipped my head back so that he could have better access to my mouth.

I ran my hands up his arms to rest on his shoulders, enjoying the slow kiss that ignited fire in my veins. When he slowly pulled away, I kept my eyes shut, savoring the moment. It was the best kiss I'd ever experienced.

# FIFTEEN

"WHERE ARE MY nude heels?" I got down and looked under the hotel bed. Pushing the extra pillows out of the way, I made sure they weren't hiding.

"I think they're out here," Max hollered. "If by nude you mean beige."

"What the hell are they doing out there?" I mumbled as I ran into the living area. "Thanks."

I plucked them from his fingers and ran back to my room. David was supposed to be here any minute and I still wasn't finished getting ready. Sliding into the bathroom, I grabbed the curling iron and added a few loose curls to my hair, giving it that careless look that was anything but careless. I checked my makeup and spritzed on a light perfume. Nothing too heavy, but just enough to know it was there.

Turning, I looked at my outfit and frowned. I didn't have a lot of options at the hotel and no time to shop. I'd picked out a pair of jeans, a dressy tank top, and a blazer. The shoes and some jewelry pulled it all together. It wasn't exactly my best outfit, but it was comfortable and I liked it. It also wasn't too dressy for the movies, but not so comfortable that it looked like I hadn't cared what I was wearing tonight.

Voices coming from the living area made me hurry, and I grabbed some lip gloss quickly and threw it in my bag. I rushed out, to save David from Max. I wasn't sure if my brother would give my date the third degree or not. He usually didn't seem to care if I dated someone, but he'd been much more interested in David for some reason.

"Where are you going?"

"The movies and dinner." David's voice was calm and polite.

"Which theater?" Max asked.

I rounded the corner in time to see that Max hadn't let David very far into the suite.

"I'm not sure exactly. I believe the bodyguards chose the one they felt was most secure." David tucked his hands in his pockets. He had dressed up, still in jeans, but in a button-up shirt under a light sweater. He had shaved too, which was the first time I had seen him that way. I liked it just as much as I did when he had a five-o'clock shadow.

No matter how you cut it, the man was mouthwatering.

"Max," I warned. He held his hands up in the air in mock surrender.

"You look great." David smiled at me.

"Thanks." Smiling I walked past Max to stand in front of David. "So do you."

"Have her home by midnight," Max grouched from behind me.

I rolled my eyes and held my hand out to David. His warm fingers wrapped around mine, and the familiar feeling of heat from his touch traveled up my arm and over my body.

The car was waiting downstairs, but at an employee entrance instead of out front. I wondered if the press would have caught on to our sneaky attempt, but there was no one with a camera in sight. Of course, that didn't mean someone with a telephoto lens wasn't hanging out in a tree.

"How did we manage to escape the press?" I wondered aloud.

"Jameson's idea. He has the car I came in idling at the front entrance." David sat next to me and turned so that his long legs were tucked into the backseat comfortably. "You know, the last time someone drove me on a date was back in middle school. Feels like I should be asking my parents to extend my nine o'clock curfew."

I laughed. "Well, despite Max's demands, I don't have a set curfew."

"Good to know." His hungry eyes ran over my face and down my body. "I want to keep you to myself for as long as possible."

A slow smile pulled at my lips. "That sounds like a good plan."

Reaching over he wrapped his fingers around mine. "Do you care what movie we see?"

"Hm. I like funny movies, action movies, or romantic comedies." I paused. "Nothing that is going to make me want to cry or want to hurt the actors."

"Right. No Nicholas Sparks movies." He nodded his head.

"Most definitely not." The last thing I wanted was to be snotty and miserable while on our first "official" date. Tear-inducing movies were out of the equation.

The ride to the theater was comfortable, and except for the driver and bodyguard it almost felt like the normal dates I had read about in books. We joked about movies, talked about our favorite actors, and even argued about music. And yet, the whole time his thumb traced circles on my palm, sending electric tingles up my arm. I'd never thought that someone who could affect my body in the simplest way would actually match me in other ways. And even the things we disagreed about seemed to make us fit. He hated pizza, I couldn't imagine life without it. I loathed country music and it was all he listened to. He thought Donatello was a turtle, and I had no idea who Bob White was, but it didn't matter.

We decided on a movie, purely because of what was about to play when we arrived. A romantic comedy that I had secretly been hoping to see but hadn't wanted to ask. I hated to pick movies, unless it was with Sam. She and I always seemed to agree, and if it was something the other hadn't seen, we trusted each other's opinion. However, I hadn't wanted to force David to sit through a sappy movie. Especially since we were finally on the date he had originally asked to do.

"You look relieved." David handed me my ticket.

"I saw commercials for this and it looked good." I tried to play it nonchalant, but he raised an eyebrow and smiled that damn smile I couldn't resist. "Okay, I was hoping we'd get to see it! Jared Sutton is in it and I'm a sucker for him. I can't help it."

"Uh-huh. Well, I really did want to see that new spy movie instead. We could wait a half hour . . ." He started to take the ticket back but I hugged it to my chest.

"No way. It's bought and paid for. A done deal."

"Well, I guess I'll have to suffer through you drooling over another man." He mock-sighed.

"Might work to your advantage." I walked over to the concession counter and ordered drinks and popcorn.

"In that case, I won't complain." He reached over and took the drinks so I could carry the popcorn.

"Smart man." I winked at him.

"I have my moments."

The theater was dark by the time we went inside and we had to duck as we searched for seats so as to not block the view of the other moviegoers.

"Excuse me," I whispered as we slipped past a couple sitting in the last row. The woman did a double take when she looked up at me, but didn't say anything, just shifted her legs so we could get through.

We had perfect seats, right in the middle with no one blocking our view. It was shaping up to be a great night. Why hadn't I gone on a regular date before? All of my other dates had been to formal occasions, or occasionally to the party of an important family or business. Never to anything normal like the movies.

David set his drink down in the arm farthest

away from me, before handing me my drink. We missed the previews, but had made it just in time for the start of the movie. At some point during the laughing and the sweet parts, David's arm had wrapped itself around my shoulders. As the end of the movie neared, happy tears slid down my cheeks and I tried to hide them. I loved happy endings. Life so often dealt us ugly blows that I wanted books and movies that left me feeling happy.

"You okay?" David ducked his head down to whisper in my ear. With his free hand he wiped away a tear from my cheek.

I nodded my head and sniffled. "Just happy."

His arm tightened around me and I savored the feeling of being held. I might be a virgin, but I was beginning to realize it wasn't just sex that was lacking in my life. Most forms of intimacy were foreign to me. Especially the kind where you could really relax and just enjoy that sense of comfort without worrying what the other person wanted.

I snuggled closer into his side, enjoying the smell of his cologne and the warmth that seeped through his clothes. Almost as if without thought, he turned his head just enough to kiss my temple, and my heart melted. It was something I had seen Alex do to Sam a million times; it was something you did when you cared about how someone felt or what they were thinking.

As the credits rolled, we stayed in our seats, not wanting to get caught in the crowd. So far no one had stopped me, or bothered us, and I was hopeful that would last for the rest of the night.

My phone buzzed in my pocket and I frowned. I sat up and pulled it out in case there was some change with Selene. The text message was from Chadwick, and it wasn't good.

"Everything okay?" David took his arm back and picked up our trash. "Is Selene worse?"

"It's not Selene." I turned the phone so he could see the screen. "We've been found."

"What should we do?" David watched my face carefully.

"Well, that's up to you." I took a deep breath.

"What do you mean?"

"It depends on what you want people to think. We could try to sneak out the back, but it's likely to be crawling with photographers." I chewed on my bottom lip for a moment, worried about what he would say. "Or we could leave through the front, let them photograph us together."

"Okay." I could see his mind working through the potential scenarios. "Being photographed together isn't a lifelong commitment."

"No." I chuckled. "But it will always be floating around in the world. It could come up at some point in the future."

"So?" He shook his head with a smile. "Anything could come up from the past." He grabbed my hand and ran his thumb over my knuckles. "Let's go."

"You're sure?" So many of my acquaintances hid their relationships from the public; secret rendezvous and hasty phone calls were all they had. Walking out hand-in-hand with David after only three dates would seem like a big deal to the media. "They're going to assume that we've been dating for a long time if we do this."

"Well, you know what they say about assuming." He pulled me to my feet. "It makes an ass out of them."

"I thought the saying went: It makes an ass out of you and me." I let him pull me along with him. There were still a few people in the theater, but none of them paid us any attention.

"Yeah, but it really just makes an ass out of them."

The press was out in full force as we exited the theater. The amount of people crammed around the doors was staggering as other moviegoers realized that there was someone famous inside. Jameson took point with Mark in the rear. It was like a madhouse, with people shoving to get a good shot, people hollering questions, and royal watchers trying to hand me presents.

David put his arm around my shoulder to try

and keep the worst of the offenders at bay, but it merely incited the reporters.

"Aren't you Princess Samantha's friend?"

"Is that how you met?"

"How long have you been together?"

"Are you pregnant? Is there a baby royal on the way?"

I stumbled on that question, caught off guard. I knew that Sam had dealt with people asking that question, but in the past there had been no reason for people to even wonder about me and my uterus.

David was a champ and never broke stride. Between him, Jameson, and Mark, I was tucked safely in my car within moments.

"Wow. Maybe I should rethink this shirt." I looked down at the flowing top I had chosen and frowned.

"They just wanted a reaction."

"When did you learn so much about the media?" I buckled my seat belt and watched him.

"You're not the only one that's had a busy week."

"Did something bad happen?" I watched his face tic as he thought about something.

"No, nothing bad. It just wears me out; the constant smiling and talking. I have no idea how you do it so often."

"You're an introvert." I shrugged. "It's harder

for you, because you need time to yourself to recharge. That's not a bad thing, but it makes it difficult in this type of job. Max is an introvert as well. That's why he does everything he can to get out of public events. He doesn't mind the speaking so much as the mingling afterward."

"And what about you? Are you an introvert or an extrovert?"

"Extrovert." I didn't hesitate to answer. "I love being around people." I hesitated for a minute. "Usually. Lately things have been different."

"You planned a huge wedding, took on more appearances, and then watched someone close to you almost die. That would wear anyone out." He shifted in his seat so he was turned slightly in my direction. "Maybe you should take a break. Surely things aren't going to just stop if you take a day off."

"I wish." I sighed. "Some of these things have been planned for months—years even. How do you tell someone that you're just having a 'me' day?"

"That would be difficult." He humphed to himself.

"It's not so bad. I usually have a weekend or two off every month. This month is just a little different." I shrugged. I didn't mention that lately I stay home on my weekends off. Then again, I doubted he would be worried about whether or not I went to clubs or bars.

"What do you do on your weekends off?"

"Normal things." I shrugged.

"What are normal things?" He chuckled. "Reading? Gardening? Robbing banks?"

"Pfft. I don't need to rob banks." I raised an eyebrow. "I do that for fun."

"Living on the edge, huh?" He smiled.

"Is there any other way?" Laughing, I rolled my eyes. "Okay. No bank robbing, but I do occasionally swipe extra desserts."

"We all have to start somewhere." He nudged my leg with his knee. "And what other dangerous activities do you take part in?"

"I run." Shrugging, I smiled at him. "It's one of the only times I'm truly by myself. No one demanding or expecting anything of me."

"They let you run by yourself?" He seemed surprised.

"Only on the property. If I run at school I have a guard with me." I couldn't help my grimace. "She keeps her distance, but it's not the same thing."

"You must really look forward to going home for just that."

"If you mean D'Lynsal, I always look forward to going home." I smiled. "There we're just a family. We hang out in front of the fireplace and if there is more than one of us we will talk or play board games. It's a nice break." I smiled thinking about it. "What's your home like? I think I remember hearing that it stays pretty warm in Georgia."

"That depends on what part of Georgia you're talking about. The northern part of the state has its share of snow and ice, but my home is further south." His eyes grew distant. "We have a lot of land that was passed down through the family and an old two-story farmhouse. It's cozy, with creaky wood floors, and a fireplace that my mother insists we use at least once a year. There's always company popping by for some reason or another and my mom cooks nonstop. There is always something in the oven or simmering on the stove." He smiled at me. "I miss it, even though I've technically been gone for nine years."

"Home will always be home." I smiled. "I'm sorry you are so far away though. Will you get to visit sometime soon? Maybe for the holidays?"

"I'm not sure. It depends on how things go here."

For a minute I thought he meant between us, but quickly realized he meant with the Future Bird Trust. "What do you think so far?"

"I think that when Sam gets back I will beg her

for a position where I don't have to do as many speaking engagements." He laughed. "Like your brother, I don't mind the actual speaking part; it's the mingling and small talk that kills me."

"The wrong people can drain you dry." I shook my head. "Like psychic vampires. Just zap all of your energy with a simple hello. It takes a lot of practice to not let it get to you."

"I'm not sure I want to even learn how to keep them from doing that. I'd rather just avoid it all." He shrugged. "I guess there's a reason I get along with animals so much better."

"That's not true. I saw how you handled the room the other day." I pushed his knee. "You were a natural. You might not enjoy it, but you have a knack for teaching people things."

"I do like to teach, but on a smaller scale. I'm really looking forward to the students that are coming to visit Victory Hall from a nearby school." He flashed a genuine smile. "They're young and there will only be around twenty or so total."

"That sounds like fun."

"I think so. We'll be able to spend more time with the animals with the smaller group." He frowned. "There were so many people at the opening, most of the animals became stressed."

"Have you had a chance to spend more time

with the raptors? Get to know them a little better?"
I remembered how upset he had been about Loki.

"I spent most of today with them. Sam had a
pretty great routine already set up, but she asked
me to tighten everything up." He shifted in his
seat, his excitement palpable. "The owls needed
a diet adjustment, but I think that was a staff
issue—not something Sam had set up. Some of
the birds are spectacular. Most of them will never
be reintroduced to the wild, but there are two
making great recoveries. You should come out
when they're ready to go."

"I'd like that."

The car pulled up to the hotel, but didn't bother
pulling around to the rear entrance. At this point,
there was no hiding from the media. They knew
we were together and had most likely either followed us, or called ahead to their counterparts.

"Ready to run the gauntlet again?" David
asked.

"Yeah, I'm pretty used to it." I undid my seat
belt. "Don't worry about getting out. I'll see myself
to my room."

"I was raised in the South, Cathy." He shook
his head with a small smile. "That's not going to
happen."

"Are you sure?" I frowned. "They can be overwhelming."

"I'm sure." His eyes bored into mine and I tried not to hope that this meant I would get a kiss good night.

"Then smile, but don't answer any questions. Just look friendly, but don't get sucked in."

"Got it." David hopped out of the car and walked around to my door and helped me out.

"Catherine! Princess!"

"David, are you dating the princess?"

"How long have you been seeing each other?"

"Princess, are you seeing the American? Will your family approve?"

David put his hand on the small of my back as we walked through the people and into the hotel lobby. I smiled but kept my head down, unwilling to meet their probing eyes. It was a real shame that I couldn't go on a date without them all jumping to conclusions.

"They are really persistent," David muttered once we were out of earshot.

"You have no idea. Will your family approve of an American?" I snorted. "They sure do have selective memory, don't they?" My brother had just married a woman born and raised in America.

"Is that an issue?" David frowned as we waited for the elevator. "Will they disapprove of you dating a commoner?"

The way he said the words, like it was such

a foreign concept, touched my funny bone, and I laughed. "Will my family care if I date a commoner? No, but I wouldn't care if they did." I shrugged when he looked at me sharply. "I do a lot of things for my family, but who I want to spend my time with is none of their business." Well, as long as it wasn't a terrorist. Or the Gene Simmons look-alike stripper.

"You'd go against your family if they didn't agree?" He motioned for me to step into the elevator ahead of him.

"When it comes to who I like or care for, I'm not sharing that decision with anyone else." I said the words firmly, but softened when I looked at David. "Not that my family would try to dictate something like that. There is some pressure from the older families to make sure the royal line isn't diluted."

"And let me guess, they have a son or nephew your age." David frowned.

"You got it." I tapped my nose. "Some are more persistent than others, but it's always the same thing. Seating me next to them at dinner events, trying to get me to join their family charity events."

The elevator dinged for the top floor and we stepped out.

"It must be difficult to find a diplomatic way of getting out of those situations," David offered.

"Selene is great at helping me avoid those events, or I try to give a donation instead of attending. School gives me a good excuse as well." I shrugged. "Max is stuck with this type of stuff too. Alex had it the worst though."

"I can imagine." David stopped outside of the door. "Speaking of brothers, is Max staying with you?"

"Yes." I dragged the word out as my heart pounded in my chest. "Why?"

"Well, I'd like to kiss you good night, but wasn't sure if he'd be waiting on the other side of the door with a bat."

I laughed. "Max is probably asleep on the couch snoring loudly."

"Good." Grabbing my hand, David pulled me against his chest and didn't waste time pressing his mouth to mine. Where our last kiss had been soft and exploring, this one was hungry. His tongue teased my mouth open to dance along with mine. His hands never strayed from my waist, but I leaned into him, desperate to be closer.

There was something about David that drove me crazy. His careful restraint that barely hid his hunger turned me on more than if he had pushed me against the wall. Knowing that he wanted me, but that he wanted me to experience it all was extraordinary. Most men would have taken the opportunity I'd presented David and not have thought twice.

His fingers dug into my sides and I moaned into his mouth. Pulling me with him, he spun so that he was leaning against the wall and I was pressed against him. I ran my hands up his arms and back down his chest while his hands inched lower ever so slowly. When he finally cupped my ass, I pressed against his leg, trying to get closer to him. I could feel his excitement through his jeans and he groaned softly.

Breaking away from my mouth, he trailed kisses down my neck while his hands massaged my behind. I tilted my head so he could have better access and ran my hands up into his hair. When his fingers slid a little lower, closer to my growing need, I couldn't help the movement of my hips against his.

His fingers squeezed tightly, pressing me against his hard on, before releasing me suddenly. When his mouth touched mine again, the kiss was soft and short.

"You're killing me, woman." David's raspy voice whispered in my ear.

"Then don't stop." I looked up at him, wanting what he had hinted at.

"Not yet." He kissed me again, slowly, tenderly

before pulling away. "I had a good time tonight."

"So did I." I fought against my disappointment. It wasn't like I could take him to my room with my brother asleep on the couch.

"I want you to know that if I hadn't made you that promise, I would be searching for an empty room right now." He grabbed my hand and brought it to his lips. "But I meant it. One thing at a time."

"What if I don't want to wait?" I raised an eyebrow. It was a bluff, though. In twenty-one years I hadn't found a man who made me feel like David and I wasn't fool enough to let that get away.

Leaning close, his lips touched my ear. "It'll be worth it."

I just looked at him, unable to find any words. I had no doubts that it would be worth it and that was exactly why it would be hard to do so.

"Good night, Cathy." He kissed my temple. "I'll see you soon."

"Good night." I watched as he walked to the elevator before digging my key out of my purse.

Max was right where I thought he would be, snoring on the sofa. Even at home he slept on the couch more than he did in his own bed. It was a habit he had developed as a child when waiting for our parents to come home. He was twenty-five, so I figured it would be a hard habit to break if he ever decided to do so. Paperwork had fallen off his chest and was strewn all over the floor.

I took my shoes off and padded across the room to pick up the mess. There were graphs of land surveys, lists of regulations, a small notepad, and a thin book about raptors. I smiled as I flipped through the notepad and looked at his notes. There were definitions with Latin names under-lined, and curse words written next to names of people he apparently had to contact. I covered my mouth to keep from laughing out loud. Appar-ently Max thought Sam and Alex needed to get another hobby.

As quietly as possible, I straightened his notes and stacked them on the side table before grab-bing a throw blanket to lay across Max.

"Good night," I whispered. Careful to not make any noise, I crossed the suite to my room. I wasn't sure I'd be able to sleep after that kiss in the hallway, but a nice shower might go a long way to helping.

# SIXTEEN

THE NEXT MORNING was beautiful. It may have been in my head, but I felt like the sun was shining a little brighter, the sky was a little bluer, and it took only a few seconds for the shower to heat up. By the time I wandered out of my room, I was happier than I had been in days. There was no denying the bounce in my step.

"Well, someone woke up in a good mood." Max was sitting at the table where breakfast was spread out.

"It's a pretty morning." I sat down across from him and swiped some fruit and toast.

"Mm-hmm," he mumbled around a mouthful of eggs.

"Did you hear about Selene?" I picked through the bowl of fruit until I found some grapes.

"They called last night to say that she was making a remarkable recovery. I think she will get to leave soon." Max looked up at me from the paper he was reading.

"I had the same message this morning." I took a big bite of buttered toast. "I think they're ready to send her away." I laughed around my mouthful.

"Speaking of messages . . ." Max folded his paper in half and turned it in my direction. "Have you seen the news this morning?"

Some of my good mood faded immediately. "Let me guess, I made the headlines."

He tapped the picture and I set my toast down and grabbed the paper.

"Oh great." I wrinkled my nose at the title.

"Frisky Royal." I'd think this was a joke, but I'd seen all of the idiotic titles about Sam and Alex. The word *frisky* would bring in a lot more attention than something about a movie date.

"It could be worse." Max shrugged.

"No kidding." I frowned, thinking about Alex and his drama.

"So you did do something more than hold hands with him?" Max narrowed his eyes. "He's not going to come waltzing out of your room any minute, is he?"

"No." I sneered at him. "And you're one to talk. How many times has some girl done the walk of shame for you?"

"Oh, that's not shame." He picked up his teacup and raised an eyebrow. "That's satisfaction."

I made a gagging noise and rolled my eyes, but my heart wasn't in it. It bothered me to see David's face and name plastered in the paper. If it wasn't for me, they'd be leaving him alone. I skimmed the article, the half truths and assumptions. It wasn't any worse than I had expected, so I folded up the paper and pushed it back to Max.

"Here." I finished my food and carried my dish to the sink in the small kitchen. "I have to get ready for a meeting in town. What's your schedule like?"

"Nothing until this evening. I was going to get some studio time in." He frowned at me. "Why?"

"Would you mind checking on Selene? I hate that there is no one there with her." I widened my eyes a little and frowned.

"Yes, but not because of your anime eyes." He shook his head. "I just like Selene."

I walked over and threw my arms around his neck. "Thanks!"

"Yeah, yeah."

I spent time making sure that I looked just like a princess should before leaving the hotel. My dress was immaculate, my suit jacket was cute in a way that was classy but sexy, and my hair was pinned in place.

While in the car to the local artisans' guild

I texted David to tell him thank you for a great night. He didn't respond for the rest of the ride, but I wasn't too worried. It was likely that he was too busy to even look at his phone. Samantha had timed it so that he was busy doing a lot of school and business visits while she was away. No one would say that my sister-in-law wasn't smart; considering how much she hated to do speaking events she must have planned this out a long time ago.

There were more reporters at the guild building and Tabitha seemed to be enjoying having them call her name. It was amusing to see her smile for the camera. It almost looked like she had practiced how to stand and where to turn. Then again, when I was younger, I'd been taught those things as if they were part of a normal education.

The guild was full of people, men and women alike, all eager to hear what I had to say. It was lovely to talk with people that felt the same way I did about art education. By the time I had finished my speech, I felt excited and hopeful. Here was a room full of people who had made a name for themselves with art; ran successful business and seemed genuinely interested in what I had to say. It validated all of my belief and hard work on the project.

"Can I set up a monthly donation?" a woman wearing a flowing green skirt asked. "I can't do a large sum, but I can do a steady amount every month."

"That would be wonderful." I held my hand out. "I'm Catherine."

"It's a pleasure to meet you, ma'am. I'm Hilda Thatcher. I run the local pottery studio." She bobbed a quick curtsy.

"Please call me Catherine." I smiled at her. "Is that the place on Portvel Road?"

"Yes, it is." Her hand fluttered to her chest. "That's my shop."

"We drove by this morning. I loved all of the wind chimes hanging out front." I folded my hands in front of me. "I bet that sounds lovely in the morning."

"Yes, ma'am, it's a wonderful way to start the day."

"I've been thinking about having people donate time instead of money. Maybe you'd be willing to be a guest teacher at a local school and teach the kids about pottery."

"I'd like that very much. Very much." Her smile grew until it stretched across her face from ear to ear. "But I'd also like to donate money as well."

"Tabitha will help you set up a payment if you'd like, or you could just send money in when you can. I can't wait to start the children's program." I reached out to shake her hand again. "Thank you so much for helping make it possible."

Hilda walked over to where Tabitha stood, her smile still planted on her face as she wrote a check and gave Tabitha her business card.

By the end of the day I had almost reached my financial goal and left with a light heart. If there was one thing I could be proud of, it was that I had planted the idea of this program into the minds of people who cared—people who would help me see it through.

"That was a very beneficial event." Tabitha was looking through a stack of business cards.

"Wasn't that great?" I smiled at her. "To know that they want to help, that they are helping?"

"Definitely." She turned her phone on and started typing. "You're going to have these kids swimming in crayons and paper in no time."

"Well, I hope it's more than that." I frowned. "I want them to experience as many different forms of art as possible—for them to experience it hands on."

"And they will." She never looked up and I tried to not be annoyed by her lack of interest. It wasn't her fault that she didn't seem to care about art. As long as she did her job, that's all I could ask for.

Watching her play on her phone made me think about mine, though, and I pulled it out of my jacket pocket and frowned when I realized there were no missed messages. I stuck the phone back in my pocket and sighed.

Busy. He was busy.

Or I had done something wrong.

Or he was just busy. Which was probably the most likely explanation—and it did nothing to ease the worry that gripped me.

When we arrived at the hospital I dismissed Tabitha for the rest of the day. I wanted time alone with Selene before going back to the hotel. My appointment had run late, so Max was gone by the time I got to the room.

Unbuttoning my jacket, I sat down in the chair next to Selene's bed and propped my feet up on a stool. The sound of Selene's soft snore and the whir of the machines worked like a sedative. I was asleep before I realized I was tired.

"Your Highness?" A cold hand shook my shoulder and I startled awake.

"What?" I sat up and brushed the hair out of my eyes. "What?"

"I'm sorry, I didn't mean to scare you." The doctor smiled at me. "I need to get to the machine behind you."

"Oh." I climbed out of the chair so he could get to the monitor.

"She's doing really well. I think just a little longer and she'll be ready to go." The old man smiled at me.

"Excellent. Thank you so much."

"It's been my pleasure."

As soon as the doctor closed the door, Selene popped one eye open. "Is he gone?"

"Yes." I sat back down and laughed.

"Good. I'm tired of answering all of the same questions." She sighed and reached for my hand. "You should have gone home. No need to sleep in the chair."

"I'm fine."

"I saw you on the news." Selene raised an eyebrow. "David looked nice and you looked very happy."

"Oh, you know how we fake it." I winked at her. My heart did a little dip at the mention of his name and I had to fight the impulse to check my phone.

"Yes, I do. And I also know when you look truly happy." She smiled at me.

"It was fun. We get along really well even though we're so different."

"That's the key." Selene smiled fondly. "I dated a boy like David once. All muscles and brooding eyes. He was a carpenter and made the most beautiful things. We had nothing in common, but that didn't seem to matter."

"What happened?"

"Oh, life. Things change, jobs change. But I wouldn't trade the memories." She patted my hand. "If you really have that special something, hold on to him."

I frowned. I thought we had that special something. Had I been wrong?

Turning away from Selene I dug my phone out of my pocket and checked my incoming messages. Still nothing. Frowning I checked my e-mail. Nothing there either.

Had I broken some cardinal rule? Texted too soon? David wasn't the kind of guy to play games. I'd dated those types of people—Kyle had been that guy. The one who thought when I said no I secretly meant yes.

Not wanting to give in to my worry, I decided to text him again. What could it hurt?

Is everything okay? Are the paparazzi bothering you?

I hit send before I could rethink it and turned back to look at Selene with a smile. "There. That's me not letting him get away. I think."

"Good for you." A nurse with a rattling cart

pushed open the door and delivered breakfast before leaving just as quickly.

I looked at the covered tray and felt bad for poor Selene. "That looks horrible."

"Trust me, I know." She picked up her cup and I moved to help her. "You should get out of here and get some real food."

"When you're done, I will." To be honest, I'd have to leave. I needed to go back to the hotel and change before a video conference.

As soon as Selene was back asleep, I was up and running. Jameson called for the car and I didn't even take the time to shower before changing. Instead I put my hair in a loose fishtail braid and freshened up my makeup just before my computer beeped.

"Hi, Mother."

"How are you, dear?" Mother's face popped up into view and I smiled. She was in a car, headed to parliament for the day. "How is Selene?"

"Good." I took a sip of the tea Tabitha brought into my room before disappearing again. "She's healing quickly."

"I'm glad to hear it. I plan on visiting her at D'Lynsal when she's released. I want to see her for myself. Oh, and I meant to tell you that your dog is doing wonderful. He hasn't used the bathroom in my apartments once." I had asked her to watch Xavier when it became apparent that I wasn't going to be back soon. Mother situated her phone so that it was off to the side while she went through her files. "I wanted to chat with you about a few things before the others join us. I hear you did an outstanding job at the artisans' guild."

And we were off to business in no time. When the prime minister joined us to talk about my program, I had to force myself to pay attention. I kept glancing at my phone, wondering why David was ignoring me.

"Catherine, have you decided on a name for the program?" Mother's voice cut into my thoughts.

"I—I—not yet. I'll narrow it down soon." My attention snapped back to the computer and I frowned.

"Excellent. Let us know once you do and we will meet again." Mother closed her folder all business. "Thank you for taking the time to speak with us, Prime Minister."

"Never a problem, Your Majesty. I'm very interested in this program." He smiled. "Please send my regards to Selene."

"I will." I nodded my head. "Good luck today in parliament."

"Thank you." They both laughed. They were

not in agreement about the newest bill, so it would be interesting to see how it worked out today. However, they had known each other for so long it was easy for them to separate state affairs from each other.

When I closed the computer I threw myself on my bed and buried my face in a pillow. My phone beeped and I practically flew across the room to pick it up.

There was a text message.

But it wasn't from David. Instead it was Chadwick.

Turn on the news.

Grabbing the remote I pointed it at the television and held my breath. I flipped to a news station quickly and cussed loudly. The reporter was talking about David's family and showing images of his youngest sister and mother being hounded in a parking lot.

Liberty Anne was crying and shaking her hands at her sides. It was obvious that the attention was upsetting her a great deal and yet the cameras persisted.

"She's a child, you assholes!" I screamed at the TV in fury.

"Whoa! What's wrong?" Max burst into my room. "Who is that?"

"That's David's youngest sister. She's autistic and they won't leave her alone."

Tears formed in my eyes as I watched the little girl start hollering and swinging her hands at the reporters. His mother dropped her bags and wrestled with her to get her away from the people.

"This is my fault." I covered my mouth. "Oh God. He must hate me."

"This is the reporters' fault." Max wrapped an arm around my shoulder.

"I should have insisted that we sneak out. The fallout wouldn't have been so crazy. It was so reckless to just walk out with him." I closed my eyes. "No wonder he isn't answering my texts."

"You do not control the media." Max looked down at me. "And if he's not answering your text messages it could be because he's trying to handle this. Or he's an asshole and I'll beat the shit out of him."

I shoved his chest. "I don't know what to do."

"Do you like him?" Max looked at me with serious eyes.

"I really do." I really, really liked David.

"Then go find him." He shrugged. "If you don't try, you won't know."

I thought about it for a minute. Did I want to put myself out there that far? It would be a long, painful fall if he turned away from me. Then again, if I didn't try, I'd go crazy just thinking about it.

"Okay." I took a deep breath and picked up my phone.

Where is he?

I waited for Chadwick's response.

**Chadwick:** Fishing.
**Me:** Fishing? Where?
**Chadwick:** Rousseau. He said he needed to think.

I looked at Max. "Get out. I need to shower."

"Okay." He walked to the door. "Remember, I'll beat the shit out of him if you want."

"Gee, thanks." I rolled my eyes. "I've always wanted to meet a nice guy and then have my brother try to kill him."

"The offer stands." He closed the door behind him with a wink.

I was ready in record time, throwing on jeans, boots, and a shirt. I braided my wet hair and had Jameson bring the car around. The ride to Rousseau was a long one and I spent it going over in my head what I would say.

What would I say?

Everything I came up with sounded so corny—so pointless. Really, if he was smart he would run from me, and fast. God, I hoped he wasn't smart.

When Rousseau came into view I bit my lip and took a deep breath. I'd just wait and see how he felt. Maybe I'd be strong enough to let him go without crying. Or at least not crying in front of him.

He was sitting on the front steps when we pulled up. I didn't know how long he had been sitting there, but when he looked up at the car my heart jerked. His dark eyes were partially obscured by his hair, but I could see the worry that worked through them. He pushed off the stairs and opened the car door for me. We stood there looking at each other without saying anything.

"I—" he started.

"Is your—"

He motioned for me to go on as his jaw worked silently.

"How is your sister?" I was thankful that my voice didn't shake.

"She's better. They took her riding this afternoon and are trying to explain things to her." He took my hand and led me back to an area on the porch where no one would be able to see us. "I was going to call you, but I had to decide what I was going to do."

"I understand." I looked down at the steps. "If we stop seeing each other now, this should blow over for your family."

"What?" He frowned.

"Your decision." I shrugged. "I figured that would be the easiest thing for you. Dating me is difficult. I understand that."

"Cathy." His sigh held a hint of frustration. "Not seeing you wouldn't be easy. Not seeing you would be the most difficult thing I could do." He reached up and touched my face. "And I'm not that strong."

I covered his hand with mine. "Then what are you going to do?"

"I was trying to decide if I should go back home for a quick trip or if that would make it worse." He let his hand fall from my cheek, but kept our fingers threaded together. "I spent some time talking to her on the phone today."

"Is she—did she understand?"

"She did. She was pretty excited that my girlfriend is a princess." He smiled at me.

My heart did a flip in my chest and I leaned forward to gently kiss him. "I'm so sorry for all of this."

"I knew it could happen." He frowned. "That's one of the things I was thinking about today."

"I don't want to see your family hurt or afraid to do their shopping." I shook my head. "I know what that's like."

"I'm not calling us quits because of some jack-ass reporters." He looked at me with a fierce expression. "I won't let someone else dictate my life."

I nodded in understanding. Relief lightened my heart.

"Besides, I had Chadwick call the producers of the news program." His teeth gleamed white in the moonlight. "I don't think my family will have to worry."

"Chadwick can be scary. Awesome but scary."

"It was brutal." He laughed and I felt the last of my nerves melt away. "We had a beer afterward."

"Now I know it was bad. Chadwick hates beer."

"Well, I had a beer. He had wine." He lifted my hand to his lips. "So, you're not going to dump me because I'm a quiet introvert who needed some time to think?"

"Nah." I shrugged. "You can balance out my need to be involved in everything."

"Sounds like a plan." He pressed his lips to mine again, slowly, tenderly coaxing my mouth open. When his tongue darted across my bottom lip I sighed and he deepened the kiss. His arms wrapped around my waist and in one quick move he had me sitting in his lap. I snuggled close, letting the heat of his body warm me up in the cool summer evening air.

I ran my hands through his hair and tilted his head back to take the advantage of our kiss. He melted under me, letting me kiss him with abandon. Gently I nipped his bottom lip and he moaned softly. His hands slid under the back of my shirt, playing with my bra clasp, but never undoing it. I knew that he wanted to, knew that he was straining against the material of his pants, but he had more self-control than I did.

When I finally broke our kiss, he pressed his face to my neck and inhaled deeply. "You smell like an angel."

"It's just soap. I didn't take the time to do anything special." I sighed as he trailed his lips down my neck.

"I like you like this. No makeup, a pair of jeans, and need in your eyes." He shifted me on his lap so that I could feel his hard-on against my thigh. "Need for me."

I didn't have words, just kissed him again. It was short, because I knew that if it went on too much longer I'd never be able to leave him and I had meetings the next morning.

"I have to go." I whispered the words against his mouth.

"I know." He kissed my forehead. "I'm glad you came to see me."

"Next time, just text me back." I winked at him to let him know I was mostly kidding.

"There won't be a next time to worry about." He stood up slowly, holding me in his arms and easing me to the ground.

"I'm going to hold you to that."

"Angel, you can hold me anyway you want to." He raised an eyebrow and flashed a devilish grin.

"Oh, I plan on it." I winked at him before sashaying back to my car.

# SEVENTEEN

*I* COULDN'T HELP MY yawn. I had stayed up all night watching movies while talking to David on the phone. It was like a long-distance date, even though we were only a couple of hours from each other.

We had watched a horror movie marathon that started with one of my favorite zombie movies. It had been more fun than I would have thought.

"You're sure it's safe for her to leave?" I looked over the papers the doctor handed me.

"She's doing excellent." He offered me a reas-suring smile. "Make sure she takes it easy, does her physical therapy, and takes her medicine."

"I'm right here," Selene grumped from her wheelchair. "You could talk to me."

"Will her mood get any better?" I looked at the doctor with wide eyes.

"Yes. She's still in a lot of pain, and the medicine can affect the patient's mood, but don't worry."

"I'm tired of being cooped up in this hellhole. You won't even let me have my phone and I hate my phone." She adjusted the blanket covering her legs with angry jerks. "Forget my heart. I'm going to die from boredom."

"Honestly, Doctor, are you sure you can't keep her?" I wrinkled my nose.

"The nurses are starting to complain," he whispered back. My mouth fell open and he started to laugh. "I'm just joking, Princess Catherine. You'll be fine. Miss Selene will be more herself soon."

"I'm going to hold you to that," I warned.

"I'm confident in my diagnosis." He patted my shoulder before handing his clipboard to the nurse. "Please make sure that she has a follow-up scheduled in three days."

"Yes, sir." The nurse made a note before moving to push the wheelchair. "Let's get you home!"

"Oh, I don't get to go home. Her Highness won't allow it," Selene grumped. "Can't I just go back to my own bed?"

"Stop whining. You and I both know that you prefer your room at D'Lynsal."

"Oh, that's nice! I've heard that D'Lynsal has amazing rooms and service." The nurse patted Selene on the shoulder. "You'll be in good hands there."

Selene frowned but didn't say anything else

as we moved through the hospital. The press had been moved farther away from the entrance so that we would be able to get into our ride without trouble. I wasn't willing to risk someone knocking over my friend in their haste to get a picture.

"Try to smile," I whispered.

"You smile," she whispered back through her teeth.

"You know, I'm not going to forget this." Shaking my head, I smiled and offered a small wave for the cameras.

Jameson lifted Selene out of her chair and slid her into her seat before reaching over and buckling her in with gentle hands. I folded up the wheelchair and put it in the trunk before climbing in next to my friend. I waved to the cameras briefly as we drove away, making our way back to D'Lynsal.

Selene was pale as we drove, obviously uncomfortable. Reaching over, I grabbed her hand and squeezed. She held on for the entire ride, not once letting go, even though she glared out the window the whole time.

After the longest car ride I had ever sat through, we were able to get Selene situated in one of the guest rooms down the hall from mine. I'd hired two nurses to stay on-site, working with Selene and attending to her physical therapy on a daily basis. While I intended to help as much as possible I had to get back to taking care of the events I had picked up for Alex and Sam. Poor Max looked like he had been put through the wringer in the last two weeks.

Once I was certain Selene was tucked into her bed and sleeping comfortably, I changed out of my "princess gear" and into running clothes. I grabbed my mp3 player and waved good-bye to Mark and Jameson where they sat near the front door.

After some stretches I set out on my normal trail. This one was eight kilometers and wrapped around the edge of the lake that abutted our property. This trail was my favorite. There was an old stone wall, dips and turns, and I loved the way the sun flickered through the leaves on the trees.

It was warm outside and it didn't take long for me to work up a sweat, but I didn't mind. After having been stuck in pant suits and dresses for two weeks, it was nice to cut loose and just run. That saying about how exercise hurt but in a good way was true. It was like I was able to run out all of my frustration and worry from the last weeks.

By the time I reached the lake I was moving at a good pace, my mind lost in thought as I listened to classical music pumping into my ears. I finally felt at peace, calm and centered. The fact that I was so content in my own mind is probably why I didn't notice David at first.

He was sitting on a large stone with a fishing pole in his hands. I slowed to a jog and then a walk. I pulled my earbuds out and let them hang over my shoulder.

"Hey." I walked over to where he was sitting and smiled down at him. We'd texted a few times since our date, but hadn't been able to match up our schedules to see each other.

"I was hoping I might see you." He held his hand out to me and pulled me to sit next to him.

"You were hoping I'd be fishing?"

"I was hoping I'd see you run past. Thankfully you stopped. I'm not much of a runner and you were moving pretty fast." He set down his pole and turned to look at me.

"How'd you know I'd be running?"

"I was hoping." His smile turned wicked and my heart rate had nothing to do with my exercise.

"Hoping what exactly?"

He reached out and twisted a strand of my hair around his finger. "I heard from a trustworthy source that no one ever comes to this part of the lake—except for a princess when she goes running. And I thought that you just might be hot enough to want to take a dip with me."

"I didn't bring my swimming suit."

He patted along his chest and shorts. "Looks like I forgot mine too."

"I guess we're out of luck." I lifted one eyebrow as he reached around me to undo the strap of the mp3 player on my arm.

"I can think of an alternative." With a delicate finger he traced the strap of my tank top before sliding it down my shoulder.

"Are you suggesting that we go skinny dipping?" My stomach did a funny little flip. He was right, no one ever came to this side of the lake, but the thought of swimming naked with him was enough to get my juices flowing.

"Oh, I'm more than suggesting it. I'm asking really nicely." Leaning forward, he pressed his lips to mine and I melted into his side. Carefully he laid me down on the rock and rolled over so that his body was partially covering mine. When he pulled back from my mouth, he pressed a kiss to the shoulder he had pushed the strap off of. "I missed you this week."

My heart was beating a million times a minute, but when he said he missed me, it froze in shock. It didn't take long before it started back again and I felt like I had melted into the rock. Touching his cheek, I made him look at me. "I missed you too."

Hunger filled his gaze as he looked at my face. "Good."

Propping himself up on one arm, he used his free hand to push the other strap of my tank top and then pressed a kiss to that shoulder. His mouth came back to mine in a slow, lazy kiss as his hand slid under my shirt to spread across my stomach. I slid my hands over his chest until I found the hem of his shirt. I tugged it up, forcing him to break our kiss and sit up so he could pull it over his head.

He looked down at me from his kneeling position, his eyes raking over my body. I took in a ragged breath when he stood and undid the button on his jeans. With slow movements he stepped out of the material and held his hand out to me. I let him pull me to a standing position and stood very still as he peeled my tank top up and over my head, leaving me standing there in my sports bra.

He kissed me again, still slow and tender, but with a barely restrained sense of urgency behind his touch as he traced the waistband of my shorts. Gently he pushed them down over my panties, his fingers tracing my skin as he did so.

Pulling away from me, he grabbed my hand and looked into my eyes. "Ready?"

"For what?" My heart beat in my chest so hard it hurt.

"To swim." Smiling, he swung me up into his arms and ran to the water.

At first I was disappointed but it was quickly forgotten after a quick look at his face. He looked happy and carefree, and it released something in me that I had been holding on to. I needed to stop waiting for him to make love to me—stop expecting it every time we were together and just let it happen. It was a freeing thought. And when he threw me into the water I came back up laughing.

"*Muearde!*" I sputtered. "*Il est frigid!*"

"What does that mean?" He swam toward me with slow strokes.

"Cold!" I splashed water at him. "Shit, it's cold."

He tsked at me. "I don't think a princess is supposed to use that word."

"I'm not a princess right now." I placed my hands on his shoulder. "I'm just Cathy right now."

"I'm starting to wonder if you have a multiple personality complex." He brushed some of the wet hair out of my face.

"You know, you might be right." I laughed. "I do feel like two people sometimes."

"Well, I have a confession." His eyes searched

my face while his lips twisted into a smirk. "I like you both. I'm not sure I can choose."

"Luckily for you, I'm not a jealous woman." Pushing with my legs, I shot out of the lake and used my hold on his shoulders to dunk him under the water.

He came up laughing and splashed me. "Sure."

"Okay, I would be upset if it was a different woman, but technically, despite all of my moaning, they are both me." I cut my eyes at him as I treaded water. "Though I'm surprised you like Princess Catherine."

"Why wouldn't I?" He swam around me. "All that self-control, just begging to be broken."

My cheeks heated at the thought. He could do it so easily.

"And then there are those skirts you wear." His next lap around me was a little closer. "What are they called?"

"The pencil skirts?" I raised an eyebrow.

"They kill me." His smile turned darker, hotter. "I can barely keep my hands off of you."

"Good thing you have some self-control. I hear the princess's bodyguards are pretty serious."

"And then there's you." He stopped in front of me. "Cathy. The girl that cracks jokes, hunts zombies, and practically begs me to take my clothes off."

My head dropped back with a laugh. "That's going to haunt me forever."

"At least for as long as you keep letting me come around." He grabbed my waist and slid my body against his. The feel of his slick skin against mine made me suck in a breath.

"Hm. We'll see." I could barely get the words out, but I didn't want him to know how much he affected me. He was already obsessed with the fact that I had drunkenly asked him to strip.

His hand slid down to grip my thigh. He lifted it so that he was pressed against my center and I lifted my other leg to wrap around his waist. In a slow movement, his hand ran up my body and over my breast before cupping my neck.

"Just something to think about," he whispered against my mouth.

His lips were teasing as he coaxed my mouth open. His tongue was soft and probing as I turned to putty in his hands. When he let go of my neck and moved his hand back down over my body, I sighed against him, but when he slid his fingers between where we were pressed together, I moaned gently.

With soft strokes, he rubbed and teased my hot center. His mouth continued to capture my moans, and when I leaned my head back in pleasure, he pressed his mouth to my neck. His teeth scraped along my skin and I groaned.

Pulling my panties to the side, he trailed his fingers between my sensitive folds, exploring softly, learning what I liked and didn't like. It was so different from the first time he had touched me in this manner. There was no fear, no apprehension at his touch, just pleasure.

My hips moved, grinding against his hand and subsequently his hardened shaft. He groaned against my shoulder and took a deep breath. With steady steps he carried me back out of the lake and laid me on a sandy patch along the edge of the water. He covered my body with his, his mouth no longer soft and gentle, but hungry and demanding. Sliding downward, his lips closed on one peak of my breast through the wet material of my bra and his hand never stopped stroking me; never stopped driving me toward a shiny edge that I'd only found by myself before.

When he pulled his mouth away I moaned in disappointment, but was quickly rewarded with a trail of hot kisses down my stomach as he made a path toward his busy hand. When he pulled away from me, I made a moue of frustration while trying to catch my breath. His hands were careful as he pulled my panties off and tossed them onto the beach next to us.

"David—"

"Shh." He moved back to me, kissing me before raining kisses down my body until he met my warm center. I took a deep breath, surprised by the gentle touch and sincerity of his kiss there. It was as if he was kissing me, my mouth, teasing me with soft strokes of his tongue. The warmth of his breath only added to my enjoyment, sending tingles over my skin, as he worked my body into a frenzy. I didn't expect it when he slowly slid a finger inside me while his mouth focused on the top of my mound. It was tight, but good. In fact, I couldn't think about it without thinking about his mouth on me, the way it felt, how I wanted more. As my hips moved faster, his mouth and hand matched pace. I couldn't help my groans of desire as I fell over the edge into pleasure. Nothing I had done for myself had come close to this feeling.

His mouth slowed, kissing me gently before he sat up on his knees and looked down at me. There was no missing his excitement as it pressed against the wet material of his boxers. His breathing was slow and steady, despite the look in his eyes.

Slowly I sat up on my knees, my body still tingling from the gift he had just done for me. I wanted to return what he had given me, but I wasn't sure how to do it, how to ask. Instead I reached out and ran a hand across his chest before pressing my lips to his. Slowly I trailed my fingers over the ridges of his stomach and down to the thick shaft protruding from his shorts.

His fingers circled my wrist and I pulled back to look at him. Had I done something wrong again?

"You don't have to do that." He shook his head. "I just—"

"I want to." I pushed his shorts down, careful to not let them get caught on his excitement. Tenderly I wrapped my fingers around him. "I don't know how . . ."

"It's okay." His chest heaved and he reached down to cover my hand with his own. He guided my hand with his, showing me where to touch him, and how to move. After a moment his hand fell from mine and he groaned into my mouth. He cupped my breast, teasing the nipple through the fabric while I continued to stroke him. The intake of his breath, the soft moans coming between our kisses, empowered me. Pushing him with my free hand, I made him sit down before finally lying back while I hovered over him, my fingers still working along his shaft.

Breaking our kiss, I moved down his body, and before my bravery could disappear, I wrapped my lips around his head. I circled around him with my tongue, enjoying the fact that I had coaxed him into this state of need.

"Cathy." My name was a gasp on his lips.

I didn't pull back. I took as much of him into my mouth as I could, leaving my hand at his base. It was weird, strange, and exciting to do this for David. To know that the sounds he was making were for me—because of me. His hands ran through my hair, pulling it back and away from my face. I met his eyes and he groaned loudly.

"Damn it." He gasped. "I can't wait, angel."

Not sure what to expect, I focused on the task at hand, sucking and pulling gently. I felt him spasm before his seed filled my mouth. I swallowed quickly, but some of it escaped my lips and trailed down his shaft, where my hand continued to move in a slow pattern. When his hips stopped moving, he reached down and pulled me up so that I was lying on his chest with my head tucked under his chin.

"Thank you." He kissed the top of my head and I smiled.

"Thank you too." I pressed my lips to his shoulder.

We stayed there like that for a while; when my breathing started to slow and grow steady, he shook me gently.

"Will someone come looking for you?"

"Oh God." I sat up and looked around for my clothes. "How long have we been here?" I wasn't wearing my watch, because I had intended on just taking a quick run.

"You've been asleep for about thirty minutes, I think."

"I fell asleep?" It had felt like half a second that my eyes had drifted shut. I found my panties and shook as much dirt out of them as possible.

"Mm-hmm. Drooled too."

"Oh no. I did not drool." I shook my head. Apparently I had slept really well for that half hour. "I don't drool. Never."

"Oh, you drooled. I have the wet spot on my chest to prove it." He sat up and wiped at one well-formed pectoral muscle. If I wasn't so worried about time, I might have been distracted by his chest.

Shaking my head, I looked for the rest of my clothing. "How long before that?" Thirty minutes wasn't so bad.

"Well, I think we spent about an hour together before you fell asleep?" He raised his shoulder in question. "I don't know how long you were gone before you found me." He picked up my tank top and tossed it to me. "But I sure am glad you found me."

His smile was so carefree and boyish that my

heart melted and a little of the worry gripping my shoulders dissipated. "Me too."

"How long do you normally go running for?" He put his shorts back on before pulling his shirt over his head.

"An hour. Maybe two. But I always let them know if I'm going to be a while." I frowned as I replaced my shorts. "Right now, I'm really regretting that habit. They're probably looking for me already."

"You don't ever just take off and spend time by yourself?" He frowned and sat back down on the rock he had been fishing from and watched me.

"Closer to the house, yes. But when I'm running the circumference of the property? No. I have to let them know in case something happens." I shrugged. "I've never really thought about it before now. I mean, if someone did try to snag me off the property I would hope someone would be looking for me pretty quickly."

"Do you worry about that a lot? I mean, is that something you really have to think about?" His face grew hard. "People threaten you?"

"Whoa, cowboy." I couldn't help but smile at his protective tone. "I'm sure there have been threats, but nothing that was a real issue. It's mainly a precaution."

"Sam has to put up with this now too, huh?" He frowned. "I thought they were honeymooning somewhere secret, but I saw pictures of them on the television this morning."

"It's part of life for us." I shrugged. I hated that their honeymoon had been crashed by the media, but there wasn't much we could do about it. We had all known it was likely to happen at some point, but I had hoped it would take longer.

"I don't like it." He looked out over the water.

"Don't like what?"

"Having people I care about stalked." He looked back at me and my heart thudded in my chest. Did he mean he cared for me? Or was he just referring to Sam?

"Lots of people have dangerous jobs." I sat down next to him and bumped his shoulder with mine. "It's not like we're police officers or part of the military. It's more like being a celebrity than anything else. And just because of the family we were born into."

"This world, this way of life, is so far from how I grew up." He reached over and twined his fingers with mine. "I would disappear on our property for an entire day. Hunting, fishing, or just exploring. No one would come looking for me until after dark, and when I got older, probably not even then."

"That's such a foreign thought, but it sounds lovely." I looked at our hands, noticing all of the differences. His hands were tanned, with calluses and cracked knuckles; mine were pale and soft. "But if you think about it, a lot of that has to do with where you grew up. You wouldn't let your kid run off in New York City for an entire day without worrying. And I bet your mom worried about you anyways."

"Mom probably did." He chuckled. "But it was still different. She wasn't worried someone would kidnap me or hold me for ransom."

"She probably worried about you drowning or being eaten by a bear."

"No bears there." He smiled. "There are alligators though."

"You know what I mean." I rolled my eyes. "There are all types of bears—or alligators—everywhere."

He sighed, but I could still see the muscles twitching along his jaw. "You're right. But those have four legs not two."

"True." I squeezed his hand.

"Catherine?" Jameson's voice sounded through the trees.

I sighed. "I'm here by the lake."

"Think they'll notice you're covered in sand?" David winked at me.

"Oh yeah, but they won't say anything." I shrugged.

"Catherine? Are you hurt?" Jameson broke through the foliage with Mark right behind him. "You've been gone for a while."

"I'm fine. Just decided to fish with David for a little while." I stood up and brushed my shorts off.

"I didn't realize I was on D'Lynsal property. Stanley, the steward at Rousseau, said I could fish anywhere around the lake."

"I saw him and decided to stop," I said again, and grimaced. I sounded guilty. "I'm sorry to worry you." There, maybe that would cover my guilt.

"Of course, that's fine." Jameson flashed me a genuine smile. "You've had a long couple of weeks. Fishing sounds like a nice way to relax."

Mark's face stayed visibly still, as if he was fighting his actual reaction.

"Yes, it's been a nice break." I turned to look at David and smiled. "I've got to get back."

"Call me when you have some free time." He stood up and came close to me. "I'm working at Victory Hall all week, so have most of my nights and afternoons free."

"I don't suppose—" I stopped, wondering if it would be too weird for him.

"What?" He grabbed my hand again.

"I have a charity auction to go to later this week. Would you like to go with me?" I held my breath while I waited for him to answer.

"Is this the kind of thing where I need to wear a suit?" He raised an eyebrow.

"Black tie." I bit my lip.

"So, a tuxedo." He narrowed his eyes. "Would I be your date or just going the same place you were?"

"My date." I smiled and was rewarded with one of his own.

"Then for you I will wear a tux."

Standing on my tiptoes I pressed a soft kiss to his lips. "I'll see you then."

Letting go of his hand, I walked over to where Mark and Jameson stood waiting. "Thanks for letting me fish with you."

"Any time." David's grin was fast.

"Later." I took a few steps backward.

"Later." His eyes stayed on me while I moved, but I had to turn around and walk the right way or I risked tripping on a tree root.

I started jogging as soon as I turned around. It wasn't that I thought Jameson or Mark would give me a hard time, it was just that I didn't want to share my afternoon with anyone else. I wanted to relish in what I'd done with David; to stay in that moment for as long as possible.

# EIGHTEEN

*I* LOOKED THROUGH THE jewelry room and frowned. I wanted something that was elegant, but not over the top. Of course, anything I picked would be over the top according to Sam. She was such a tomboy when it came to clothes and accessories. If Chadwick didn't keep her in line she would probably wear jeans and boots to all of her meetings.

Thinking of boots made me wonder what David would look like tonight. He hadn't worn a tuxedo at the wedding, but he was tonight for me. I had a feeling that was a much bigger deal than he had let on while we stood at the lake.

I settled on a pair of diamond drop earrings and a bracelet that Alex had given me for my eighteenth birthday. I'd skip the necklace so it wouldn't compete with the neckline of the dress. The dress itself was a soft, petal pink that flowed behind me as I walked. The tiny cap sleeves barely sat on my shoulders and were covered in crystals. I hadn't worn this dress yet, because of the amount of cleavage it displayed, but tonight was a date, and I was going to wear something date worthy. It wasn't an outrageous amount of breast, but enough that I questioned it while appearing somewhere as Princess Catherine. But, damn it, if David was going to wear a tux, I could take the risk of wearing something that showed a little more skin.

I put on the bracelet and checked my hair in the mirror to make sure nothing had fallen or come loose before I left my room. I could hear Selene talking to someone in her room so I knocked instead of just walking in.

"Come in." Her voice was steady and it made my heart sing to know she had recovered so much in the few days that she had been home.

"How are you feeling?" I walked in and sat down on the edge of her bed.

"I'm fine! Fine. Too bad these women won't let me out of bed." She sighed dramatically and I laughed.

"Oh hush. Stop giving them such a hard time!" I smiled at the two nurses in apology. "She's usually much better behaved."

"She's fine, Your Highness." The older nurse

smiled. "And she's not getting past me. I know it still hurts her to walk around more than a trip to the bathroom."

"Call me Catherine, please."

"Ha! See, I can't even use the bathroom on my own."

"Rotten." I poked her leg. "You don't want to fall and hurt yourself any more."

"This is just payback for when you had your tonsils removed." Selene smiled. "Do you remember that?"

"I demanded ice cream for every meal for a month." I laughed.

"Exactly. You went on an eating strike and would cry when I tried to give you soup." She shook her head. "So, if I'm not an easy patient, it's because I learned from you."

"Ouch, that hurts, Selene." I laughed before turning to look at the nurses. "Would you mind giving us a few minutes? I promise to not let her do jumping jacks."

"Yes, ma'am." They left and pulled the door shut behind them.

"You look lovely." Selene smiled.

"Thank you." I preened.

"I don't think I've seen that dress before."

"You told me I should stop being so careful, so

I figured I'd show a little boob tonight." I winked at her.

"Is it for anyone in particular?" She narrowed her eyes.

"David is coming as my date tonight."

"Ah, I see." She cocked her head to the side. "And how much of your boobs has he seen already?"

"Selene!" I stared at her, shocked, while she cackled.

"Don't play coy. You've practically been whistling while walking around the house. Something has happened."

"I'm not sure I like this side of you. It's so . . . so . . . weird!" I laughed.

"Get used to it. I don't think it's going away when I get off this medicine. Especially if you cut back on my hours." She mock-glared at me. "Which we still need to talk about."

"How is Tabitha doing? She seems to have everything in hand. Even with all of the extra media attention lately." I fiddled with one of my earrings that felt loose.

"She's doing an adequate job."

"Wow. Don't lavish so much praise on one person, Selene. It'll go to her head." I frowned.

"She is very worried about your media presence, which could be because of all the attention you're receiving with Alex being out of town, but I think she should be paying more attention to the events that are behind the scenes. She hasn't rescheduled your investment meetings yet, and since I'm not even allowed to *think* about working, no one will give me a phone so I can do it myself."

"To be fair, I asked for a couple of days off."

"You needed some time?" Selene looked at me with worried eyes. "Are you okay?"

"Yes, I was just tired. I didn't sleep much while you were in the hospital."

"I'm sorry—"

"Don't you dare apologize for being sick!" I poked her leg again. "That couldn't be helped and I'm just grateful that you're doing so well now."

"I do hate that I caused you to worry so much." She smiled sadly. "But I do appreciate the fact that you took such good care of me."

"Just returning the favor." I felt tears well up behind my eyes. "You've always been there for me."

"I will be for as long as I can." She reached out to me and I grabbed her hand. "I heard that you told the surgeons that I was your family."

"You are my family." I squeezed her fingers gently, still worried I might hurt her. "And there is nothing more important than family."

"I want you to know that you're my family as well." She smiled. "And I couldn't have asked for a better one."

I couldn't find words to respond, just held on to her hand and fought the tears that wanted to fall.

"Don't you dare cry!" Selene let go of my hand and pointed at me. "You'll mess up your makeup, and you look so lovely and polished."

"Stop saying sweet things then!" I sniffled.

"You just got on to me for being a grump!"

"I didn't mean it." One tear slid down my cheek as I chuckled. "You can be whatever you want as long as you're here to do it."

"Good. Then get out of my room. I'm tired and I don't want to see you cry." She made a shooing motion at me. "And tell those nurses that I'm ready for my gruel and water."

I laughed. "It's not that bad."

"Not that bad? Have you seen what they are feeding me? It's colorless, smells awful, and tastes even worse." She made a disgusted face.

"But it seems to be helping."

"I think they're drugging me. I always fall asleep after I eat." She frowned.

"Could you blame them?" I stood up and laughed. "It's not like you could just be tired and worn out from eating. No. Not after nearly dying from a heart attack."

"You're a cheeky princess. I'm not letting you get away with that any longer."

"I'm going." I opened the door and turned back to look at her. "I know I said I didn't, but I do like you like this. All cranky and pushy. It suits you just as well as your clipboard."

"I miss my clipboard." She sighed as I closed the door.

"We're taking good care of her, miss." The younger nurse smiled at me.

"I know you are. She's healing quickly!" I touched her shoulder in gratitude. "She's not normally so prickly."

"I think it's a defense mechanism," the older nurse offered. "She doesn't want people to treat her like a frail, broken thing. So she's pushy and grumpy. Makes her look stronger."

"I think you're right." I nodded my head. "But I kind of like it."

"Your brother said the same thing." The dreamy look on the younger nurse's face made me smile. Despite Max's antisocial tendencies, he had a way of making hearts flutter.

"He would know." The doorbell rang and I smiled. "I believe that's my ride."

"Have a good evening." The older nurse smiled. "I think you're going to knock your date over in that dress."

"Do you think so?" I looked down at the material.

"Oh yes, ma'am." Her smile grew. "You're practically glowing."

"Thank you. Have a good night!" I turned to run back to my room to fetch my purse. "And don't let Selene bully you."

David was waiting by the fireplace by the time I made my way downstairs. His back was to me, but I enjoyed the way his tuxedo pants hugged his backside. Tabitha was chatting animatedly with him and I found myself frowning. Instead of wearing a nice dress that would fit in with the rest of the auction and partygoers she was wearing a ball gown that left little to the imagination.

I didn't enforce a dress code for the people who worked with me. That seemed cruel and unfair. I would hate being told what I could and couldn't wear. But if I was being honest, Tabitha looked like a call girl. And she was busy pushing her cleavage in David's direction.

Okay, maybe I was being catty, but the dress was well on the side of ridiculous. And her cleavage put the little bit that I was showing to shame.

"Hello." I stayed by the sofa, not wanting to compete for space next to the low fire.

"Wow." David turned to look at me and his eyes drank me in. "You look amazing."

"What a beautiful dress!" Tabitha cut off any response I had. She put a hand to her bosom and I tried not to roll my eyes. It was likely she didn't know what to wear to the event, and I hadn't thought to offer any advice or ask what she was thinking.

I bit my lip. "You look nice too."

"Thank you. I was just telling David that my friend is a designer." She ran her hand over the material. "She made this for me when I told her I couldn't find anything that I liked."

"I'm going to grab my wrap, would you like me to get yours as well?" I motioned toward the closet. I really hoped that she was planning on covering up a little bit. Or a lot. A lot would be good.

"Oh, no thank you. I'm warm enough."

I eyed the cutouts at her waist and bit my lip again. Taking out a silk wrap, I started to drape it over my shoulders, but David's hands stopped me.

"Let me help." He tucked the soft material around me. "You really look amazing."

"So do you." I eyed the way his shirt hugged his chest under the jacket. "The tux looks good on you."

"Chadwick made me buy one when I asked where I could rent one." He touched the tie at his throat. "It was a scary experience with tape measures and a little man with straight pins."

I chuckled. "Then pass my regards to Chadwick. He did a good job."

"I'm sure he will appreciate them. He said that if I was going on a date with you, I had to look the part." His eyes clouded for a minute before clearing with a smile. "That you would be wearing the latest in fashion."

"I like having you with me no matter what you're wearing." *And not wearing*, I thought. I liked that idea a great deal, but I kept the thought to myself. If Tabitha hadn't been watching us closely I might have offered it up as a flirty line, but now wasn't the time.

"So, tonight you are Princess Catherine, and I'm her date." He reached up and touched one of my earrings gently. "Maybe Cathy can come out and play later."

I laughed. "Tonight you are Dr. David Rhodes, trusted confidant of Princess Samantha, and I'm the lucky girl that gets to hang on your arm." I leaned close. "But Cathy would like to get out of this uncomfortable dress eventually."

"I knew I liked you." He leaned forward and

pressed a gentle kiss to my lips. "And now we've gotten the kiss out of the way. Our date can proceed without inhibition."

"Hm." I smiled. "Not a bad idea."

He walked me to the door, which he opened. The limousine sitting in the drive was running and ready for us. There were glasses and a bottle of champagne waiting for us inside. Before the door closed, Tabitha slid into the back with us, and I felt myself frown again. While I had known that she would be attending the formal function with us, I hadn't planned on her crashing the date part of the night.

"There will be several journalists when we arrive. Is there one that you would prefer to speak to?" She pulled her phone out of a small satchel.

"I'd prefer to not speak to any of them." My voice was a little sharper than I intended.

"It would be good publicity for your upcoming charity. Let them know about what you have in the works." She eyed me over her phone, the slit in her dress showing most of her leg.

"If you're worried about me, don't. I can stand in the background while you answer some questions." David smiled at me.

"Very well." I frowned at the list she showed

me. "Let me talk to Yvette. I've spoken with her in the past."

"I'll let her know." She tapped on her phone. "How should I explain David?"

"Excuse me?"

"What do you want me to say about him?" She smiled at him, but her words annoyed me. As if he was an object that needed a backstory.

"He's my date." I shrugged. "That's all they need to know."

"Should I tell them you're in a committed relationship? Or that you're friends?" Tabitha persisted.

"That's none of their business." I looked at David, worried. He was watching, his mouth doing that thing when he isn't sure if he wants to say something.

"Well, they're going to ask."

"That doesn't mean we need to answer." I shook my head. "Tabitha, it's your job to talk around those questions, so you decide how you want to not answer."

"I can do that." She frowned. "But what about the pictures from the hotel?"

"What pictures?" My blood froze and my stomach twisted.

"I got word today that there are two magazines

in possession of photos with you and David kissing at your hotel."

"What?" I practically shouted the word. My stomach did a nasty flip. After Alex's ex-girlfriend had released sex pictures, it had been my worst nightmare to think it could happen to me. It was one of the reasons I had been so careful.

"Are they security tapes?" David squeezed my fingers. I wasn't sure if he knew about Alex and his ex or not, but he was quick to offer comfort.

"I'm not sure. Maybe cell phone pictures." She shrugged. "If you don't want them knowing about your relationship, you need to be more careful."

"What magazines?" I took a deep breath.

"*Stylish* and *Celeb First.*" She shrugged. "They're releasing them tomorrow."

"Why didn't you tell me about this before now?" I glared at her.

"I thought you knew."

Deep breath. One. Two. Three. Four. Five. Six. Seven. Eight. Nine. Ten. Another breath. My chest hurt. And another shallower breath. "How would I know if they contacted you?"

"The e-mail said they were going to offer you the chance to buy the pictures from them."

"I can't do that." My words sounded raspy. I

looked at David. This touched him as well. "I'm sorry. I can't."

"It's okay. I'm more worried about how this will affect you." He touched my cheek.

"If I pay their blackmail money, it will only get worse."

"It's just a kiss, Cathy." David cupped my cheek. "It's not like what happened with your brother."

So he did know.

The air left my lungs and I fought to catch my breath. My hands started shaking and tears rushed to my eyes. It was like catching the flu in a second flat and I had no way of getting better. In that moment I felt like I was dying. It was as if my worst nightmare had just jumped out of a closet and was dragging me down to the pits of hell and no one, especially myself, could save me.

David was watching me with worried eyes, but Tabitha just looked interested. As if this whole thing was an amusing story—that my reaction was overboard and insane. The derision in her gaze amplified that feeling of helplessness and I gasped loudly for air.

"Cathy?" David covered my shoulders with his hands.

"I can't. I can't do that." I tried to take a shallow breath and then another. I meant paying off the vultures. "It's us. Us. Our moment and they're going to publish the photos in trashy magazines like they're porn." I couldn't get enough air and I was starting to feel light-headed. "I can't pay them off. I know this. I know it. I can't but they'll—"

"Take a deep breath." His eyes focused on mine and didn't flinch away when a tear ran down my cheek.

"I can't. I can't breathe." I sniffed and covered my face with my hands. My breath rattled in my chest. The only thing I could think, the only words I could say, were *I can't.*

"Take us back to D'Lynsal." David looked at Tabitha.

"She's supposed to be at the auction." Tabitha shook her head. "And Yvette is expecting her." She picked up a wineglass. "Here, drink this."

I shook my head violently and for a brief moment thought that I was going to be sick all over David. The feeling of being trapped, suffocated was almost overwhelming. Like I was drowning, but there was no water, no way to pull me out.

"It's going to be fine, Cathy. Do you hear me?" David squeezed my shoulders. "I'm right here with you. We're in this together. Do you understand?"

I shook my head no. I didn't feel like anyone

was with me. I was alone in a way I'd never been alone before—singled out in the media for the sole intent of being embarrassed; for someone's perverted gratification. The only thing I knew was that there was no way I could walk out on that red carpet and face those vultures.

"I can't." The tears were running down my face, and the embarrassment that came with them only made it worse.

"Cathy, you're having a panic attack." He lifted my chin so I could see his face. "My sister has them—has since she was a little girl. You're going to be okay."

That made sense, but it didn't help. Knowing what was happening didn't stop it from happening. It just made me feel worse that I couldn't control it.

"Maybe I have a Xanax." Tabitha started looking through her purse. "You'll be fine and ready in no time. Fashionably late."

"No!" I shouted the word. The last thing I wanted was a pill that had been floating around in Tabitha's bag. If the doctor had prescribed it for me, then that would be a different matter, but I wasn't taking medicine that wasn't mine. David let go of me. I thought I had scared him, but instead he rolled down the window between the back and the driver.

"We need to go back to D'Lynsal. The princess isn't feeling well. Hurry, please."

Mark looked back through the window at me and frowned. "Princess, are you hurt? Can I help?"

I shook my head, not trusting myself to speak. Each time I opened my mouth the crying became worse. It was pictures—just pictures—and yet I felt as if my life was over. How had Alex handled the pictures sold of him having sex? He was so much stronger than I.

"This is a nightmare." Tabitha started typing on her phone and I had to fight the impulse to take it from her and throw it out the window. She didn't know what a nightmare was and if she thought I was being a diva now, she had no idea what I could do.

"Tabitha." David's voice shook with anger and I was glad it wasn't directed at me. "I haven't been around royalty long, but from what I know, your job is to take care of Cathy. And right now, your priorities are fucked up."

"I am taking care of Cathy." She frowned. "This could hurt her image. And the pictures aren't that bad. In fact, it will make her even more interesting. People will love that she's dating Sam's best friend. It will show she's just as desirable as her brothers."

"You can worry about the PR later." He glared at her, but his fury was so intense I could barely keep from shaking uncontrollably just being near it. "Right now, you need to be thinking about helping her calm down."

"Please." I whispered the word, ashamed of needing help. I was the person who took care of everything, who planned events and rolled with the media. I wasn't the person who had breakdowns and hysterics. I took another breath and wiped at my face. "Please tell them I came down with something. I'll make it up to them later."

"No you won't." David turned me back to look at him. "The only thing you're going to do is relax and not worry about this. They don't deserve to have you do anything nice for them." His eyes cut to Tabitha. "You tell them she's sick and leave it at that."

"I don't take my orders from you," she said. Her eyes narrowed.

"I will see to it that you don't take any orders from anyone at all if you don't put Cathy first," David growled. "If you think Sam and Alex are going to let you keep your position when you're endangering the princess's health, you're very confused."

She shut her mouth with a loud snap. While

I watched, she took the wineglass she had originally offered me and took a long drink. The limo used one of the local roundabouts to take us back in the direction of D'Lynsal. The closer we came to the house, the more Tabitha drank, and the easier I could breathe. As long as she was being quiet I could put up with the nasty looks she kept shooting my way. I wasn't better but D'Lynsal was my safe haven. The one place I didn't have to pretend—didn't have to feel threatened by people out to get something from me.

When we arrived, Tabitha exited the car before the bodyguard or the driver could get out. She didn't stop at the door either, just disappeared inside.

I dabbed at my eyes, trying to school myself into a semblance of normalcy before climbing out of the limo. David moved closer and cupped my face in his hands. Using his thumbs he brushed the tears off and leaned forward until our foreheads touched.

"You are not alone. I'm right here with you and am not going anywhere. Do you believe me?" He waited for a response, needed an answer, so I nodded my head. "This feels like a huge thing because of what happened to Alex. It's intrusive and thoughtless for someone to take the pictures, much less publish them. But it's a kiss. A kiss I would gladly give to you in front of a million people if you asked for it. Do you understand? I don't care if people know that I've kissed you, that I'm with you as whatever you want to call me. The only thing I care about is you. And right now, I'm worried about you."

I opened my eyes to look at him. Honesty rang through his words and sincerity shone through his eyes. Reaching up, I touched his jaw with my fingers.

"You're right." My fingers danced along the stubble. "It was a kiss and I would have wanted your kiss no matter what."

"What happened to Alex is not going to happen to you," he whispered the words. "Whoever you choose will not do that to you. Your trust is too important to risk losing."

"I've already chosen." I whispered the words quietly, aware that there were people outside waiting for me. "I chose the night I saw you at Sam's, I just didn't realize it. You're the first man I've wanted that way."

"Then when it happens, you will have nothing to worry about." His lips touched mine softly, and I melted into his arms before burrowing my face in his chest.

"I'm so sorry that I've exposed you to this type of thing. If you had been with any other woman, no one would have taken your pictures." Guilt filled my heart and I could feel the panic spiking again.

"I told you, I don't care. I would have rather that moment stayed between us, but I plan on making a lot of memories that no one else will have their hands—or eyes—on."

"That would be nice." My mouth twitched slightly into a small smile.

"Let's go in and do something silly or boring." He let go of my face and coaxed me out. "A board game or maybe a television marathon. How do you feel about infomercials?"

"Infomercials? Where they try to sell you things." I shook my head.

"Those are the ones. Great for putting a person to sleep."

"Your Highness, are you well?" Mark stepped forward, his eyes running over my body in a quick check. "Should I call for a doctor or one of the nurses?"

"I'm just feeling under the weather. I'll be fine." I nodded my head and didn't bother to force a smile. It would be wasted on him anyways. He had known me for so long that he could tell when I was being sincere.

"If you have need of me, please let me know."

He nodded his head in a quick bow before walking ahead of us to open the door of the house.

"Thank you." I nodded my head to him while David and I walked past.

"Where's the kitchen? Why don't I make us a snack?" David leaned down to whisper in my ear.

"The cook should still be up, you could ask her." I stepped out of my shoes and bent over to pick them up. "I'd love a hot cup of tea."

"Okay, I'll go see what I can do." David led me over to the armchair closest to the fireplace. "Have a seat and I'll be back."

I curled up in the chair and propped my chin in one hand. It felt odd to be taken care of, but I was so tired and worn out from the panic attack I didn't have the energy to argue. I could feel that anxiety dancing just on the edge of my consciousness, waiting for me to fall into its dark pit of fear. Instead I watched the flames of the small fire dance across the logs and let my mind blank. Any time my brain started to even touch upon the idea of pictures . . . No, I couldn't go there. I just focused on the flames.

"Well, I found a cook and a maid." David walked back into the room with a cup of hot tea on a saucer. "And Jeanine, the maid, said she would bring us some board games."

"Thank you." I took the cup from him.

"Oh, I didn't make it. The cook wouldn't let me even open a cabinet." He cleared a spot on the table in the center of the sitting area when Jeanine brought out several boxes and a pack of cards. "What will it be? Monopoly?"

"No!" I laughed at his surprised face. "Alex has ruined Monopoly for me. Take my advice and never play with him."

"Good to know." He looked at the other boxes. "It looks like the rest all require more players, so how about a card game?"

"That sounds good." I set my cup down. "How about Go Fish?"

"Go Fish?" David blinked in surprise. "If that's what you really want to play—"

I burst out laughing. "I'm joking. I can't believe you fell for that."

"That's it. Your choice has been revoked." He shuffled the cards before starting to deal them out. "Crazy Eights. Do you know how to play?"

"I do." I slid out of my chair so that I was sitting on the floor next to the table. "Are you any good?"

"It's a game of luck. I'm as good as anyone else." He shrugged out of his jacket and undid his tie before joining me on the floor.

"Yeah, you keep telling yourself that." I raised an eyebrow in challenge. If there was anything I had picked up from my brothers, it was their competitiveness. My nerves were still shot, but just being next to David seemed to help. He had a way of making everything important seem unimportant. He put things into perspective, and right now, Crazy Eights was much more important than anything lying photographers could make up.

Though there was one thing that bothered me and I couldn't shake it. Where had the photos come from and just how bad were they? And why? Why had someone taken pictures of such an intimate moment? It had to be for the money they got when they sold the photographs to the magazines.

After I beat David three times in a row, he conceded defeat and packed up the cards. Sitting on the couch, he patted the spot next to him and I took the seat. With a comfortable ease, he tucked me against him.

"I loved hearing your laugh."

"I loved seeing you lose." I giggled when he mock-groaned.

"I just wanted you to be happy." He smiled at me.

"Riiiight." I shook my head, but scooted close against him. "Whatever you have to tell yourself."

"That's how it's going to be, huh?" In a swift movement he had lain back on the sofa and shifted me so that I lay on his chest.

My ear rested just above his heart and I closed my eyes to listen. There was something soothing in the rhythm combined with his steady breaths. The fire crackled and popped as it slowly faded from existence and I found it hard to keep my eyes open.

"Will you stay?" I tucked one of my hands under my cheek. I felt safe in his arms, and even if those photos made an appearance in the morning, it wouldn't feel so bad with him here to keep me calm.

"Yes." His answer was quick. "Go to sleep."

"Are you comfortable?" The words came out in a mumble.

"I'm fine." His arm tightened around my waist.

"Thank you." *For holding me. For keeping me calm. For staying.*

"You're welcome." He dipped down to kiss my head.

# NINETEEN

"Why DIDN'T YOU tell me?" Selene stood on the stairs, her voice angry. The younger nurse stood beside her with big eyes.

"What?" I rubbed my eyes, confused. Was I at the palace?

"The pictures. You could have let me know. I have people sending me e-mails left and right." She was using a cane, but the expression on her face was fierce.

"I didn't want to upset you." Fat lot of good that had done for me. I was tucked next to David on the couch, his arm still over my waist. I sat up and let his arm fall to the side. "Who let you have a computer?"

"I got out of bed and took it. I'm not asking for permission anymore."

"Why are you up? I can deal with this." But the truth was that I could taste vomit in the back of my mouth. The pictures were out and people were seeing me with David in a very private moment.

"Because I know." She shook her head sadly. "I know what you're feeling right now." Taking the steps slowly, she made her way down to me.

The nurse was helping her, but I hopped up to assist her myself. "You're going to kill yourself."

"Sitting in that bed, stressing over not knowing what is going on, will kill me faster." Selene grabbed my arm and looked into my eyes. "It's going to be okay."

"I don't know what to do." Tears prickled at the backs of my eyes. "What do I say?"

"Nothing right this minute." She cupped my cheek and I was reminded of when I was a child. "We think about it and handle it with a clear head."

I led her to a seat across from where David was sitting on the couch. "Sit here and I'll get you some tea."

"I'll get it, ma'am." The young nurse disappeared.

"She's probably going to slip drugs into it." Selene frowned. "Good morning, David."

"Good morning, Selene." David smiled at her, his hair sticking out in different directions. "I'm sorry you woke up to this."

"This is my job. To make sure Cathy doesn't panic or make the wrong move." She shook her head. "Where is Tabitha?"

"Are you not taking your medicine?" I glared at

her. "Why do you think they are drugging you?"

"Because they're tired of me complaining." She waved her hand. "They probably aren't, but I bet they wish they could. Now, where is Tabitha?"

"I don't know. She disappeared last night." I shrugged. At the time it had been a relief. Of course she did drink an entire bottle of wine in the car, so it was likely that she was still snoring in her bed. "Maybe in her room."

"We need to talk about the photos." Selene said the words quietly. "Have you seen them?"

I shook my head, my stomach rolling. I remembered the kiss, the intense need, the way he had cupped my ass. I didn't want to see that splattered in a tabloid.

"They aren't that bad." Selene leaned back in her chair. "They're actually sweet. David, can you pull them up on your phone?"

"Yes, ma'am." He fiddled in his pocket until the phone was free, and he pressed buttons until he had pulled up the file. He looked at the pictures for a minute, but I refused to look down. Instead I watched his face as he decided what he thought. "They aren't bad. Just personal."

"No, and what I'm most worried about is where the photos came from." Selene said the words calmly, but it sent my heart racing.

"What do you mean?"

"Those are cell phone pictures. Who else was staying on the floor with you?" She frowned. "I don't remember much from the hospital, but I know that you would have been in a penthouse. Were there other rooms on the floor?"

"I don't think so." I shook my head.

"No, that's not right. There was a door on the opposite side of the hallway from yours." David narrowed his eyes.

"I thought that was a janitorial closet."

"It would have been large enough for someone to hide in." He looked around the room angrily as if he could spot the perpetrator walking through my living room.

"Who would have done that? The staff? How long did they hide in that closet? Just for the chance of a photo?" My mouth worked for a minute as I watched Selene's serious face. "Who has time for that?"

"Someone that could make large sums from selling the pictures."

"A hotel employee?" I shook my head. "Can we call the hotel and figure out who it was?"

"I'll have someone look into it." Selene took a sip of her tea.

"Not Tabitha." David's voice brooked no argument.

"Okay." Selene watched him carefully. She wasn't used to taking orders from people other than the royal family. "Why?"

"She tried to insist Cathy go to the auction last night after she dropped the bomb about the pictures in the car." His voice was a growl. "Cathy had a panic attack."

"Are you okay, dear?" Selene looked at me with worried eyes.

"I'm better this morning." I took a deep breath as if to prove it. "David kept me calm." I smiled over at him. "But I think I ruined this dress." My smile turned into a frown as I looked at the material hanging around my legs. There was mascara on the pale pink skirt.

"You still look amazing." He reached out and tucked some of my hair behind my ear.

"I hate that I wasted the dress." I sighed. "I had been saving it for a special night."

"Playing Crazy Eights wasn't a special night to you?" He mock-frowned. "I'm heartbroken."

"Oh hush." I pushed at his shoulder. "Chadwick will be glad you loved your new tux so much that you slept in it."

"Remind me to thank him for insisting on the extra tight pants. They were so comfortable last night." The snark was palpable.

Selene was watching us with a small smile. "Not to interrupt your adorable banter, but what do you want me to do with Tabitha?" From the sound of her voice, she had a few ideas of her own.

"I don't know." I shrugged. The truth was that despite the laughs we had shared, I'd be just fine if I never saw her again. But that seemed unfair. She had done her job for the last two weeks, even if she was a bit confused about what that entailed.

"I'm going to say something that Cathy will probably disagree with, but I think it should be said." David turned to look at me. "I don't trust her. I've been thinking about this all night and I don't see why it couldn't have been her that leaked the photos. Somehow the media has been following you relentlessly since she started working for you. She could be leaking information."

"I don't want to jump to conclusions." I shook my head. "The media could have simply found us at the movie theater, and let's not forget that with Alex and Sam being out of the country, they needed somewhere to focus their attention."

"I happen to agree with David." Selene cleared her throat. "It would be almost impossible to prove, but I can't overlook the fact that she has ignored your basic needs. She should have approached you with the information about the pictures in a much better way."

"She's only been working for me for a couple of weeks. She couldn't know how it would affect me." I frowned. I was defending her, but I remembered some of the evil, hate-filled looks Tabitha had shot my way. Especially when I insisted on going home the night before.

"Anyone would have been upset about the pictures. And she shouldn't have insisted that you go to the auction when you were obviously distraught." David wrapped his fingers around mine. "Give her a different job, demote her without calling it that. Put some distance between you both. Don't let her put you in a bad position."

"I'll tell her that I've decided to let Selene pick up some of the work," I said. "To keep you from tormenting the nurses." I shot my old friend a look.

"Honesty is the best policy." Selene shot me a devilish smile. "She's still going to suspect that she's in trouble."

"Good." David was obviously not on Team Tabitha.

I slapped his leg. "If she is leaking stuff, we don't want to alienate her."

"Friends close, enemies closer." David nodded his head.

"Exactly." Selene sipped more of her tea. "I'll take care of Tabitha."

"What about me?" She walked out into the

living room, still wearing her dress from the night before and carrying her shoes.

"Where have you been?" Selene set her cup down on her saucer. "You should be up dealing with today's turn of events."

"I was busy this morning." She shrugged, and one of her breasts almost popped out of her dress. "A friend came over."

"You invited a friend into my home?" I stood up, shocked.

"Yes, my boyfriend came over to comfort me last night."

"To comfort you?" My ire was white-hot. "To comfort you where? You aren't coming from your room. Where is he?"

"We slept in one of the guest rooms. And he left out the back, where his car was parked." She set her shoes down on the floor and stepped into them. "Now, what is it you want me to do this morning? I tried to make things right last night, but you weren't having any of it."

"I want you to pack your shit and get the hell out of my house." The words flew out of my mouth before I could censor them.

"Excuse me?"

"You disappeared last night, you got drunk on the job, invited a stranger into my home during a difficult time, and then did God knows what in a guest room that is reserved for visiting dignitaries." I clenched my hands at my sides. "Get your stuff and get out."

"You might as well clear out your desk at the palace as well," Selene added. "I'll let them know you have limited access for the next two days."

"You're firing me?" She put her hands on her hips and I had to fight a violent urge. Apparently I'd spent too much time with my sister-in-law.

"Yes."

"For having my boyfriend over." She started laughing. "Fine. Fire me for having my boyfriend over to your freaking house. Fire me for being driven to drinking by your emotional baggage. Do you know how much money you cost me yesterday?"

"What are you talking about?" David stood up and put a hand on my shoulder.

"She bailed on an interview. I was going to make five thousand euros just for getting *Her Highness* to talk to someone." She pointed at me and I froze. "I didn't complain when you chose one of the lowest bidders, but then you started crying like a giant baby. I've been helping you! You're boring, you do nothing, and your charity was going to fizzle."

"Did you take those pictures?" I squeezed the words out from between my teeth.

"How could I have taken those pictures? I was a floor down with the peasants, remember?" She sashayed toward the stairs.

"If I found out you took those pictures, you will never work in Lilaria again." I could feel the explosion building under the surface, fighting to get free of my tight hold.

"Is that a threat, *Princess*?" She turned to look at me. "Are you threatening an ex-employee?"

"I'm reminding you of the contract you signed." I sneered at her. "The one where you agreed to never release revealing or damaging information about the royal family and their staff."

"Well, it would be impossible to prove that I took any pictures."

"It's not impossible to find out who leaked them." David laughed. "And from what I can tell from your face, you're going to have something to worry about all the way back to whatever hellhole you came out of."

She turned to go back to her room and I broke. "Get out. Don't get your stuff. I'll have it shipped to you. Get out of my home right now."

"This isn't your home. This is your mommy's home." She laughed. "You're just a floating figurehead. You have no real title or job. You have nothing but your boy toy—"

"ENOUGH!" I shook with the need to hurt her. "I may be a princess, but I can get my bitch on when I need to. Take your slutty ass and leave right now." She started to respond and I held up my hand. "If you don't want to be escorted out by Jameson and Mark, you will keep your lying mouth shut."

Jameson had come to stand by the door with crossed arms. His face was impassive, but just his large bulk was threatening. You could feel his desire to throw her out vibrating in the air.

Turning on one heel she marched to the door and yanked it open. Without a look back she disappeared, but not before slamming the heavy wood panel.

I stood there shaking, unable to say anything while my blood boiled with rage. The only other time I had been this angry was when I found out Sam had been mobbed by the paparazzi. I had let Tabitha into my home, into my life, and she had sold pictures of me to people who would use them to damage my reputation.

The sound of clapping caught my attention and I realized that Selene was applauding me. "I didn't think you had that in you."

"I guess we're surprising each other this week." I shrugged.

"Wow." David touched my hand and I turned to look at him. "That was really sexy." His eyes ran over me hungrily, but there was a small smile playing along his lips that softened the comment. "I really like you as an angry princess."

"Off with their heads!" Selene cackled.

I turned to look at her and couldn't stop my own laughter. She was holding her chest, but otherwise looked happier than I had seen her in years.

David pulled me into his arms and rested his chin on top of my head. "Are you okay?"

"I think so." I melted against him, glad that he was there to comfort me. "I wanted to beat her face in."

"I could tell." His chuckle vibrated in his chest under my cheek. "She deserved it."

"Hell yes, she did." I shook my head. "I can't believe she sold those pictures. I can't believe she was auctioning off interviews with me."

"She was evil," Selene said from her seat. She looked a little paler and had slumped in her seat. "I'm the one to blame. I hired her and thought she would match well with you when it was time for me to retire."

"Are you okay?" I knelt down at her chair. "David, get the nurse."

He disappeared in an instant.

"I'm fine. Just tired." She shook her head slowly. "I made a very bad mistake."

"It just means that you have to live forever and never retire." I grabbed her hand and squeezed it.

"I'll see what I can do." She smiled at me.

"Time to get you in bed." The nurses came out of the kitchen.

"Okay." Selene let them help her out of the chair, and she wasn't feeling well if she wasn't complaining about being told what to do.

"Will you stay awhile?" I looked over at David.

"I'll call Chadwick and let him know." He smiled. "I told you, you're not in this alone."

"Thank you," I whispered as I followed the nurses upstairs.

Selene collapsed in her bed and I sat next to her while the nurses checked her blood pressure and the incisions on her chest.

"Is she okay?"

"She's fine, just worn out. I think you surprised the hell out of her." The nurse winked at me before giving Selene some medicine. "Can't say that I wouldn't have done the same in your place."

"I suppose that everyone heard that, huh?" I cringed.

"I didn't hear anyone complaining." The nurse winked at me. "I'm going to step outside for a few minutes, but Selene really does need to sleep."

"I understand."

"You did the right thing." Selene's fingers squeezed mine. "I'm sorry."

"Don't be sorry." I shook my head. "I should have trusted my gut, but I thought I was just reacting to all of the change that was happening."

"Well, we both learned some lessons this month." She smiled at me. "Tell Chadwick what happened. He'll get you taken care of until we find a replacement."

"I think David is already on the phone with him." I smiled.

"I like him."

"Chadwick?" I laughed.

"David. He's good for you. You've been so quiet and careful lately. It's good to see you reach out to someone else." Her eyes drifted shut slowly.

"I like him too." I leaned over and kissed her head. "Get some rest. I'm willing to bet that Chadwick is already on his way here."

Downstairs I found David on the phone, pacing in front of the fireplace.

"Yes, I will be in tomorrow." His back was to me, so I didn't disturb him. "Make sure the cages have all been cleaned and the birds have been fed. We don't want the kiddies to see the blood." He turned to look at me and smiled. "Listen, I have to go. No, don't worry. I'll be there tomorrow for the presentation. Yes. I'll remember. Bye."

He hung up his cell phone and stuck it in his pocket.

I frowned. "If you need to go, I understand."

"No, there isn't anything that they can't handle without me today. Really, Sam could have left it all in their hands. I'm just a formality."

"I saw how they paid attention to what you had to say." I walked over to him. "They feel better having you there, and you have a lot to offer."

"I'm proud of you." He looked down at me and brushed some of the hair out of my eyes.

"Why?" I felt my eyebrows rise. I had lost my temper, screamed at an employee, and even cursed. My mother would be so disappointed. Oh God, my mother. She would know about the pictures.

"Because you stood up for yourself. You told her what you were really thinking and didn't hold back." He closed his mouth and chewed on the inside of his cheek for a moment. "I haven't seen you do that when you're being Princess Catherine. Today your two sides merged. It was something else."

"So, a little bit scary?" I laughed.

"Scary was Chadwick on the phone." David shuddered. "I got yelled at for not letting him know what happened last night. Then I listened as he yelled about what he was going to do to Tabitha if he ever saw her, and I quote, uneducated, badly dressed ass, again."

My giggle was honest and I leaned into David a little more before letting go. "I'm going to go change out of this dress."

"Want some company?" His eyes darkened and I felt my body flush.

"When is Chadwick going to be here?"

"He was on his way to the capital but is turning around." He cocked his head to the side and I knew what he was thinking, because I was wondering the same thing. Was that enough time?

"Then we should have a while." I grabbed his hand. "C'mon."

As we walked into my room, I undid the earrings that had somehow managed to stay on through my night on the couch and dropped them in a dish on my nightstand.

"You know what I want more than anything?" I raised an eyebrow and smiled.

"I hope we're thinking the same thing." His eyes ran over me.

"A shower."

"Thank God. I was scared you were going to say sex." He mimed relief.

Laughter burst out of my mouth. "Well, I wouldn't mind some company."

"I'd be happy to scrub your back." He started undoing the buttons of his shirt. When he sat down in a chair to pull his shoes off, I took a deep breath and turned my back to him. Carefully I slid the zipper down and over the swell of my backside. When I reached the end, I was surprised to feel his hands slide up the dress, spreading the edges open so that the little sleeves slipped off my shoulders and I let the dress fall to the ground.

I didn't say anything, waiting to see what he would do. The feel of his hands on me sent my heart into overdrive. I couldn't get enough when it came to David.

His hands moved up over my shoulders and into my hair, where he pulled out the pins that held the bun in place. Gently he worked the knots out with his fingers until my hair fell softly against my shoulders. I leaned my head to the side when he stepped close enough that I could feel him pressing against my lower back through his pants. My entire body was alive, and it took all of my willpower not to turn around and melt into him. He pushed my hair to the side and touched the pulse point under my ear with a feather-light kiss.

His hands slid between us and undid the snaps

of my bra. I slid the straps off of my shoulders and let it join the dress on the floor. When his fingers teased along the edge of the tiny lace panties I was wearing, I sucked in a deep breath.

He continued to kiss along my neck and down my shoulder until I couldn't take it any longer. I turned in his embrace so that I could work the rest of his clothes off. His pants were already undone, so I only had to push them off of his hips. I traced the length of him with my fingertips and he sucked in a deep breath.

"Cathy." He pressed his mouth to mine hungrily. "You're beautiful."

I opened my mouth, eager to taste him. It was dark and heady, enough to make me want to forget everything else in the world. When he did pull away, it was only to remove his shirt.

He stood there, letting me look at him in all of his naked glory as I pushed my underwear down to my feet. I held my hand out to him with a small smile. He laced his fingers with mine and I led him to the bathroom.

The stand-alone shower was in the corner and I stepped inside before turning on the water. There was no wait time for warm water, which was my favorite part of my bathroom. I hated cold water more than I hated Tabitha. Well, almost.

There was no talking as we cleaned our bodies, just hungry glances and touches. It wasn't until he pressed me against the wall and kissed me that I realized this was it. There was no turning back and I was more than ready.

He dropped to his knees and picked up the sponge I had dropped. Without looking away, he ran the sponge between my legs, gently cleaning me. My breathing got heavy when he worked that area for a little too long, but I couldn't look away from his gaze. When he pushed me gently into the water to rinse off I tried to calm down, but he had other plans for me.

Once I was clean he pushed me back a little further until I was pressed against the tile wall once more. He was still on his knees when he leaned forward and nuzzled me gently. Carefully so I wouldn't fall, he spread my legs apart with his hands until he had the access he wanted. Darting his tongue out, he caught some of the water that ran down my inner thigh and I shivered in anticipation.

His hot breath was already making my knees weak and I braced my arms against the shower walls. He continued chasing water drops until he was right where I wanted him to be. His mouth was hot and wet as he turned all of his attention on me. There was no teasing, no pulling away here. He was giving me the full treatment, no holding back. My head slammed against the shower wall and I moaned as his tongue stroked me over and over again. No one had ever made me feel the way David did.

"Right there, David. Yes. There. Please. There."

My groans grew with each touch and my hips chose a rhythm, moving against his face the best they could while he pleasured me. His arms were getting a workout, because the closer I came to finishing, the weaker my legs became. Soon, he was lost in his task, the sounds of what he was doing speeding my journey along. I braced against the wall as my release flashed through my system. Lights exploded behind my eyelids and I felt light-headed. I slid down the wall and melted into a puddle in front of him. He waited patiently while I caught my breath and my limbs started to work again.

"You're really good at that." I pushed off the tile and moved toward him on the floor. I straddled his lap and looked down into his eyes while I reached between us, stroking him gently.

His mouth found mine and I enjoyed the way our tastes mingled together. It was intimate and honest. A real part of the experience I hadn't thought about before it had actually happened. When I moved my hips against him, he groaned loudly and fought to stand up while holding me against him.

I was too busy kissing him to think about what was happening until the shower door flew open. David carried me back into the room, still covered in water and hot with need. When he laid me down on my bed I watched him with hungry eyes as he climbed over me. His mouth captured one of my nipples and sucked it into his mouth. I groaned loudly and bucked against him. He only released my breast to move to the other, before finally trading that one for my mouth.

His tongue was hot and hungry as it explored my mouth. I held nothing back as I returned his kiss, just as hungry for him. With gentle hands he spread my legs and positioned his cock at my entrance.

"This might hurt a little, angel," he whispered in my ear.

As he slid in inch by thick inch I concentrated on his kiss. It was tight and my breathing was fast, but I was already loose from my orgasm in the shower. Once he was pressed all the way inside, he stilled, his breathing ragged.

I ran my hands over his back, tracing the muscles before squeezing his ass.

He groaned into my ear. "God, you feel good."

Slowly he moved against me, barely rocking as I got used to his body. It hurt, but in a good way. And then it didn't hurt at all. It only felt good. He kissed me slowly, keeping a steady pace until my body began to move against his. Slowly he increased his rhythm, and my breathing increased right along with my pleasure.

It didn't take long before I was gripping his back and moving against him in eagerness. The feel of him sliding in and out, his hot breath on my shoulder, the way one hand cupped my breast was enough to send me over the edge.

"David!" My eyes slid shut as wave after wave of pleasure swept through my body. He stiffened on top of me with one thrust and he filled me with his hot orgasm.

Gently, he rolled so that I was tucked against his chest, his weight no longer pressed on top of me.

"Are you okay?" He kissed the top of my head.

"Are you kidding?" I leaned up on one elbow and raised an eyebrow. "I'm fucking fantastic right now."

He laughed and pulled me back down to his chest. "I meant, are you sore?"

I thought about it for a minute. "A little, but not much. Different. Is that normal?"

"I think so." He shrugged and I could hear

the embarrassment in his voice. "You're the first virgin I've made love to."

"Oh." I thought about it for a minute and then started laughing.

"What?"

"Out of all the men, I picked the one that had never been with a virgin before." I shook my head. "Go figure."

"I don't think I did too bad." He frowned.

"Actually, I think you did an excellent job." Leaning forward I pressed a kiss to his lips. "I'm glad I waited for you."

"Was it too fast?"

"I don't think so." I lay back down with my head on his chest. "I know everything about you that I needed to know."

"You can ask me anything." His voice rumbled in my ear.

I thought about it for a minute, but there wasn't anything I wanted to ask. There was something that I wanted to say though.

"Anything?" I bit my lip.

"Anything."

"What if . . ." I took a deep breath, not sure how to word the question.

"What if what?" He turned so that his chin brushed the top of my head.

"What if there is something I want to say, but I'm not sure I should say it yet?" I cringed, waiting for his response. Would he know what I meant? Would he tell me to wait? Could I just tell him?

He rolled over so that I was cradled in his arm and he was hovering over me, and his eyes traced my face slowly.

"I love you, Cathy. I love every angle, every side, every part of you."

Tears filled my eyes. "I love you too."

# TWENTY

$\mathcal{I}$T WAS ALMOST unfair to compare Tabitha to Selene or Chadwick. Well, it would have been unfair if she hadn't turned out to be a crazy, money-hungry whore.

Chadwick swooped into D'Lynsal with a bag of clothing for David, a laptop, and a bottle of brandy. It took minutes for him to talk me into looking at the photos, which I hated, but it eased some of the anxiety I felt. The pictures were intimate, with one of David's hands on my ass, but other than that, they were pretty tame. What I hated knowing was that there were sickos out there who would get a real kick out of the images—and that they would be brought up any time there was a news story where I was concerned.

I held the phone to my ear and sighed.

"Are you okay? Should I come to D'Lynsal?" she asked. "Those pictures were everywhere."

"No, Mother. I'm fine." I tried to keep the frustration out of my voice.

"I don't expect you to not date, dear, but please be more careful." The disapproval in her voice hurt.

"Yes, Mother." I frowned. "You know, we were in what we thought was a private area. But from now on I will check the broom closet first."

Her chuckle surprised me. "The air vents too."

"God, what about the drains in the bathroom?" I laughed.

"That might be stepping over the line and into the realm of paranoia." She tsked again, but I could sense the humor under her words.

"I'm sorry," I said. "I've tried so hard to keep myself clean the last couple of years. I just—"

"I know. You needed to live a little." She sighed. "We live under a microscope, but that doesn't mean you shouldn't live at all."

"I love you, Mother." I whispered the words in Lilarian.

"And I love you." I could hear her smile through the phone. It was in the way the words came out of her mouth. "When are you bringing this young man to meet me formally? Not just a rushed hello during your brother's wedding."

"I'm not sure. He's working at Victory Hall, Sam's newest project. When he has time I'll drag him along with me for a weekend." I switched the phone to my other ear. "We should keep it informal. He's a lot like Sam and hates to dress up."

"My children." She chuckled. "You certainly managed to find your opposites, didn't you?"

"I think so." I said the words with pride. I loved the fact that we were opposites but that we complemented each other.

"Don't worry about the photos." Mother's voice turned to business. "Once I can prove that Tabitha leaked the photographs, we'll take legal action against her. I'm tired of people trying to use my family to further their careers or to fatten their pockets."

"Have you heard from Alex or Sam?"

Sam had contacted Chadwick when she saw the images of David and me on the television. She said Alex was livid and that he was ready to come home and help if I needed it, but I had called and told them to stay their asses on the beach. Not only did I not want Alex glaring at David the way Max was right this minute, but I didn't want them to think I couldn't handle myself. Max had shown up right behind Chadwick and hadn't stopped glaring at David the entire time.

"Yes, he called." She sighed again. Not that I could blame her. Alex was a handful. "But they are not coming home early."

"Good."

"He's just worried about you." I could hear someone in the background whispering to her.

"Yeah, I get it. Could you tell Max to stop giving David the evil eye? He's been giving him the third degree since he got home."

"Oh no, dear. That's a brother's right. Besides, I have it on good authority that David warned Alex about Sam when they first met."

That didn't surprise me in the least. "I bet he did."

"Yes. So I wouldn't be surprised if your oldest brother isn't prodding Max along."

"Aha." That made entirely too much sense. I could see Alex finding it all very humorous. Not that I could blame him. Who would have guessed that David would end up falling in love with Alex's sister when he was defending Sam?

"I have to go, sweetheart. I'll see you soon?"

"Yes. I have to get back to deal with the art charity."

"Have you come up with a name for it yet?" The noise in the background meant she was on the move.

"A name for my art charity?" I had been toying with the thought for a while. "I have." I paused, unable to keep the smile from coming to my lips.

"The Liberty Anne Foundation." It was my way of honoring David's sister after the trouble she had been put through by the media.

"That sounds lovely. It will be easy to remember for people too."

"I think so." I blew a kiss into the phone. "Go do queenly stuff. I'll see you soon."

"Love you." The phone clicked and I looked out across the field behind D'Lynsal Manor.

Knowing that Mother wasn't upset with me eased a lot of my tension. I was worried she was going to freak out over the photos. Especially since we had all been instructed to be careful after what happened with Alex. I also thought she might pull a normal mom moment and be upset about seeing how David was holding me. I could only guess that I was old enough now that she accepted the fact that I was a grown woman.

"How'd it go?" David opened the rear door facing the patio and watched my face with careful eyes.

"It went well." I laughed at his look of relief. "The queen is not going to order you be thrown in the dungeon."

"That's a relief." He walked over to me and wrapped his arms around my waist. "You don't really have a dungeon, do you?"

"Our palace was originally built in the fifteen hundreds. Of course we have a dungeon."

"Yeah, but you don't really use it as a dungeon?" He raised an eyebrow, a half grin lighting his face.

"I'll give you the tour next time we're there." I stood on my tiptoes and kissed his cheek. I loved the way his stubble felt against my skin. It was so coarse and manly. "How are your parents?"

"They're okay. My mother was a bit . . . shocked by the pictures." His low chuckle warmed my body. "I wouldn't call her a prude exactly, but living in the South, there are certain things that come with the culture. And anything sexual can be a bit taboo."

"Well, I hope she knows it's not my fault you grabbed my ass." My cheeks heated at the realization that his family and friends had seen the pictures as well. At this point they were probably floating around the entire world in some fashion or other.

"Oh, it was your fault." He leaned down and nuzzled my neck.

"How do you figure that?" I tilted my head so he had better access and was rewarded by the touch of his lips on my pulse point.

"You can't look that good in a pair of jeans and

expect me to not grab your ass." As if to demon-strate he reached around and got a handful. "It's too perfect. I can't help myself. It looked great in that dress last night too, but there's just something special about an old pair of jeans."

"I hadn't noticed." Reaching around, I tucked my hands into the pockets of his pants and laughed when he made a pleased sound deep in his throat.

"So, tell me, is Max preparing to kill me while my back is turned or is he just a protective older brother?"

"Protective older brother." I narrowed my eyes. "But I also heard that you did your own little bit of protective brothering for Samantha once upon a time."

"Alex ratted me out, huh?" He laughed. "And I thought we were finally getting along."

"That was before you decided to date his sister," I reminded him.

"True." His warm eyes traced my face. "I couldn't help but overhear part of your phone con-versation."

"I'm sure you tried really hard not to, with your head sticking out the door."

"Pfft." He cupped my cheek and turned my face up to his. "You're naming your charity after Lib?"

"I think that there are a lot of benefits for children in art programs. And Liberty is a good example of that. It lets her express herself in a way she wouldn't otherwise be able to do."

"You're an amazing woman." His lips touched mine softly, almost reverently. "I love you, Cathy."

I wrapped my arms around his neck and sank into his kiss. There were few things in the world that made me feel like all was right in the world, and his touch was one of them.

"Love you too."

# EPILOGUE

"*T*HAT'S BEAUTIFUL!" I smiled down at the little boy holding up his drawing. I wasn't exaggerating. The pencil sketch he was proudly displaying was a breathtaking rendering of one of the birds he had seen earlier that day.

"I made it for you." Brandon grinned, and I knew this was a rare moment for him. He so seldom smiled for anyone, it made my heart soar.

"Thank you." I knelt down and looked at the picture. "I'm going to hang it in my office. Is that okay?"

"That sounds good." He ran the back of his hand across his nose three times and then smiled. "Hang it where you can always see it."

"That I can." I wanted to hug him so badly, but I knew that might push him over the edge. So instead I held up my hand for a high five. After three quick slaps on my palm he ran back to the craft table and picked up his pencil.

David was watching me from where he sat surrounded by seven little girls all giving him googly eyes. He was holding the small merlin that Alex had given Sam as a wedding present.

"Help!" he mouthed at me, and I giggled.

"You'd think he'd be used to it at this point." Sam stood next to me, shaking her head.

"It's kind of cute, right? All those little girls in love with him." I chuckled when he frowned at me.

"You bet. And he might just be the reason they go into wildlife studies when they get older." She leaned against the wall and tapped her gloves against her thigh.

"I don't think that will make him feel any better."

"Wah." Sam rolled her eyes. "In the end we're all winning because he's a cutie."

"That he is." I eyed her with interest. "Tell me something."

"Something."

"God, you're bitchy today." I bumped my shoulder against hers. "Did you think I would end up with David that night we were talking in your kitchen?"

"I thought it might happen when you gyrated your hips and told him to take his clothes off." She laughed while I groaned.

"Did you tell Mom about that?"

"Um, that's a negative." She shook her head and turned green.

"Someone did and let me tell you, she was not amused when she thought I had hired a stripper." I reached out and touched her arm. "Are you going to be sick?"

"No!" She put a hand to her mouth. "I don't think so."

"I thought you were going to wait a year before you tried." I looked down to where Sam had her hand on her stomach.

"It's almost been a year." She frowned. "I don't know. Alex . . . he just talks circles around me sometimes and before I knew it, BAM! First try."

"Bam, huh?" I laughed loudly, drawing some looks our way, and Sam dropped her hand. No one knew that my brother and best friend were expecting a baby. It was a family secret for now.

"Yes, and now all I want to do is sleep and puke." She frowned. "Sometimes at the same time."

"Are you happy?" I leaned close so no one could hear us.

"Very." She smiled and her face practically glowed. "I'm scared to death but so, so happy."

"I wonder if you'll have a boy or girl."

"Won't know for a while." Her hand fluttered to her stomach briefly. "So tell me something."

"Something. Hey!" I chuckled when she smacked me with her gloves. "What?"

"When are you two going to make things official?" She glanced to where David was sitting. He had finally been saved by one of the other workers and the girls were asking questions instead of just staring at him.

"We're taking our time." I shrugged. "Besides, with you making little heirs, I don't have to rush."

"I noticed you moved your stuff to Rousseau." She smiled.

"Well, with you at D'Lynsal it made sense." I shrugged. "Besides, it's a long drive in the middle of the night just for a booty call."

"Tell me about it." Her laugh was infectious.

"Really, I want to finish school first. Then, we'll see." I watched David lean over and place the merlin on the gloved arm of a girl. "We talked about it. I hope we'll get there someday."

"Pfft. You're there, you're just killing time at this point." Sam shook her head. "But I get the degree thing. It was painful to give that up when I moved to Lilaria."

"I want to accomplish something first. Have something that I *earned* for myself, not just something I was born into." I shrugged. It was hard to explain but I wanted to feel like I had done more than just been a figurehead.

"Uh-oh." Sam stood up from the wall she was leaning on. "He's coming and I think you're in trouble." She darted away from me quickly as I turned around to see who she was talking about.

"You left me for the vultures." David leaned close and whispered in my ear.

"Oh, I didn't know you had those here." I widened my eyes and tried to look innocent.

"Oh, that is not going to work on me." He traced my cheek with one finger. "They were just staring at me and didn't hear a word I said."

"Well, it's your fault for being so cute." I placed my hands on his plaid-covered chest. "The whole lumber jack think really works for you."

"It did snag me a princess." His eyes twinkled.

"That is true." I toyed with the pocket on his chest. "And now that you have one, what are you going to do with her?"

He leaned down so that his mouth barely touched my ear. "I can't say what I'm going to do because there are too many kids around."

"Are you sure that said princess will go for your plans?" I raised an eyebrow as he moved his face so that his lips were a mere breath away from mine.

"She did this morning." Ever so softly he pressed his mouth to mine.

"You know, I always thought I wanted a knight

in shining armor." I broke away from his kiss and looked up at him with a smile. "But I like my dashing rogue much better."

"Angel, shiny armor just means the knight never went to battle." He kissed my temple. "And I'd fight dragons for you."

# ACKNOWLEDGMENTS

Writing a book is a bit like raising a child. It's been said that it takes a village, and in this case, that couldn't be closer to the truth.

A huge thank-you to my agent, Rebecca Friedman, who has stood beside me through this endeavor and held my hand the whole way. I'm very lucky to have her on my side. I also have to tell KP Simmon thank you for listening to my crazy blatherings and random thoughts. She never once laughed at me.

I'd owe my family an apology for all of the fast food we ate while I was writing this book, but they probably preferred it that way. In all seriousness, I will never be able to thank my husband enough for his love and support while I pound away at this career I'm carving out. His strength and belief in me gets me through the toughest of days.

My daughter is a whopping four years old and she told me the other day that she wanted to write books. While that made me tear up, I'm positive that she will do wonderfully at whatever path she chooses in life—though I will always tell her to take the one less traveled. Thank you, sweet potato, for being so patient while Mommy turned her imaginary friends into characters in a book.

A huge and massive thank-you to my friends and family for supporting me while I was writing this book. My sister, as usual, is my rock and source of confidence. She never lets me down. My mother, father, and stepfather have been my cheerleaders from the get-go, constantly cheering me on from the sidelines. My best friend was there to listen to me cry and laugh, and to lift my spirits or just commiserate.

A big thank-you to the Thorntons, our adopted family, for being a ray of sunshine and constantly pushing me forward. (And for putting up with all the craziness that goes with having a pirate ship in your backyard. Argh.)

Thank you to Tessa Woodward for taking a chance on me and my books. It's been a fun and interesting journey, and I'm so glad that I get to work with you.

For the readers who have followed me from the beginning, thank you. It's because of you that I do what I do.

**Want to see how it all began?**
**Keep reading for a glimpse**
**of Sam and Alex's story,**

# SUDDENLY ROYAL

# ONE

**Royal Donors Cause Congestion on Campus**
—*COLLEGE DAILY*

To SAY MY day was not going well, would be like saying the French Revolution had been a bit troublesome for Marie Antoinette. My truck had coughed and sputtered all the way to school. I couldn't find my gloves, so my fingers had turned into frozen sticks by the time I reached my classroom. Only half of the students in my first class showed up, and then I couldn't find the tests I had spent the entire weekend grading. My entire day was turning into a bad country song. By the time lunch rolled around I had been more than ready for a break. I snagged a sandwich and ate it on my way to the library. The server for our building was down and I needed to do some research.

Crossing campus, I had to wade through a

crowd of people. It was like the entire student body had gathered in the middle of the school for a pep rally. Hordes of giggling freshmen were pushing their way to the front and one of them elbowed me, making me drop the notebook I was carrying. The fraternities and sororities had painted signs and hung them on trees to welcome someone. I grimaced when I realized one of them was actually a sheet that didn't look very clean. I looked from the signs to the crowd and realized I would never be able to make it up the stairs to the library. Standing in the middle of the steps was a group of people, but my eyes focused on the tall blond man. I couldn't pull my eyes away from him. He was joking with a girl while she batted her eyes and twirled a lock of hair around her finger.

I tried to see exactly why everyone was so excited, but none of it made sense. Donors came to the school all the time and most of the self-absorbed student body never noticed. The man on the steps was attractive enough to be a movie star and that had to be what had brought the mob out.

"Do you see him, Sam? The prince?" One of the girls in my first class pulled on my arm.

"Prince? Yeah, I see him." A prince? A real-life prince with a crown and throne? No wonder the masses were out in the snow. A royal donor would bring out everyone. Movie stars were one thing, but a prince? That wasn't something you saw every day. I wondered why royalty would be donating to our school, but standing out in the cold watching some guy flirt was not part of my plans. I only had a little longer before I had to be at the research center and a lot to get done in the meantime.

"He's gorgeous," the girl gushed while her friends made noises of agreement.

"Yeah, I guess." I rolled my eyes.

"Even you have to admit he's hot." She laughed at me. What the hell did that mean? I wasn't blind. Of course I noticed he was hot. What the hell kind of good would that do me? I'd never see him again. He was a freaking prince!

Spinning on my heel, I headed for a side entrance, only to see it was blocked by police. Gritting my teeth, I stomped through the snow to the back entrance. It took forever, because I was dodging mobs of people. I almost tripped on a cord and the news reporter hollered at me. I gave him my best eat-shit-and-die look, but he wasn't fazed. By the time I reached the back steps I was ready to murder someone.

There was a group of cops standing at the door,

but I didn't care. I marched up and went straight for the entrance.

"You can't go in there, miss."

"Why not? I pay tuition so I can use this library."

"It's closed right now. Should be open again in an hour or so."

"I'll be busy in an hour." I gave him my best imitation of puppy eyes. "I just need to use the Internet and check out some books. Please? I'll be good. One of you guys can come in with me."

"Sorry."

I took a deep breath, the cold air stinging my lungs, and turned back toward the parking lot. My angry breath caused plumes of fog as I stomped across the pavement. I went straight to my truck, cranked it up, and headed for the center. The stars had not aligned and I wouldn't be doing what I had needed to, so I might as well throw myself into the other part of my work.

I weaved through the campus traffic, careful to not run over any of the people that seemed to see vehicles on icy roads as anything but dangerous. Thankfully, the closer I got to the wildlife center, the fewer people were out to annoy me. My old truck slid into a parking spot, coughing noisily. Ready to move on to the favorite part of my day, I hurried inside and immediately felt better. Working with the birds brightened my mood. After checking through the cages to make sure there were no problems, I moved to weighing and measuring the birds. When I got to Dover, an owl who had been hit by a car, I cooed softly. She had lost an eye, so tended to be nervous when people approached her mew.

"Hi, sweetheart. Time for some food." I unlocked the cage door and stepped in slowly. I untied the string that held her to her perch and gave her a good look-over.

Once I had her in the office, I weighed her, careful to note the exact amount in our logs before getting her food.

"Eat up. You know you want it." I lifted the mouse to her beak but she turned away. "Aw, c'mon, Dover. It's yummy mouse guts. Your favorite."

She ruffled her feathers and sighed. Dover was beautiful, but getting her to eat was always a frustrating process. I lifted the mouse to her beak again, making sure she could see the food out of her good eye. Delicately, as if she was doing me a favor, she took a small bite.

"That's it," I hummed. "Eat up."

Slowly she lifted her claw and grasped the mouse. I sighed in relief. She needed to eat to keep her weight up. It was also how we administered her medicine. Dover was a smart bird and I suspected she knew we were putting something in her food.

Once she was done, I took a few measurements and took her back to her mew. I checked the cage quickly and then cleaned up any mess she had made. I checked all our logbooks to make sure nothing had been missed, made a few notes about a Harris hawk with an injured wing, and closed up shop.

I felt much better by the time I was ready to leave. The annoyances from earlier didn't seem like such a big deal and I was looking forward to getting home. After double-checking the medicines and the food for the next day, I flipped the lights and headed out the door. I fished out my keys to lock the gate as I neared the entrance. No one else would be in until the morning.

"Samantha Rousseau?"

I looked up at the man standing just outside the gate to my research center. Dark pants met with a black blazer and an equally boring tie. The only thing remarkable about him was the expensive pair of sunglasses sitting on his nose and the little gizmo tucked into his ear, complete with a curly cord running down into his shirt collar.

"Yeah?" I finished locking the bottom of the gate and stood up. He wasn't a very tall man, possibly my father's age, but he radiated power. Since I tend to have issues with authority, I immediately disliked the guy. He hadn't really given me a reason to not like him, but people that think they're better than you or know more than you make me itch.

"Are you Samantha Rousseau?" he asked again. He didn't introduce himself or make an attempt to appear friendly. No offer to shake hands.

"Who wants to know?" I slung my bag over my shoulder as I headed toward the old pickup I drive. Authority dude followed close behind, making my hackles rise even farther.

"If you are Samantha, I need to speak with you privately."

I threw my bag into the back of my truck and turned around to look at him. I didn't bother to keep the annoyance off my face when I realized how close he was standing to me. "Well, if I was Samantha, you're in luck. There isn't anyone else around." I motioned toward the unoccupied parking lot. We were the only two people.

His frosty expression seemed to crack a little and he gave me something that could almost pass as a smile. "Miss Rousseau, I would like to ask you to accompany me. I have someone who would like to speak to you downtown."

"Uh, yeah. That's not going to happen, Mr. Uptight. Look, if you're here about my father's medical bills, I made a payment today. If he could make any more payments, then we would, but since he can't work I doubt that's going to happen anytime soon." I yanked open the door to my truck and started to climb in. A hand landed on my shoulder and I reacted without thinking. Grabbing his fingers, I twisted as I turned and swung my other arm around in an attempt to clock him. Unfortunately he seemed to be expecting this move and countered smoothly. Taking his hand back, he ducked under my swing and danced out of the way.

"Who the hell do you think you are?" Brushing some of my brown hair out of my eyes, I glared at him. The fact that his weird smile had grown made me even more irritated.

"Nicely executed, Miss Rousseau. You almost had me." The FBI wannabe nodded his head at me. I clenched my fists at my sides to keep from trying to cream him. What a snide little—

"Here is my card. My name is Duvall. It would please my boss a great deal if you could meet us for dinner tonight. She is staying at the Parallel and has dinner reservations set for eight-thirty at the restaurant downstairs." I looked at his card and then back to his face. What on earth could this be about? The Parallel was the nicest hotel in town. I looked back at his card and noticed the odd crest at the top. A small bird rested on a branch that wrapped around a blue shield. Who was this weird little dude wearing an earpiece?

"Who's your boss?"

"The Duchess Rose Sverelle of Dollange."

I looked at him for a moment to see if he was joking. Nope, his face was still set in that frosty, serious expression. I blinked slowly and looked back at his card before returning my eyes to his face.

"I think you have the wrong Samantha. There is no reason a duchess would be looking for me." I climbed into the driver's seat and he closed the door once my leg was in, attempting a smile. It looked weird on his face, as if he wasn't used to doing it very often. I rolled down the window and tried to hand him back his business card, but he waved a hand to signal I should keep it.

"You are Samantha Rousseau, wildlife biologist specializing in raptors? Graduate student, daughter of Martha Rousseau?"

"Uh, yeah, but—" I shook my head when he stepped a little closer to the window.

"I am very good at my job, Miss Rousseau. I was told to find Samantha Rousseau, and I have. The duchess's reasons are her own." He shrugged. "Of course, falconry is a large sport in our country. Perhaps it has something to do with that."

"And what country is that?" I looked back at his card as if it might offer some answers.

"Lilaria." He stepped away from the car and nodded to me. I looked at him for a moment in confusion. Eventually I threw the business card onto the pickup bench next to me and stuck my key in the ignition.

"Okay, Duvall. I might be there, but I'm a pretty busy person. Got to check the calendar first." With that, I threw the truck into reverse and backed up.

"Of course." He nodded at me as I switched to drive and pulled out of the parking lot. From the way he smirked at me, I was pretty sure he knew I was lying about being busy.

I watched him get into his black sedan, noticing for the first time the little flags on the hood. What on Earth would a duchess want with me? How had I ended up on some royal's radar? I hit the switch for the radio and leaned back into the old driver's seat. My mind worked through reasons that someone from a country I barely knew existed could possibly want to speak to me. Maybe she was interested in the research center. But why would she come to me? Wouldn't it make more sense for her to contact Dr. Geller? He would be the one to handle donations or any sort of involvement on her part. He was out of town; maybe he forgot to tell me this lady was coming.

The truck coughed as it switched gears and I entered the on-ramp for the highway. The clock on the dashboard said it was almost five-thirty. Dr. Geller would still be in the field, so there was no point in calling him to find out what was going on. I'd just have to wing it. I snorted and sped the truck up. I didn't have much time to change and make it back downtown.

It wasn't like I had anything else to do and she might be able to help the research center. The staff was making do with half the supplies they really needed to rehabilitate the injured raptors in their care. The cages were much smaller than they needed to be, and medical supplies were expensive. We're always cutting out things from the budget to afford more medicines or training equipment.

When I pulled up to the little house I shared with Jess, I sighed and parked at the curb. Her boyfriend was parked in my spot again, not that it mattered since I was leaving soon. Yanking the key out of the ignition, I hopped out and grabbed my bag from the truck bed. When I opened the front door, the smell of fresh chili wafted to my nose and I groaned. It smelled delish. I dropped my bag and kicked off my boots before walking to the kitchen.

Bert was wearing a flowered apron and stirring the chili with a large wooden spoon while Jess sat on the counter next to him. He held up the spoon for her to taste and she laughed when some of it dropped onto her legs. The little TV was on and there was some type of news show playing, which surprised me. Jess liked to watch all the pregame shows.

"We made chili! Ready for the game?" When she saw me she smiled and waved me over.

"I forgot about the game." I looked over Bert's shoulder at the chili and my stomach growled. "I made plans."

"Sam!" Jess groaned. "What could be more important than this game? It's the most important game of the year."

"Every game is the most important game of the year to you." I rolled my eyes and looked back at the TV. "What are you watching?"

"Don't," Bert whispered. But it was too late.

"Some idiot prince and duchess are in town

and all the news stations are acting like it's some kind of big deal." Jess glared at the old television set. "It's not like they're from an important country or anything. I mean, I'm missing the stats from the other games!"

"Oh." I looked back at the TV, interested. There on the steps of the university's new museum were the good-looking guy and an older, dignified woman. She used a gold pair of scissors to cut a red ribbon and waved at the people around her. The prince was speaking to a blond coed near the front door. He was definitely not a frumpy prince. Nope, not frumpy at all. Short blond hair, long legs, and broad shoulders. Even without the royal credentials, he would probably have snagged all the female's attention. And from the cocky grin, it was obvious he knew it. I really hoped he wouldn't be at dinner. Mainly because I didn't want to stare at him like a dumbass. I was already nervous about meeting royalty.

"So?" Jess's voice cut through my thoughts and I tore my eyes from the screen.

"What?"

"I asked what your big plans were." Jess frowned. "Quit staring at Prince Yummy and pay attention."

"Prince Yummy?" Bert pulled off the apron and frowned at Jess. I tried not to laugh.

"That's what the undergrads were calling him. It's annoying, but it stuck in my head." Jess hopped down and wrapped her arms around Bert's neck. She wasn't a short girl, but she looked petite next to her boyfriend. I started to leave to avoid their PDA, but she wasn't ready to let me escape. She leaned back and frowned at me. "You didn't answer!"

"I'm going to dinner with Prince Yummy's dear old relative." I smiled at her shocked expression and made my way to my tiny bedroom.

I started flicking through the clothes in my closet as Jess banged in after me. She was looking at me like I was crazy, so I just shrugged.

"You're serious."

"Yeah. I've got to be at the Parallel in less than three hours."

"Oh my God. You're going to have dinner with a duchess? Is Prince Yummy going to be there too?" Her eyes were huge and I frowned. It would be much better if someone like Jess went to this dinner. She was gorgeous and people tended to like her immediately. I, on the other hand, rarely dressed up and couldn't remember the last time I painted my fingernails. What was the point if I was going to be scraping dirt out from under my nails in a few hours?

"I don't know about Prince Yummy." I shook

my head. I needed to find out his name so I didn't accidentally refer to him that way.

"Why?" She sat down on my bed and watched as I pulled out the few dresses I owned. I held up a bright summer print and she shook her head.

"I don't know. Some guy showed up at work and said the duchess wanted to have dinner with me. I guess Dr. Geller forgot to tell me she was coming." I looked at the dresses in my hands and put the blue back. Black was probably the safest option. That way if I spilled anything on myself, it wouldn't be overly obvious.

"Some guy said she wanted to have dinner with you. Why do you think this has anything to do with Dr. Geller?" Jess crossed her legs and I realized she wasn't leaving. "Seems pretty fishy. Are you sure he is who he says he is?" Jess was pretty practical when things boiled down to it.

"I think so. And if not, then I'll have only wasted one night." I shrugged. "Why else would a duchess want to talk to me? And she was at the school earlier. Maybe she's a donor or something." I laid the dress out on the bed and thought about jewelry. "I have no idea how to talk to her. I mean, do I address her as Duchess? My lady? Your Highness?" This wasn't something I'd grown up knowing. It wasn't like I was from England.

"The Internet is our friend!" Jess grabbed my laptop off the bedside table and popped it open. She typed for a moment and then looked up at me. "They are from Lilaria, right? Says here they're big into birds, so I guess it makes sense."

"Okay. What about their royalty?" I turned to look back at my closet, realizing I didn't have an appropriate jacket.

"Just the usual stuff. A prince is addressed as His Royal Highness." Jess skimmed through the link she was reading. "Address the duchess as Duchess Whatever. But it says you should adopt their type of formality."

"So, I shouldn't call him Prince Dude or her Royal Lady?"

"I think you nailed that one on the head." Jess closed the computer. "You'll be fine. Just be the charming person I know you can be."

"Note to self: Don't eat with fingers or burp in their faces. Got it." I smiled at Jess and she laughed.

"We'll save you some chili." Jess got up and looked at me. "Text me when you get there and let me know it's legit."

"Sure." I smiled at her over my shoulder as I headed for my bathroom. Time to make myself presentable. Thank God, I had time to shower.

# TWO

**Royals in Rags**
—*CHICAGO GAZETTE*

$\mathcal{M}$y truck sounded like it was on its last leg as I pulled up to the hotel. The traffic had been terrible, so I didn't have time to park the thing myself and avoid the embarrassment of valet. Cursing under my breath, I tried to stuff some of the garbage from the bench under the seat before the attendant opened my door. Looking up I smiled at the young guy.

"Sorry, the Bentley is being detailed."

"Looks to me like you traded up, ma'am. This is a classic." He held his hand out and helped me out of the car. I smiled gratefully at him because I had let Jess talk me into wearing heels tonight. He handed me my ticket and I gave him my keys.

I tried to not cringe as my truck made a cough-

ing noise before it pulled away. The hostess wa
watching me through the glass doors, so I took
deep breath and held my head high, all the tim
quietly praying I wouldn't end up busting my as
in the damn shoes. The doorman opened the doo
for me, but even he had a look of disdain as h
studied me.

Chili was already sounding much better. Hope
fully the food would be decent. And not overly ex
pensive. I'd just sent three hundred dollars to th
hospital for my dad's monthly payment. To say
was scraping the bottom of the barrel would b
putting it nicely. I smiled at the hostess, hoping tha
being polite would smooth over the truck fiasco.

"Hi. I'm meeting Duchess Sverelle for dinner."

"Does she know you're coming?" The blonc
woman's voice grated on my ears. It was high anc
nasally. Why would they want that for their firs
impression? There are lots of blond, modelesqu
women who would love a job like this. Her eye:
narrowed and ran over me in disgust.

"Since she's the one who invited me, I woulc
assume so." Operation Nice was over.

"Uh-huh. And what's your name?" The
woman looked down at the list in front of her witl
so much seriousness you would think it was ful
of people waiting for a heart transplant.

"Samantha Rousseau." I watched her as she looked at the list and then back to me. "I'm from the university."

"I see. Just a moment." She walked away, her hair swishing behind her like she was walking in a wind tunnel for a photo shoot and I found myself wondering how she did that.

She returned a moment later, accompanied by a man with a bored look. He was tall, thin, and older, and reminded me of Alfred from the Batman movies. But without any of the humor or intelligence. His eyes traveled over my big winter coat and glimmered with disgust. He lived here, didn't he? How could he think it was weird to wear a big winter coat?

"Miss . . ." He looked at me expectantly.

"Rousseau. Samantha Rousseau."

"Miss Rousseau, your name isn't on the list."

"I'm sure it was a simple mistake." I narrowed my eyes at the man. "Perhaps you could go check with the duchess."

"I'm sure the duchess would have informed me had she been expecting someone else for dinner." He smiled at me and I had to take a deep breath before answering.

"Well, as close as you apparently are with the duchess, it must've slipped her mind." I leaned forward. "Look, I'm just trying to keep an appointment here. Can't you go ask her if she was expecting me?"

"I'm afraid it is against policy to bother guests while they are dining."

"You've got to be kidding me." I brushed the hair out of my eyes and glared at mini-Alfred. "Just go ask her."

"Miss Rousseau, this is a very respectable restaurant. I suggest you leave and not cause a scene. I will call security if I need to."

"I suggest you go ask the duchess if she's expecting me, or go ahead and call security and you can expect a scene. Then when she sees you escorting me out of the restaurant, you can explain why you sent me away."

"I'll go. This once." He eyed me for a long moment before sighing heavily. "If it turns out you are not an invited member of their party, I will be returning with security."

"And you can apologize when you get back with your tail between your legs." Operation Pissed was coming into play. I had a hard time holding my tongue when I got into that mode.

The man sniffed again and I was tempted to offer him a tissue but bit the inside of my cheek instead. "We'll see."

He walked away from the little podium and

the blond hostess took his place. She ignored me as if I wasn't there, and that was just fine by me. I slid closer and looked at the sheet in front of her. Just before she covered it with her arm, my eyes landed on my name.

"Oh, now that's just rude." I turned away and quickly followed the old man to a table in the center of the room. Those petty jerks were trying to keep me out because they thought I didn't belong? Because of my truck or my clothes?

My furious stride made quick work of the space between the door and the table Alfred was standing next to. I caught up to him in time to hear the last of his words.

"She looks rather questionable."

"The 'rather questionable' woman is standing right behind you." *You stupid little dildo.* I glared at his head, barely registering the people at the table until they stood up.

"I was told the Parallel, and I would assume its restaurant, was used to hosting dignitaries and royalty." The woman's voice was calm and cool. "Your tone would be embarrassing no matter who you thought Lady Rousseau was."

My eyes jerked to the woman and I wondered if the duchess was losing her mind. Perhaps it was appropriate to address people by Lady or Sir in their country. Her mouth twitched in amusement as she watched the man grovel and I decided she must be teaching him a lesson. She might be my hero.

"I'm so sorry, I had no idea. . . ." The Alfred wannabe was sputtering apologies and it took all my willpower to keep from rolling my eyes.

"No, don't apologize to me. Apologize to Lady Rousseau." Her eyes twinkled when she looked at me.

"My apologies, Miss—I mean, Lady Rousseau."

I bowed my head a little. "Accepted. Perhaps you shouldn't be so quick to judge next time."

"Yes, my lady. May I take your coat?"

I shrugged out of my coat and that's when I felt his eyes on me. Looking up, I realized Prince Yummy had indeed come for the dinner. Jess and the undergrads had been wrong. He wasn't yummy, he was delicious; a feast to be savored. Dark blond hair hung a smidge too long, eyes so blue it was like looking into the heart of a glacier. Built like the statue of David; the contours of his suit hugging every delicious muscle. Laugh lines around his mouth and eyes brought him into the realm of humanity, and gave him a personality. As his eyes ran over my face and down my body slowly, heat washed over my skin. When I handed the jacket to the maître d' I felt naked. There was something about his bright blue eyes that left me feeling exposed.

"Thank you, Alfred." I mumbled the words, feeling completely off guard by the look I'd just received. The man left without a word, and I really hoped he didn't do anything nasty to my jacket.

"Alfred?" The prince's mouth quirked on one side, revealing a dimple, and I wondered if a dimple could kill a person. It was possible I was having a heart attack right now. "Is that his name?"

"Oh, you know. He looks a bit like Batman's butler, but without the wicked sense of humor." I winced. I was speaking to a prince, a real live prince, and my first interaction was describing a comic-book character. At least I wasn't a slobbering mess looking at him.

"I vaguely recall something about Batman and his butler." The prince's eyes glittered mischievously. I felt my mouth twist a little, relieved he had gotten my ill-timed sense of humor. "I would have pegged him more as Jarvis. Slow, annoyed voice."

"Samantha, it's a pleasure to meet you." The duchess held her hand out for me, and for a brief moment I panicked, not sure if I was supposed to bow over it or shake it. I decided if she was in

America I was just going to shake it. Her fingers were dry and warm, her grip surprisingly tight. "I'm Rose."

"It's nice to meet you." Jesus. I should have read that article myself. I had no idea what to say or how to act.

"This is my nephew, Alex." I turned toward the outstretched hand and hoped my palms weren't sweaty.

"An honor to meet you." As soon as the words had left my mouth, I regretted them. Why had I said that? Why didn't I just say it was nice to meet him? Surely it hadn't sounded like a come-on. I was just being paranoid. How had I lost control of this evening already? Who was I kidding? I'd lost control as soon as that weirdo Duvall had approached me.

"The honor is mine. Trust me." Instead of shaking, he lifted my hand to his mouth and his lips brushed across my knuckles gently. They were warm and full, and my body tingled at the contact. I stopped breathing for a moment and had to remind myself that oxygen was important. When he lowered my hand, his thumb ran over my knuckles. He knew how to affect a woman, that was for sure. Stepping around me, he pulled my chair out. I don't think anyone has ever pulled a chair out for me. It was weird. What did I do with my feet? The stupid heels caught on the floor and almost came off, so I just lifted them up until he was done.

He moved around to his aunt and helped her into her chair as well. She was watching me with bright, intelligent eyes and I wondered what she was thinking. I felt a bit like she was measuring me. She motioned to the waitress standing off to the side and I was offered a glass of wine. I took it, but only to be courteous. I was already feeling out of my element.

"I apologize for that terribly inappropriate behavior, Samantha." Rose frowned.

"It's okay, Duchess. I'm sure he was just trying to keep people from bothering you." I was being generous. I was mentally debating egging the hotel.

"Please, call me Rose." She smiled at me and I smiled back.

"Thank you, Rose."

"Are you ready to order?" The waitress was back, her white button-up shirt was undone a bit and she stood close to the prince. The question had been addressed to him and only him. Rose looked at me and winked as if amused, but when I noted his uncomfortable expression I couldn't help but feel bad for him. His face had transformed from friendly and thoughtful to stony.

"Actually, I haven't had a chance to look at the selection." I cleared my throat and picked up the large red menu.

"I'll give you a little more time."

"Could you turn the heat up a little?" The waitress started to turn, but his voice stopped her. His blue eyes locked on mine and for a minute I wondered if my clothes had caught on fire. Or maybe his accent had managed to make it hotter without turning up the heat. "I noticed your hands were cold."

"No, no. I'm fine really." It was cold in the restaurant, not that I noticed right this minute. Or maybe that was just the dress I was wearing. It wasn't exactly designed for winter wear, but it was the nicest dress I owned. When my mother passed, it was one of the things I had made sure didn't disappear. I wasn't much of a fashionista, but I loved the vintage Chanel.

He looked at the waitress and smiled. "The heat, please."

"Of course, Your Highness." At her use of his title, the corners of his mouth twitched down briefly and he looked back at his menu.

"Thank you, but I really was fine." I looked at him and narrowed my eyes. I didn't care for men that ordered food for their women and picked out their clothing. Even if he was hot as hell.

"No reason to be uncomfortable." He smiled, his eyes moving back to my face. I felt heat creep into my cheeks and I looked away. Squinting, I stared at my menu, not really seeing the words, and tried to crush the odd effect he seemed to have on me. This was a business meeting and it needed to stay professional.

I could feel his gaze like a hot touch. It had been a while since I had been with a man, but that was fixable. They made toys to replace men. However, I had a feeling Prince Alex could do things that would make my toy wholly inadequate.

"Have you been here before, Samantha?" Rose's voice drifted to my ears and I was glad for the distraction.

"No, this is the first time I've eaten at the Parallel, but I've heard the food is wonderful." I smiled over my menu at her. Sometimes there's a feeling when you meet someone, a sense of understanding and connection. I felt it with Rose. "Dr. Geller comes here occasionally for business lunches. Speaking of Dr. Geller, I wasn't able to get in touch with him before coming to dinner, so please forgive me for being unprepared. I'm not sure what exactly we're discussing tonight."

Rose smiled at me for a minute as if amused. I looked over at Prince Yummy—dang it, Alex—

and frowned. His eyes were moving back and forth between me and his aunt, a small smile playing along his delicious lips. They both looked like they were hiding something.

"Let's order and then we'll talk about it. I'm starving." Rose set her menu down, so I quickly looked through and picked something to eat. Something weird was going on here and I was going to figure it out. I looked for the waitress and smiled, hoping that would bring her to the table a little faster so we could get down to business.

She glared at me as she sauntered back to us and I wondered why the staff here seemed to hate me so much. What on Earth had I done? Shown up to dinner with the duchess and the prince— Oh. The prince. She was glaring at me because I was eating dinner with Prince Yummy. Sheesh. It wasn't like we were alone. Who brings their aunt on a date?

The thought brought heat to my cheeks— again. I was never going on a date with Alex. We were from different worlds. He wore expensive suits and probably never got his hands dirty. I wore blue jeans and flannel shirts. My hands were always dirty. Okay, not always dirty. I washed them, but I never met a bird that hadn't at least thought about pooping on me.

"You're ready?" The waitress once again turned her body and ample cleavage toward Alex and leered.

"Ladies first." Alex leaned forward so he could look around the waitress. "Samantha, what would you like?" My name spoken in that accent made it sound much sexier, but it was the glint in his blue eyes that made my skin burn.

"I'll take the chicken, please." There were no prices on the menu, but I was certain that had to be the cheapest thing on there. Chicken would certainly fall under lamb or duck. I hoped.

"Got it." If the waitress had been chewing gum she would have popped it in her mouth at me. I was torn between laughter and being offended. She smiled at Rose, though. A disgustingly sweet expression that made her look sick. Or maybe it just made me nauseated. "And for you, Duchess?"

"I'll have the same thing Lady Rousseau is having." Rose pushed her menu toward the waitress, but the girl didn't notice. She was looking at me with a worried expression. I shrugged, not sure what to say. A deep chuckle made me sit up straighter in my seat and look at Alex. He was watching me, an amused gleam in his eyes as if he was in on a secret.

"I'd like the rib eye, please. Rare." He handed

his menu to the waitress without looking at her and leaned forward, his hands clasped in front of him, and smiled at me. "Samantha. Are you from here?"

"I'm a transplant. My family moved here ten years ago for a job. Thankfully, the college I wanted was nearby."

"Is that so?" Alex leaned forward and looked at me intently. "I would think most people going off to college would want to get as far away from home as possible."

"My mother passed away and I didn't want to leave my father." I didn't like where this conversation was going. He seemed almost too interested. Like in my private life there were secrets that he had to know.

"How is your stepfather? I understand he's been sick." Rose's eyebrows drew together. "I can't say I care very much for the way that health care is handled in the States."

"He's handling everything very well, thank you." I guess my outburst with her lackey earlier hadn't gone unreported. "But we're not here to discuss my family. What kind of questions do you have about the center and our program?"

Rose leaned forward. "Actually, your family is exactly why I am here."

# THREE

### How to Lose a Royal
—*PERRY TALKS*

"**M**Y FAMILY?" I felt my eyebrows rise and tried to control my expression. What the hell was going on?

"Why did you decide to keep your mother's maiden name when she married your father?" Rose folded her hands in front of her and her eyes bored into mine.

"I'm not sure why that would be any of your business." I looked at Alex, but his face gave nothing away. "I thought I was here to discuss the raptor program for Dr. Geller."

"Yes, I realized that earlier. However, I was hoping to discuss something else." Rose leaned back as the waitress and several helpers delivered their food to the table. "I was hoping to discuss you."

"I can't imagine why." Shaking my head, I leaned back so the waitress could set my plate in front of me. "Thank you."

"Do you know much about Lilaria?" Rose took a sip from her glass before picking up her fork and knife. "We're a small but proud country."

"No, I can't say I know much about your homeland."

"Let me tell you a bit about it. We control a rather large portion of Europe's oil resources, which brings a great deal of wealth to our citizens, but it also brings trouble. In the late eighteen hundreds, a royal family of the name Malatar felt it was time for a change; however, they didn't want an outright war. You see, they didn't have many supporters. The country was flourishing and the people were happy." Rose looked at the waitress, who seemed to be taking longer than needed to deliver Alex's plate. With annoyance, I realized she was buttering his roll while pushing her cleavage into his face. I don't know why I cared, but it bothered me. Here we were trying to have an important conversation and this chick was acting like a dog in heat. He didn't look exactly happy about it, but also looked like he wasn't sure how to stop it without a fuss.

When the waitress stood up with a smile on

her face, I pushed my dinner roll in her direction. "What exceptional service the Parallel offers. Thank you." The waitress's eyebrows pulled together, but there wasn't much she could do. Taking the butter knife off my dish, she generously slathered the roll with butter and set it back on the plate.

"I haven't seen bread buttered that well in a long time." I smiled at her sweetly and heard Alex chuckle. The waitress turned around and stormed away. Narrowing my eyes at Alex, I frowned. "Don't take this the wrong way, but maybe you should practice telling people to leave you alone. I thought she was going to maul you."

"Occupational hazard. If I'm rude, there's a story in the paper about me mistreating the staff. If I do nothing, it could go either way." He raised an eyebrow. I was obviously not cut out for diplomacy. "But thank you for stepping in. I was afraid to breathe or I might fall into her shirt."

"No problem." I shook my head, amazed by how people behave, and looked back at Rose, who was watching us. "You were telling me about the family trying to take over."

"Yes. Well, they didn't have much support, so began going after the royal families they thought would put up the most resistance. Several royal families died in bizarre accidents and that's when everyone became nervous. There was a lot of anger and finger-pointing, but no hard evidence. Our family was left with no way to legally arrest the traitors." Her sigh was laced with frustration. It was obviously something that had caused her relatives a great deal of stress, although how something that happened over one hundred years ago had bearing on this conversation about me was still a mystery. "Eventually, some of the families felt threatened enough to leave the country. At times with no notice, leaving everything behind like they would be back any day." Rose leaned forward, her keen eyes brightening. "One of the largest families to leave was that of Duke Rousseau."

I was glad I didn't have anything in my mouth, because I was pretty sure I would have spit it out on the table. "You think I'm part of his family?"

"I know you are part of his family." Rose's grin was victorious. "My sister, the queen, has been searching for all the families for years in hopes of bringing them home. We've traced your family all the way back to the day they set sail from the French coast for America."

I sat there for a minute, completely unable to form a coherent thought. Images of my mother passed before my eyes. Snippets of conversation repeated themselves. I knew that at one point my family had come from money, but my great-grandfather had gambled most of it away. Now there was the fact that my family had supposedly run. Run away and deserted our homeland.

"Why? Why are you telling me this?" I looked up from the plate of food I was no longer interested in.

"We want to reinstate your title and lands, Samantha. They are yours and have been kept in trust until we could find you." Rose watched me, apparently not sure of my reaction.

"It's true, Samantha. My mother has been searching for the missing families for years. If my aunt says you're from the Rousseau line, then you are." Alex reached out and touched my hand, the one that was clutching the fork so tightly my knuckles had turned white. Heat washed up my arm and I met his eyes.

"Why? Why would she want to find the people who abandoned their country?" I couldn't wrap my brain around this being about my family.

"Samantha, in our country, the most important thing to us is family. Not just among the royals, but all our citizens. Our work laws are geared to protecting families. Duke Rousseau did what he did to protect his family. There was

o legal way of safeguarding themselves, and
e knew they would be targets." Alex squeezed
ny fingers and I looked down at our hands. His
vas much larger than mine, and somehow, even
hough I had just met him, I found his touch
omforting.

"What does this have to do with me? What do
ou want?" I thought I'd come here tonight to dis-
:uss a donation for the raptor program.

"As I said, the queen wants to reinstate your
lands, Samantha." Rose calmly folded her hands
in her lap. "She wants to reinstate your title."

"Title?" My mind was mush. I couldn't make
sense of what they were telling me.

"Yes. By all rights, you are the Duchess of
Rousseau. You are the legal heir."

I stared at her and tried to wrap my brain
around what she was telling me. "That can't be
right. There must've been a mistake. I'm not a
duchess. I'm a grad student." I gently pulled my
hand out from under Alex's.

"Samantha, ask yourself this: Why did your
mother keep her maiden name? Why did she
not take your stepfather's last name for you and
herself?" Rose sat patiently, her face blank as she
waited for me to think about it.

Unbidden, my mother's voice filled my mind.

*There are two things you must never forget. One, you are a Rousseau and you should always be proud of that. Two, family always comes first. Always.* She had told me those things a hundred times, but I'd always thought she was telling me to be proud of who I was, it didn't matter that I didn't know my father. And we were a family until we met Dean, my stepfather. And then he too became family. The saying never changed. Family comes first.

"Did she know?" I looked at Rose and hoped she didn't notice the tears in my eyes. Mom had been gone for five years, but it still hurt when I heard her voice in my head like that. And now, to find out this, I wasn't sure what to do. What to think.

"I'm not sure. It's likely she knew a little, but I don't believe she knew everything." Rose frowned. "I'm sorry we didn't find you sooner. I would have liked to have met your mother. I understand she was a brilliant biologist."

"She was." My eyes slid around the room as I tried to regain my composure. How could she not tell me? Did she know the truth? Part of the truth? And what about my dad? My feet started to itch and I wanted to run out of there and demand an answer.

"I'm leaving in a couple of days to head home. I'd like it very much if you would return with me." Rose leaned forward. "The Rousseau family was a very important one and my sister is extremely excited to meet you."

"In a few days?" This was insane. "I can't. I have school. Projects. I can't just leave." I shook my head. "What would I do?"

"Aunt, surely we can give her more time to consider everything." Alex looked at Rose, his bright blue eyes serious. "That's a lot to put on her all at once."

"True." Rose picked up her fork and knife and cut her chicken. "But the world has a way of throwing us curve balls. We have to decide whether to swing or strike out. This is your moment, Samantha. You're up to bat."

I snorted. I couldn't help it. The duchess had just made a baseball analogy about my life. I picked up the glass of wine, deciding I needed a sip or maybe a whole bottle to help calm my jangling nerves. "How long would I be away?"

"That would depend on you. There is a ceremony to be performed. Legalities to be followed through with. Of course, once you take control of the estate and become the family head, it would be pertinent for you to stay in the country as much as possible. You would be your family's voice on the council to the queen."

"You've got to be kidding me." I looked at her, my mouth hanging open. "Holy shit. You're serious." Rose's mouth twitched and I realized I had just cursed in the presence of royalty. "Sorry. A seat on the council to the queen? You guys know nothing about me!"

"That's not true. You've made the dean's list at your school every year. You were the top student to be chosen for your graduate program. You are dutiful to your family and take good care of your stepfather. You are a remarkable young woman our country would be proud to have."

I knew my mouth was still agape. I didn't care. Rose had just outlined my life, but instead of making it sound boring, she had made it sound like I was a saint.

"I can't just leave school. My degree is very important to me." I'd worked so hard to get to where I was. The scholarships alone had taken countless hours of work.

"Raptors are incredibly important in our country. Each of the noble houses has one as their symbol. Your family is the merlin. As you know, a small but fierce bird. There are several well-known schools and programs that would be pleased to have you.

And you would have the added benefits of our medical system for your father." Rose looked up from her food. "There are many treatments available overseas your government has not allowed here."

More than anything she could have said tonight, that was the one thing that would make me seriously consider this craziness. From the look in her eyes, she knew it too. I was being maneuvered. I didn't like it, but at the same time, she made a good case. And I knew about merlins. They were amazing birds.

"I need to think about this." I picked up my fork and pushed the potatoes on my plate.

"Of course." Rose smiled and I caught a hint of victory in it. "Like I said, I will be here for a few more days. And if you decide to come, we can push it back a little so you can accomplish any tasks you'd need to do first. I'm sure you will want to speak with your father, as well."

"Thank you, but I'm not sure I'll be going." I took another sip of wine. And then another. Oh good God. What would Dad say?

"I hope he will be able to come for the ceremony." Rose sipped from her wine. "If you decide to take up the mantle, of course."

If I decided, of course. I had a feeling it wouldn't be that easy to say no.

"If you come out, you'll have to go hunting with me." Alex nodded toward me.

"I'm not much of a hunter." I racked my brain, wondering why he would think I would want to go hunting, but found it a little difficult to get past the fact he had asked me to do something with him at all. "I've only shot a gun a few times."

He chuckled, and the sound sent a wave of goose bumps down my arms. "No, I meant with birds. I own several hawks that are excellent hunters."

"Oh." That made much more sense. I scooped some of the food into my mouth, enjoying the flavors. Despite the crappy—or inappropriate?—service, the Parallel's food had lived up to the hype. "I've been a few times, but don't have a bird of my own."

"I'd be happy to lend you one of my birds. I've been away for a while, so it would be good to have help exercising them." The corners of my mouth pulled up a little. He was being nice. There was no way he didn't have a gamekeeper to help him take care of the birds while he was away.

"What do you have?" I pulled apart some of the bread I had asked the waitress to butter.

"Three Harris hawks."

"Alex is a bird advocate, as was his father." Rose tilted her glass toward her nephew. "He presented his first bill to the Lilarian council when he was twelve. He called for stricter punishments for the purposeful deaths of raptors and endangered birds."

I looked over at Alex and felt my first true smile of the night. "That's a pretty big proposal. Good for you."

"Didn't do it for me." Alex sipped from his glass and grinned.